A Killing at Ball's Bluff

"Picaresque adventure." —*Publishers Weekly*

"Kilian is definitely on to something. . . . [His] use of historical detail is accurate and pertinent without detracting from what is, essentially, a tightly constructed, well-written, and suspenseful whodunit. Raines, a relentless but all-too-human hero, is an intriguing character who can withstand the scrutiny of subsequent episodes in what promises to be a fine series of novels. Both Civil War and mystery fans will appreciate Kilian's grasp of the genres of historical fiction and mystery." —*Booklist*

"A can't-put-it-down book. The plot is like a jigsaw puzzle, and you are never sure where the pieces fit. The characters are many and the conflict constant. Harry is intelligent, sensitive, and loyal. . . . A sense of urgency keeps the pace racing." —*Rendezvous*

"Kilian takes the facts of the death of Colonel Baker and creates for his readers a fictional scenario that entertains and educates at the same time." —*Civil War Book Review*

The Ironclad Alibi

"The series seems on the whole a promising notion." —*Kirkus Reviews*

Jazz Age Mysteries
by Michael Kilian

THE WEEPING WOMAN
THE UNINVITED COUNTESS

THE
UNINVITED
COUNTESS

MICHAEL KILIAN

BERKLEY PRIME CRIME, NEW YORK

This is a work of fiction.
Names, characters, places, and incidents either
are the product of the author's imagination or are used fictitiously,
and any resemblance to actual persons, living or dead, business
establishments, events, or locales is entirely coincidental.

THE UNINVITED COUNTESS

A Berkley Prime Crime Book / published by arrangement with
the author

PRINTING HISTORY
Berkley Prime Crime mass-market edition / August 2002

Copyright © 2002 by Michael Kilian.
Cover art by Hiro Kimura.
Cover design by Tree Trapanese.

Visit our website at
www.penguinputnam.com

ISBN: 0-425-18582-6

Berkley Prime Crime Books are published
by The Berkley Publishing Group,
a division of Penguin Putnam Inc.,
375 Hudson Street, New York, New York 10014.
The name BERKLEY PRIME CRIME and the
BERKLEY PRIME CRIME design
are trademarks belonging to Penguin Putnam Inc.

PRINTED IN THE UNITED STATES OF AMERICA

10 9 8 7 6 5 4 3 2 1

*For the inimitable Kitty Lorentzen,
of Bedford, Bermuda, and the Bowery;*

*with special thanks
to Christopher Knapp Haynes.*

CHAPTER 1

I **HAVE** news," said Sloane Smith, Bedford Green's famously tall and lovely assistant, as she came through the door of his Greenwich Village art gallery more than an hour late on a disagreeably hot summer morning in 1925.

Bedford, seated at his desk, lowered his newspaper. "And what is that? Have we actually sold a painting?"

He brushed a speck of street dust from his white duck trousers, and then another from his navy blazer. The motorcar traffic in New York was becoming impossible.

"Yes, we have," Sloane said. "I have. But that's not the news."

She sat down on his desk, crossing her long legs. Even without shoes, she was equal to his six foot of height, and her legs traversed a considerable distance. Her pale yellow sleeveless summer dress had a shockingly high hemline, even by the provocative standards of the time. Bedford flushed a little, keeping his eyes on her face.

Sloane was very fair of complexion, and wore her dark hair in a chic, sleek, fashionable bob. She had highlighted her gray-green eyes with a matching eye shadow. In all, she was flawlessly groomed, though she'd been at their neighborhood speakeasy, Chumley's, as late as he had been—matching him and his friends whiskey for whiskey.

"How could you sell a painting without opening up the gallery?" he asked, pointedly but unnecessarily consulting his wristwatch.

"If you were one tenth as perceptive as you're reputed to be," she said, lighting a cigarette, "you would have noticed that I did indeed open up this much-neglected establishment this morning. I went through the mail, took delivery of two paintings from overseas, tidied up generally—which has not been done in some days—and sold one of the Gerrit Beneker Cape Cod oils to an elderly woman from Patchin Place. Then I closed up again, all before you finally arrived."

"Which Beneker?"

"The one of Provincetown harbor."

"How much?"

"Seven hundred fifty dollars."

"Gosh, Sloane. Bless you."

"Don't thank me," she said. "Thank Mr. Beneker."

"Thanks and blessings to Mr. Beneker. Now tell me the 'news.' "

She leaned back, turning her head to look at him, but then became distracted by his copy of the *New York Day*, the ratty morning tabloid where Bedford had once labored as a celebrity and society columnist. Her eyes fixed on a headline, then she swiveled around, turning toward him, and picked up the paper.

"Golly Moses," she said. "William Jennings Bryan has died. The poor old coot."

A week before, Bryan had been on the witness stand at the Scopes "Monkey" trial in Tennessee, undergoing the most merciless imaginable questioning from his nemesis, Clarence Darrow, on literal interpretation of the Bible. All Greenwich Village had followed the proceedings with great interest and amusement.

"Died defending his faith," Bedford said.

"Perhaps he just died of embarrassment," Sloane said. "The way Darrow humiliated him. It was close to torture." She put the paper aside. "I wonder though if he just succumbed to the heat. I couldn't survive three days in Tennessee."

Sloane was from Chicago. Her family had a huge house in Lake Forest on a bluff overlooking breezy Lake Michigan.

"Now your news, if you please," Bedford asked. "And could you tell me where it is you went when you were gone from the gallery?"

"It might be none of your business."

"If that's the case, you needn't tell me."

She got to her feet, smoothing down what there was of her skirt.

"I went just down the street, is all—to Gertrude Vanderbilt Whitney's studio. She rang up and asked me over for coffee."

"Was she showing off her latest sculpture?"

"No."

"She gave you this all important news you still haven't told me about."

"Yes."

"And it is?"

"It is, Mr. Green, that you have become socially acceptable."

He stared at her, wondering at the game. "Impossible. You've been grievously misinformed."

"How can you say that? Just because you're stone broke; consort with gamblers, showgirls, racetrack touts, and other lowlifes; and once actually worked as a newspaperman."

"You left out artists. I consort with artists."

"Artists are beyond society. But you, sir, for once, have now achieved genuine social status. We have been invited up to Gertrude's place in Newport. You and I—the both of us."

"By Gertrude's 'place,' you must mean that monstrous Vanderbilt mansion—'the Breakers.' "

"All she said was, 'her cottage.' "

" 'Cottage,' indeed. It has seventy rooms."

"Would you rather spend the weekend in some egalitarian Lower East Side tenement?"

"Not particularly. Neither would most of the tenements' inhabitants. But she actually invited me?"

Bedford came from a very old New York family, but one so old it had long before run through all its money. His parents had died leaving him nothing but a large farmhouse in Cross River up in Westchester and the wherewithal to open his gallery—though not enough, alas, to keep it in business.

The Vanderbilts were comparative newcomers to the New York social scene, but now ruled it as the richest clan in the city. If they wished, Bedford supposed, they had money enough to buy the whole of Greenwich Village outright. Some contemptuous local bohemians treated Gertrude as though she had a secret plan to do just that as part of some capitalist, monopolist plot, though all she owned or planned to in the neighborhood was her studio building on West Eight Street, a few doors down from Bedford's gallery. And she was as much a friend to her fellow artists as there was to be had in the city.

"She's inviting us both," Sloane said. "I suppose I'm to tag along to keep you from committing some gaffe, such as poking at the gold leaf to see if it's real." She got up and went to a painting on the wall near the front display window, straightening it.

"Of course their gold leaf is real," Bedford said. "I'm surprised they haven't covered their lawn with it."

Sloane laughed. "That's probably the next Newport *dernier cri.*"

He glanced at his newspaper again, then folded it neatly and set it on the cabinet behind him.

"There's a reason for this invitation," he said. "Something lurking in the weeds."

Sloane was still fidgeting with the painting.

"Clever man," she said. "Yes, the Vanderbilts do have a problem. Or so Gertrude says."

"Does it involve art? Or is she interested in my pick for the next Belmont Stakes?"

"It involves Hungarians. Do you know of a noble Hungarian family named Zala?"

"The only Hungarians I believe I've ever encountered outside of André Mohar's restaurant on Hudson Street were Austro-Hungarians in the war—and they were shooting at me."

"That's not true. Your actress friend Claire Pell—she's half Hungarian."

"Yes, that's right. She is."

"Is she speaking to you again?"

"I'm not sure. But what sort of Hungarians is Gertrude interested in?"

"This Hungarian countess named Zala. Gertrude is very worried about her. You might even say scared. She wants to know more about her. She's of the opinion you know everybody and can help her in this."

"Why didn't she ask me herself?"

"I think she wanted to sound me out about it first. She was afraid you'd resent being invited to Newport for what amounts to an ulterior reason."

He shook his head, wishing a customer would come in. "Sorry, I do believe I am the wrong fellow for this. Much as I like Gertrude, I'm not much good with aristocrats. Not the Hungarian kind, or the Vanderbilt kind."

Sloane returned to the side of his desk, and smiled. "Gertrude says this countess is very beautiful."

He pondered this observation, and what it might mean

for the Vanderbilts, brushing another speck from his white trousers. "Were you supposed to tell me about this countess now, or was I to learn upon arriving?"

"A bit after that, I think, so you wouldn't think the invitation was extended under false pretenses."

"As in fact it was. Or will be."

"You wouldn't think that if I hadn't told you."

"True enough. Why did you?"

"You're my friend, Bedford. I don't keep things from you. Not if they concern you."

"Has Gertrude officially tendered the invitation?"

Sloane pondered this as though it were some weighty matter. "Actually, I guess not. She said she might talk to you later."

"So in the meantime I'm to pretend I've heard nothing about Hungarian countesses."

"Just be your sweet old well-mannered and highly circumspect self, and everything will be all ticketyboo."

She leaned down and kissed his cheek, which she did about once a year, and then went to the rear alcove that was their office and workroom to wrap the Beneker painting. Bedford tilted his chair back against the wall, recalling his childhood visits to Newport, Rhode Island. He'd been intimidated by the Vanderbilts and the other robber barons even then.

His last visit there had been in the company of someone considerably more intimidating, though for a different reason. It had been aboard a motor yacht, full of smuggled scotch. Bedford had been a guest of his old Great War flying comrade, Liam O'Bannion, who had prospered greatly as a trans-Atlantic bootlegger.

"Do you really want to accept this invitation—presuming she ever extends it?" he asked.

"Yes. Of course."

"I thought you told me all these society swells bore you silly."

"They do. I just like to run barefoot on their lawns. They always have such wonderful lawns."

"Fine, but much as I like Gertrude, I think I will decline," he said.

"I really wish you wouldn't. I want you to go there."

He stared at her, in a way he seldom did. "You want me to run barefoot over their lawn with you?"

"Don't get the wrong idea, Bedford Green. I want you to come with me because I think Gertrude's really worried about something."

"What makes you think that?"

"She asked if you had a gun."

CHAPTER 2

BEDFORD suggested that Sloane quit work early, as they'd had no other customers and she'd certainly earned her pay for the day. A few minutes after she was out the door, he closed up the gallery and, straw boater in place, headed east down Eighth Street toward Gertrude Vanderbilt Whitney's studio.

The sun was still fairly high in the sky and the day's summer heat as yet little dissipated. Ever mindful of his appearance, Bedford walked slowly to keep down perspiration. Reaching the lady's building, a two-story structure with marble pillars to either side of the front steps and only a few windows facing the street, he stopped, hesitating before the door.

He was indeed resentful. He felt he was being summoned out to the Breakers like some hired tradesman, only paid in canapés. To be sure, he was a tradesman. No matter how grandly his fellow art gallery owners tended to view and conduct themselves, they were all in essence shopkeepers—paintings and sculpture as much commodities as produce, however lofty the language of commerce.

Mrs. Whitney's disingenuousness angered him. It was

wholly unnecessary. If she had simply asked him for this favor as a friend, he'd gladly have attended to it without any need of weekends in Newport.

He decided he would do precisely that. He'd learn what he could about the mysterious Hungarian lady and then present the information to Gertrude before she had a chance to extend any Newport invitation.

He moved on, happier now, strolling south toward Washington Square. The park was full of people, many of them mothers with small children. He walked around the central fountain, then turned north again and passed through the arch, heading up Fifth Avenue. He had time to call upon several people in what remained of this day.

It started with Dayton Crosby, the curmudgeonly Wall Street lawyer he'd inherited from his parents along with the family's weathered country house in upper Westchester. The old gentleman had largely retired from the law firm where he had for years been managing partner, devoting himself now to more interesting pursuits, including books he authored about notable New Yorkers and the animal welfare charity he had founded. A habitually rumpled fellow who resembled more a sort of shaggy bear than the proper gentlemen his Knickerbocker forebears had been, Crosby had a fondness for animals of all sorts. He lived with a small menagerie of dogs, cats, and more exotic creatures in a shabbily genteel townhouse facing Gramercy Park.

Bedford walked there, perspiring uncomfortably, only to find the man not at home. Presuming Crosby would be at one of his many clubs, he set out first for the Masters Chess Club down on Mercer Street. There the old gentleman indeed proved to be, sprawled in a comfy leather armchair at a table near the back, waiting with carefully restrained impatience while a younger, bearded opponent stared at the board in grim frustration.

"Should I resign?" the opponent asked as Bedford joined them.

"Well, I am surely not about to," Crosby interjected.

He looked up at Bedford and grinned, the cat in possession of the mouse.

"Do you see it?" the bearded man said to Bedford. "I'm not sure."

"I do see it, I think," said Bedford quietly. There were several games in progress in the room. "Checkmate in three moves, depending."

"Depending on what?"

"On what you do, sir."

"What would you do?"

Crosby leaned back in his chair, folding his arms. "Asking advice is against house rules."

"I would resign," Bedford said.

The bearded man nodded, taking his king and laying it on its side. He rose, and shook Crosby's hand, then walked away, pulling at his curly beard. When he was gone, the old man got painfully to his feet, and suggested whiskey in the club's back room. He was afflicted with arthritis, and it plagued him when the weather was muggy. He claimed the occasional cocktail or two helped.

"Would you have resigned?" Crosby asked when he had reseated himself and their drinks were poured.

"I wouldn't have gotten as far as he did," Bedford said. "You'd have checkmated me long before."

Crosby scowled. "That's rubbish. You'd have lasted at least two moves longer than he did. I don't suppose you've come by for a game?"

"No. I came by to seek out your extensive knowledge of Hungarian aristocracy."

"You have been seriously misinformed, my boy. All I know of the Hungarian aristocracy is that you don't notice so many of them driving cabs and waiting on tables as you do of the Russian aristocracy nowadays. But then, the Hungarian revolution had a more salubrious outcome."

He meant that Hungary's leftist revolutionaries had failed in their uprising, allowing the monarchy to return to the throne.

"Could you suggest where I might go to become better informed?" Bedford asked.

A sparkle came into Crosby's eyes. He raised a forefinger.

"The very place. Budapest!"

Bedford sipped his drink. "Thank you, Dayton, for the sage advice. As it happens, I won't be in Budapest anytime soon. I'm about to be invited by Gertrude Vanderbilt Whitney out to her family's place in Newport."

"Well, then, your problem's solved. You can ask around there about Hungarian aristocrats."

"How so?"

"The old Commodore wasn't much, in the beginning, don't you know. Skippered a garbage scow out of Staten Island. Then he moved to steam ferries from New Jersey and from there to ships, railroads, and real estate. Thus does America grow its aristocracy. Some of his descendants have hankered for the real thing, and Gertrude's sister Gladys married one—His Excellency Count Laszlo Szechenyi."

"I'd forgotten. Is he a fortune hunter?"

"On the contrary. He's a diplomat—since 1921, His Royal Hungarian Majesty's minister to the United States. I met him at a dinner once at the Coffee House Club. Nice fellow. And he's made Gladys a countess. Their children won't have to settle for having a garbage scow skipper as their most illustrious ancestor."

"I never quite understood the point of a titled American."

"Neither did the Europeans, until they got a sniff of American money. Do you know the General?"

"Gertrude's brother?"

"Yes indeed. General Cornelius Vanderbilt III. Very nice fellow, too. And intelligent. Won the Croix de Guerre in the war—just like you. Surprised you didn't run into him."

"It was a very large war. But I do know him. I mean, I know of him. I certainly know his wife."

"Who does not know the inimitable Grace Wilson Vanderbilt?"

Very blond, grand, flamboyant, and socially ambitious, that particular Mrs. Vanderbilt had become one of the most celebrated—and photographed—figures of the New York social scene. She always seemed a bit too flamboyant for the tall, spare, distinguished, and cerebral General, with his neat European beard and inquisitive mind. The General's parents had thought so, too, according to wide report, but he'd married the Wilson woman anyway.

Interesting man. Bedford recalled that he held several patents for railroad car design and had given his huge steam yacht *North Star* to the British upon the outbreak of the Great War.

"Dayton, I already know about Vanderbilts. What I need to know about is Hungarians."

"But why?"

"To help Gertrude. She's trying to find out what she can about this Countess Zala. The woman is apparently causing her some worry."

"And why is that?"

"I don't know."

"Gertrude didn't say?"

"Gertrude hasn't actually talked to me about it. She told Sloane she hoped I might be able to find out something, but she hasn't asked me to do that directly. It's all very peculiar."

"Indeed. The Vanderbilts have enormous resources. They could hire an army of detectives. Why turn to you?"

"I've no idea. Maybe because I used to write a newspaper column, and know a few people."

Crosby rubbed his chin. The matter of the Countess Zala was apparently almost as intriguing as a game of chess.

"Not as many people as the Vanderbilts do," Dayton said. He signaled for more whiskey. "It's something else in your background, m'boy. Perhaps your time in the war."

"I don't think so."

The whiskey came, but Crosby ignored it, rubbing his chin some more.

"No," he said. "It's your time as a police reporter. You have police connections. You are acquainted with criminals. You have access to information about criminals. Perhaps this countess is a criminal. That would explain Gertrude's worry."

Bedford shrugged.

"As you say, Dayton, the Vanderbilts could hire an army of detectives—or ring up the police commissioner. They could find out anything they wanted about any criminal. They certainly don't need me."

Now Dayton drank. "But they do, Bedford. You possess a quality no policeman or hired detective would have."

"And what would that be?"

"Discretion, sir. Discretion. You are Gertrude's friend. She thinks you an honorable gentleman. You can be counted on to find out what she needs to know without the whole world finding out about it. Can't depend on the police for that."

"I see."

"That's why she's inviting you out to Newport."

"This doesn't help me find out about the mysterious Countess Zala."

"No, it does not."

Bedford drank his whiskey.

"Good night, Dayton."

"Good night, Bedford. Next time you come by, I will insist upon a game."

TAKING the rattling Third Avenue elevated train to Forty-second Street, Bedford got off and walked west toward Times Square. In a few minutes, he was at Lindy's, where in the boisterous crowd of patrons he found two Broadway types of his long acquaintance—the gambler Arnold Rothstein, notorious for having fixed the 1919 "Black Sox" World Series, and homicide detective Lieutenant Joseph D'Alessandro, an honest but sometimes winking cop given to purple suits and spats and known up and down Broadway simply as "Joey D."

The two were dining together at Rothstein's usual table. It was the gambler who invited Bedford to join them.

"Hungarians?" Rothstein said after Bedford had explained his quest for information. "If you're talking about rum-running or the rackets, I can't say as I've ever heard tell of any bohunks in the trade."

He looked to Joey D, who nodded.

"Italians, like me," he said. "Jews, like Mr. Rothstein. Germans, Irish. Maybe some Negro numbers runners up in Harlem."

"And Anglo-Saxons, like our honorable mayor," said Rothstein.

"If there were Hungarians, I'd have heard of them," Joey D said. "I think maybe some of those anarchists we keep rounding up have been Hungarian, but nobody in the rackets."

"Well, gentlemen, if you do hear of anything, I'd appreciate it if you could let me know." Bedford started to rise.

"Sit," commanded Rothstein, putting his hand firmly on Bedford's arm. "Eat."

"No thanks."

"What's this all about?" Joey D asked.

"I'm not sure. A friend of mine is worried about a Hungarian lady. A certain Countess Zala."

"Bedford," said the police detective. "If you're looking for countesses, try Delmonico's. Not here."

LINDY'S was around the corner from the theater where Bedford's sometime girlfriend Claire Pell was starring in a mindless musical called *Home Town Girl*, which was on its last legs and near to closing. He stopped in front of the theater, appreciating the poster picture of Claire affixed to the wall by the doors. She was dressed in costume, her blond hair cut short and marcelled, a long leg extended in a high kick, and her face radiant in smile. Her soft brown eyes, even in this silly pose, reflected her intelligence. He missed her. They'd had no contact for weeks.

He took out his pocket watch, an heirloom from his railroad executive grandfather. It was thirty-five minutes before curtain. She would be in her dressing room.

The man at the stage door knew him—too well.

"You two make up?" he asked.

"I'm trying," said Bedford.

"Good luck."

Bedford knocked, two quick raps—a habit.

There was a long silence, then—"Bedford?"

"Yes."

"Go away."

"Please, Claire. I need your help."

Another long silence, then the door opened. She was wearing a dressing gown, but had finished applying her makeup. The poster in front did her small justice.

"Need my help with what?" she asked.

Candor was imperative. "Something about a Hungarian."

"What?"

"May I please come in?"

Her eyes narrowed.

"I'm very, very happy to see you again," he said, smiling. "You've simply no idea."

She stepped back, opening the door wider. "All right, come in."

"Thank you."

He waited for her to seat herself at her dressing table, then took his usual chair, sitting on the edge and leaning forward, a supplicant.

"Do you want a drink?" she asked, crossing her legs.

He observed the fall of her dressing gown.

"No thank you."

She swiveled about to look at her face in the mirror, reaching for a powder puff. "Last time, you wanted to know something about some criminal in Little Italy, asking me to impose on my father's relatives because you presumed they knew people down there."

"You were very helpful."

"Bedford, the curtain's in twenty minutes."

"Will you have dinner with me? After the show?"

She stared into her mirror a moment, then shook her head. "No, Bedford. No thanks. Sorry."

"You sure? The Café Très Vite?"

"I'm sure."

"Very well." He rose, boater in hand.

She dabbed at her nose with the powder puff. "What's the Hungarian woman's name?"

"Zala. The Countess Zala. Young, and apparently very pretty."

Claire put down the powder puff, but continued to face away from him.

"Bedford, my mother was a cook."

He remembered a festive, food-filled evening out in the Long Island suburb where Claire had lived as a child. "A most excellent cook."

"They didn't mix with countesses."

"Oh."

"Not even as servants."

"Sorry." He went to the door.

"But there was a party," Claire said, halting him. "A couple of years ago. A Prince Skorzeny threw it—at the Astor Hotel. A really swell affair. Someone told him I was part Hungarian, so he invited me. The party turned bad—a lot of people going wild—and I left early. But there was a woman there. Dark-haired, very pretty. She called herself a countess. I thought the name was Lala—but now that you mention it, it could have been Zala."

"What do you know about her?"

"Nothing. Except that, of all those going wild, she was the wildest."

"Was she Hungarian?"

"I presume so."

He opened the door, but hesitated. "When can I see you again?"

"I'll let you know."

"Not tonight?"

"Sorry."

He took a step.

"Bedford, who's this friend who needs to know about the Countess Zala?"

"Gertrude Whitney."

"Gertrude Vanderbilt Whitney?"

"Yes. Why?"

Claire turned around. The blush had gone from her face. "Good night, Bedford."

❖

MARGARET O'Neill, owner with her brother of the *New York Day*, had left instructions at the front entrance to the newspaper's offices not to admit Bedford under any circumstances. It was not simply a matter of a soured employer-employee relationship. Margaret had for a time been his fiancée. The rupture of that arrangement had not been pleasant.

He entered now from the loading docks at the rear. It was hours before the first edition, so there was no one about down there.

Taking the stairs, he climbed to the fourth-floor city room, waving to an acquaintance or two as he moved quickly to the door that led to the newspaper's morgue. He had enemies at the *Day*, reporters and editors always anxious to please the management, and his appearance would likely be reported. He'd have to be quick.

Ruby, the elderly, chain-smoking, whiskey-toting, card-playing boss of the morgue, was in residence, seated at a back table where she was going over the turf sheets for the next day. Ruby ran a bookie operation out of the morgue that rivaled some of Mr. Rothstein's enterprises.

"Hiya, Bedford," she said after a quick glance. "You got a horse at Belmont?"

He hadn't thought to look. "Who's the favorite?"

"Yankee Clipper."

"Sounds good." He had twenty dollars. Finding a saw-buck, he placed it on the morgue front counter.

"That's all?"

He looked at his watch. He probably had no more than five minutes before someone would come by to expel him from the premises.

"Ruby, could you check the clips for me? A Countess Zala?"

He spelled the name. She nodded. Rising, she went to a file cabinet, took out a bottle and two shot glasses, and filled both, pushing one toward Bedford. Then she disappeared into the maze of file cabinets.

He took a sip of whiskey. "Good hootch," he said.

"Got a new bootlegger," she said, from the shadows. "Here you go. 'Zala, Countess Esme.' Right where I thought."

"We have a story on her?"

"An obit. She was killed, in Paris. Right after the war. Some kind of bomb."

"The Countess Zala I'm looking for is alive."

"Not according to the *New York Day*," said Ruby, setting the clip down in front of him.

There was a photograph accompanying the brief article. The woman was aristocratic, dressed as though for an audience at a royal court, and in late middle age.

Bedford squinted at the copy, then handed it back.

"Thanks, Ruby," he said. "I appreciate it."

She downed her own whiskey.

"Miss O'Neill should never have let you go, you know," she said.

"Yes, she should have," he said, tipping his boater, and heading out the door just as the night city editor entered.

"Bedford," he said. "Miss O'Neill's brother is upstairs. You'd better skidoo."

"Consider me skidooed."

THERE'D been no dinner in all this. Walking on to Times Square, he stood watching the milling crowd of assorted shopgirls, office clerks, soldiers, sailors on leave, theatergoers, tourists, prostitutes, and pickpockets. The evening sky had turned from twilight to dark, though one could scarcely notice in all the glare of light.

Goulash. He stepped forward to the curb and, to his

amazement, saw a vacant cab in almost the same instant. He raised his arm.

H̲E̲ had met André Mohar at Dayton Crosby's chess club. The restaurant owner was a very honest, straightforward player and a likable man, though his circus strongman's build and huge moustache gave him something of a menacing air. He'd been a soldier in the war and had been involved in some way in the brief 1919 revolution. The latter experience had been more telling on him than the former, though he didn't talk about it much.

Mohar came up and hugged him.

"Captain Green," he said. "Where have you been?"

"Business has been slow," said Bedford. "I've been eating in, mostly. But we sold a painting today, so I'm flush enough to splurge on a dinner in your overpriced but splendid restaurant."

"Then this is an important occasion. I give you the table by Nadia."

Nadia was a violinist with a vast repertoire of Hungarian music. She smiled as Bedford approached, then switched from the classical piece she'd been performing to a livelier gypsy tune. He nodded his hello—and thanks.

"André," Bedford said, "Hungarian people come here a lot, don't they?"

Mohar's eyes widened slightly at the obviousness of the question.

"Sure. Hungarian restaurant. Hungarian food. Hungarian diners."

"How about a Countess Zala? Dark-haired. Young. Said to be very beautiful."

Mohar's brow furrowed. "Many Hungarian girls come here. And many are beautiful. There is one here tonight."

"Dark-haired?" Bedford glanced around the room.

Mohar nodded in a different direction. Bedford turned to look at a table in the corner, where a woman with a cigarette holder seemed to be vamping an older, overweight man.

"She is not a countess," Mohar said. "She is a dancer. And her name is not Zala."

The woman caught Bedford's stare. He looked back to Mohar.

"Well, she certainly is beautiful."

The restaurateur patted him on the shoulder. "Enjoy your dinner, Bedford."

However inappropriate for such a hot night, the goulash was very good. The waiter, an amiable, long-haired man named Sandor Petofi, lingered by the table when Bedford was finished.

"You look for Countess Zala?" he asked.

"Yes," Bedford said. "Do you know her, Sandor?"

Petofi shook his head. "She is dead." He turned and went away to the kitchen. Another waiter brought Bedford's check.

H E stopped for a last drink at Chumley's, the leftist, literary speakeasy near his flat on Grove Street. The wooden street door was unmarked and the front windows painted over. To enter, one had to mount a short flight of stairs, turn at a landing, and then descend more steps. Bedford did so in anticipation of at least finding Sloane there. But he was surprised to find the place all but deserted. Crossing to the bar, he asked if there'd been a police raid. Leland Stanford Chumley, the proprietor, was a local leader of the International Workers of the World and frequently a target of the local Red Squad.

The bartender, a small man of Asian extraction, shook his head.

"Slow night anyway, but there was an argument," the man said, pouring Bedford a whiskey. "Edna St. Vincent Millay and some other people. They all got mad at each other and left."

Bedford sipped his drink, then glanced about the establishment's Old English interior. The young magazine writer Edmund Wilson was seated alone at a corner table, the only other customer there.

"I don't suppose you ever heard of a Hungarian countess named Zala," Bedford said to the bartender.

Another shake of the head. "Whoever she is, she wasn't here tonight."

Bedford thanked him, then went over to join Wilson, who seemed forlorn. He looked up, smiled to see a friend, then launched into a retelling of the barroom dispute, which had something to do with a dadaist/surrealist French writer named Louis Aragon. Wilson then commenced a critique of a book of poetry Aragon had written called *Feu de Joie*, which he said was too calculatingly experimental. He went on and on about it, quoting verses and eloquently arguing his point.

Bedford listened, much impressed with Wilson's erudition, then finished his drink and wished the other a good night. Wilson downed his own glass of scotch, stood up, and then fell forward like a great tree. Bedford managed to catch him by one shoulder and was able to lower him to the floor, where he went immediately to sleep.

It was a perfect metaphor for the unsuccessful evening.

CHAPTER 3

IN the morning, leaving the gallery in Sloane's highly capable charge, Bedford went up to the New York Public Library on Forty-second Street and sought the assistance of a kindly-looking lady behind the main desk of the cavernous reading room. After some search, she produced a book on Hungarian heraldry, wherein Bedford found the Zala coat of arms and a brief caption noting that the family went back to the fourteenth century, but nothing more about them. There were volumes on Polish, Russian, and Austrian nobility, but none on the Hungarian, save for a biography of King Matthias Corvinus, a nineteenth-century monarch who had led the renaissance movement in Hungary.

As a young police reporter, Bedford had been far less feckless. Recalling his news-gathering enterprises, he asked for a telephone directory and found three Zalas, one in Manhattan and two in Queens. He also discovered a listing for a Hungarian Popular Front and a Hungarian Cultural Association of Greater New York. Finding sufficient nickels in his pocket, he went downstairs to a pay telephone and commenced calling. The two Zalas who answered the residence phones knew nothing about any countess. The number that did not respond was one of those in Queens.

A man answered at the Hungarian Cultural Association but did not appear to speak English. A telephone operator informed Bedford that the phone at the Hungarian Popular Front had been disconnected.

He'd wasted the morning. Taking a Fifth Avenue bus, he got off at Eighth Street and walked glumly west to his gallery, becoming at once all the more glum. Three people were standing just inside the door and one of them was Gertrude Vanderbilt Whitney.

She'd been talking to Sloane, who stood slouch-hipped beside Bedford's desk and gave him a peculiar look as he entered.

"Bedford, darling!" said Gertrude, turning to embrace him.

She kissed him lightly on the cheek and then stepped back, studying him speculatively. Bedford was not a little intimidated by Mrs. Whitney. Her immense wealth, high station, and equally considerable talent as an artist were part of it, but there was something more. That she had become his good friend made things worse.

It was well she had so many artist friends, for she had an eminently paintable face—large, full lips; a prominent, straight-angled nose; large brown eyes beneath thick dark eyebrows; and short, curly hair fluffed out at the sides in the manner of an eighteenth-century court wig. She wore a silk blouse over pants and espadrilles.

"Hello, Gertrude," he said. "What a surprise."

There were two men with her, one a dapper, elegant fellow in straw boater and pin-striped suit Bedford thought he recognized, and a smaller, shy, mild-mannered-looking man whom he did not. She introduced the former as Guy Pene Du Bois, a New York newspaper art critic and also an artist, and the latter as Edward Hopper, a magazine illustrator and painter who had exhibited in the famous New York Armory show twelve years before.

DuBois gestured sweepingly at the art Bedford had on display. "A splendid collection."

"Is there something in particular that interests you?" Bedford asked. He'd taken on a young artist from Katonah, New York, named Stanley Tucci, whose exquisite work was due some worthy critic's attention.

"Actually, Bedford," said Gertrude, "it's you we'd like to interest in something. Mr. Hopper has done a painting. I have it in my studio."

Bedford recalled that the man a few years before had exhibited some remarkable watercolors he'd done in Florida and the Caribbean. They'd received enthusiastic notices despite the fact they were not considered "modern."

"A watercolor?" Bedford asked.

The man spoke his first words. "No. It's an oil."

Bedford looked to Sloane.

"I've seen it," Sloane said. "Earlier this morning. You go on over, and I'll keep watch here."

GERTRUDE had the painting, still unframed, on a easel set in the middle of a small drawing room off the main hall of her studio building. The work was poorly lighted, but compelling nonetheless, though it was the simplest of scenes—a flat bit of countryside, a railroad track, and an old Victorian house.

There was not a human figure to be seen on the canvas, yet the picture was haunted by a mysterious presence, an apprehension of something about to happen. In a way, it made Bedford think of a stage set at the opening of a play—perhaps a dark, cynical tragedy. He had a sense of both promise and dread.

"It's brilliant," he said.

"Indeed," said Du Bois. "His best so far."

"What do you call it?" Bedford asked.

" 'House by the Railroad,' " said Hopper. He looked away after he spoke.

"Would you like me to try to sell it?" Bedford asked.

"Oh no, dear boy," said Gertrude. "I'm hoping to have it prominently exhibited and I'm seeking the good word of as many of you 'experts' as I can before I take it uptown. I was wondering if you might interest your friend Mr. Stieglitz in it?"

Alfred Stieglitz had moved his famous Fifth Avenue gallery to a room in a large commercial gallery on Park Avenue, but it was still the center of all things avant garde in New York. Hopper's painting was very different, to be sure, but it was not avant garde, not dadaist, not abstract, not modern. Still, Bedford wondered what Stieglitz's new wife, Georgia O'Keeffe, would think of it. He suspected she'd rather like it.

"I'll talk to him," he said. "At all events, I'd say it certainly deserves an exhibition. Too bad you don't have your own museum, Gertrude."

"Perhaps someday," she said.

"Thank you," Hopper said softly.

Gertrude had coffee served and they stood for a few minutes talking about art, with Gertrude and Pene Du Bois doing most of the talking. There was something flirtatious about the way the two of them dealt with each other. Bedford enjoyed watching the conversation.

But it didn't lead where he'd expected. There was not a word about Hungary, countesses, Newport, or invitations. When he had finally finished his coffee and turned to bid his leave, Mrs. Whitney was affectionate in her farewell. But she did not draw him aside.

◆◆◆

BY midafternoon, having failed to sell anything all day, Bedford told Sloane he was going to close up the shop. He was just pulling down the window shade over the door when a messenger appeared before him, proffering a small but fancy envelope. He tipped the boy a dime and turned to open it. Sloane stood before him, grinning.

He read the contents quickly, then handed it to her.

"Oh, goody," she said.

The invitation had come at last.

SURPRISED to find her in when he called, but very pleased nonetheless, Bedford made a dinner date for that night with Tatty Chase, the other actress in his life and a woman with whom he was on much better terms than Claire Pell.

Blond, blue-eyed, with high Slavic cheekbones, and an English, upturned nose, Tatty had a trim, athletic figure, boundless enthusiasm, and an aristocratic self-assurance that had seen her through the worst humiliations that New York theater critics could devise.

For all her patrician beauty, Tatty had a natural flair for broad comedy. Bedford thought her perfect for those immensely popular Mack Sennett films they were making out in California, but Tatty insisted on confining herself to dramatic roles. If she managed to work as frequently as Claire did, it was due more to her generous financial backing of the plays she was in than the reception given her by the critics. They, too, appreciated Tatty's talent for comedy, even when she was playing Lady Macbeth.

Still in her twenties, though barely, Tatiana Olga Marie Anastasia Chase was the daughter of a wealthy New York banker and a Russian ballerina who had belonged to the nobility before her fortuitous move to a land now far beyond the reach of the Bolsheviks, who were shooting aristocrats the way British gentry did grouse.

Because of her father's wealth and prominence in the city, Tatty had been "debutante of the year" in 1914, but had quickly tired of "all that" and her family's politics and culture. She came to worship the late progressive President Teddy Roosevelt and was so vociferous in her condemnation of the Republican Party's conservative wing that Bedford's socialist friends in the Village sometimes took her for one of their own.

"Dee-lighted," she had said, with Rooseveltian vigor, when he had called to invite her out, and "dee-lighted" was how she appeared when she swung open the door of her stately townhouse on Seventy-sixth Street, just east of Fifth Avenue.

She was dressed in black chiffon, a sleeveless, scoop-necked, short-skirted dress with ruffles and matching shoes, and a black velvet hair ribbon. Her only jewelry was her customary pearl necklace that she claimed had been given her mother by Czarina Alexandra and which she wore everywhere, even in the bath.

"You are indeed the cat's pajamas," said Bedford, stepping inside.

She kissed him on the cheek, smiled, and then proclaimed: "Gin." Then, with a clatter of heels on parquet, she disappeared around a corner.

Returning with a tray bearing a martini shaker and two glasses, she set it down on a wall table. Shaking the shaker three times, she poured two drinks, then kissed Bedford warmly, this time on the mouth.

"I do adore you, darling," she said. "Sometimes." Then she handed him his drink.

There were some, including Sloane and at some moments himself, who wondered why he didn't ask Tatty to marry him. But he always recalled his father's advice to him on why never to marry a rich woman.

"She will never be able to understand," he said, "why you can't go sailing on Thursdays."

He'd had in mind for them that evening a small, cheap French restaurant a few blocks down Madison Avenue. She overruled him in favor of the Russian Tea Room.

"You said you wanted to talk about the aristocracy," she said. "What better place? One of the waiters there was an officer in my grandfather's regiment."

Even with the previous day's sale of a painting, Bedford's resources were limited. Perhaps if he lunched at his gallery and dined at his home and skipped the speakeasies for a week, he could manage it.

Tatty sensed his discomfort.

"And this is on me," she said. "You can pay me back when you're head of the Metropolitan Museum of Art. Drink up, and I'll call Albert."

"Who is Albert?"

"My driver. I had to hire one because the wretched State of New York has taken away my driving license."

"Any particular reason, or have the Bolsheviks taken over the Motor Vehicle Department, too?"

"I hit a police car."

"Whatever for?"

"It was sitting in the entranceway of my garage. At least, I thought it was my garage."

"Couldn't you wait for it to leave?"

"I was distracted."

Tatty owned a beautiful yellow Packard phaeton that, heretofore, had somehow managed to escape serious damage.

"And your car?"

"Oh, it will live. It's in the hospital, but it comes out in a day or two. In the meantime, I bought a nice Pierce-Arrow, so Albert will have something to drive."

I was a very long automobile, with a black top and crimson sides. The passenger compartment, commodious

enough even for Bedford to stretch out his legs, was separated from the driver by sliding glass, which Tatty pulled
shut. Though careful of her dress, she snuggled close to
him.

"Let's spoon," she said.

T**HE** short drive down Fifth Avenue along the park didn't
allow for much of that. As they turned west on Fifty-
seventh Street, Tatty sat up straight and tended to her hair
and pearls, which had gone askew.

"Are you still seeing Claire Pell?" she asked.

"I think we're still friends," he said, "but she is still not
seeing me."

"And your former fiancée?"

"Still former. If Margaret O'Neill were Queen of England, I think I'd be in the Tower of London at this point."

"So now you're taking up with some countess."

"No. Not at all. I've never met the woman. I'm trying
to find out about her, is all—for a friend."

"What friend?"

"Gertrude Vanderbilt Whitney."

Tatty tossed back her head. "Oh yes. The garbage scow
and ferry boat people."

"Now, Tatty. Don't be a snob."

"I'm not a snob, Bedford," she said, moving to the side.
"But you know what those people are like. One of them
lavishes the inside of a house with gold and marble and the
other says, 'Whatever she has, double it.' "

"The Czars lived so humbly."

"This is America. There is no aristocracy here. There
shouldn't be. And the first Vanderbilt did haul garbage. I
know it for a fact. How is this aristocracy?"

Bedford spoke gently. "Because this is America, they

no longer have to haul garbage. In Russia, they'd be in garbage for life."

"At the very least, if they're going to make so much money, they should share it. Think of all the people who *are* in garbage for life. I could take you down to the Lower East Side and you'd see plenty."

"I'm sure they give generously to charity."

He shouldn't have been chiding her. Tatty was the principal means of support of a settlement house near Hester Street.

"And these grotesque mansions," she continued, taking a slightly different tack. "Seventy rooms. A hundred and fifty rooms. My grandfather's estate in the Ukraine was larger than the entire state of Rhode Island. And what good did it do the family? The Bolsheviks took it and killed everyone they could, including the servants and farmhands. People like the Vanderbilts, they had better watch out. All that gold they splash around is going to cost them someday."

He could just imagine Tatty at the barricades, protest sign, pearl necklace, and all.

"Yes, Tatty," he said.

He took her hand. She did not pull it away.

"Sorry," she said. "Didn't mean to get into a blaze."

"No matter."

"But I actually do like your friend Mrs. Whitney. She's done something with her life. A few of her sculptures are really first rate."

THE headwaiter, doubtless a former grand duke, greeted Tatty with all the deference and effusion due the highest nobility, and led them to a favored, plush booth near the window. When she was a leading lady in a play, she got exactly the same swell treatment from the headwaiters of most Broadway joints, but didn't appreciate that as much as this.

As usual in such places, Tatty ordered for them both, then set elbows on the table, and leaned forward.

"Now tell me all about this countess," she said conspiratorially.

"I know practically nothing. I was going to ask you for advice on where I might go to find out something about this woman. I've exhausted all my possibilities. Every avenue."

She leaned still closer, her blue eyes bright with curiosity, and a little mischief. "I don't care about this Countess Zala. The mystery here, m'dear, is why the almighty Vanderbilts are worried about her, don't you think?"

"That they haven't made clear."

"And why are they calling upon you? Gladys Vanderbilt is married to this genuine Hungarian count, isn't she? He should know more about his fellow aristocrats than you or I could ever find out."

"It is puzzling."

"No it isn't. They obviously aren't interested in your finding out something for them. They're interested in having you go out there to do something for them."

"Do you think?"

"Of course I do. I'd love to go with you."

"I'm afraid the invitation was for me and Sloane."

Sloane was the only woman in New York who intimidated Tatty.

"Well, I hope you two will have a lovely, lovely time."

"It's nothing to do with romance. Sloane is a better friend of Gertrude's than I am."

The waiter brought two bowls of beet soup, bowing in courtly fashion afterward. Tatty rewarded him with one of her dazzling, curtain call smiles. Then she turned back to Bedford, serious now.

"As you know," she said, "I belong to the Russian Nobility Association. I am sure that among our many members there is someone related to Hungarian nobility. I will find out what I can."

"Well, thank you."

"And I don't want you arriving in a taxi cab, Bedford Green. I'll send my Packard around as soon as it's out of the garage. You and Sloane take it to Newport. I want you to arrive as befits your station."

"Tatty, I don't have any station."

"Bedford, if you arrive in my Packard—you will."

CHAPTER 4

THOUGH nearly all the route was over paved highways, and they were able to make particularly good progress on the Boston Post Road through Connecticut, it took a full day and evening just to reach the Rhode Island line. By the time they arrived on Jamestown Island, the last ferry across Narragansett Bay to Newport had left, and they were compelled to pass the night in an inn. It possessed few agreeable accommodations but provided them with a lovely if frustrating view of their destination across the water.

There was only one vacant room. Sloane had no objection to sharing, as they had found it necessary to do on a recent trip to France. But as in France, she insisted that one of them sleep in the room's only chair. Bedford naturally but unhappily volunteered to be that person.

As the car journey had diminished Sloane's enthusiasm for the Newport visit, the uncomfortable night at the inn had a similar effect upon Bedford. They barely spoke to each other at breakfast. On the ferry, they stayed in the Packard, again without speaking, until the breezy little sea voyage began to gentle Sloane's mood.

"Do you know, I've never been to Newport before," Sloane said. "Even when I was at Smith College."

"It's a Navy town in which the sailors are treated abominably by the millionaires whose way of life they defended in the late, great war."

"It looks pretty. From out here."

"That's especially true down where the mansions are. I don't know why more artists haven't painted here. Can't think of a one who has, actually."

"Money isn't a very attractive subject for a painting. Or greed."

"There's wealth and greed in Maine and on Cape Cod, and they get hundreds of painters every year."

"Would that I were at either place now."

"You'll feel better once we get to Gertrude's."

She lolled her head back against the seat. "No I won't. I've changed my mind about coming here. I think we've made a big mistake."

"Why?"

"It's just all too much." She closed her eyes. "Do you suppose they'll let us go straight to our rooms and just sleep?"

"Gertrude would let us do anything, but I don't suppose her sister Gladys will. It's she who's to be our hostess, I believe, not Gertrude. I suppose there'll be a full schedule of socially acceptable summer fun and games."

"Swell."

She turned away, looking off to the right, where some enormous sailing yachts could be seen at their moorings just past Goat Island.

"Good grief," she said. "What monsters."

"With full canvas, under sail, they look like moving mountains."

"Mountains of money."

Bedford hadn't yet decided whether Sloane was simply following the leftist political cant of Greenwich Village or this was a deep-seated antagonism. At all events, it did not auger well for their weekend.

"That boat with the green trim looks almost as big as one of those old clipper ships," Bedford said, indicating a long schooner with two raked masts. "Nothing like that on your Lake Michigan, I guess."

"Nothing that isn't carrying wheat or pig iron. What's the point of these things?"

"Amusement, and a singularly flagrant way of displaying wealth. J. P. Morgan liked to say that you can do business with anyone, but you sail only with gentlemen."

"That certainly sounds snotty."

"It was meant to be."

"Someone with a nose as grotesque as his ought to be more circumspect."

"That's unkind, don't you think?"

"You were never a *yachtsman*, were you, Bedford? You haven't been hiding that dirty little secret from me?"

He laughed. "When I was young, I once won the annual Wellfleet catboat race up on Cape Cod. And I've done a bit of sailing around here."

"And how big is a catboat?"

"These were about nineteen feet long." He smiled. "Not many staterooms."

"I suppose the Vanderbilts have one of these mountainous yachts."

"Doubtless several," Bedford said. "Gertrude's brother, the General, had a gigantic steam yacht called the *North Star* that he gave to the military during the war. But I'll bet he replaced it."

"What did the government do with it? Sail it back and forth along the German coast to make the Kaiser feel bad because he didn't have one?"

"He's Gertrude's brother, Sloane. Let's not hold it against him that he isn't a verse libre poet who hangs out in Chumley's."

THERE were two sets of gates in the high, wrought iron
fence that separated the Vanderbilts' "Breakers" from
the other mansions on Newport's Ochre Point Avenue.
Only one stood open and Bedford drove the big Packard
through it with care, thinking of how Tatty Chase would
have made her automotive entrance in a great spew of
flying gravel. As he proceeded down the diagonal drive,
he noted in the rearview mirror that someone had appeared mysteriously from the bordering trees and was
closing the gates behind him. He wasn't sure why, but
that made him uncomfortable.

Reaching the wide gravel court by the porte cochère of
the main entrance, he parked as far out of the way as possible, then pulled on the heavy hand brake and turned off
the car's big engine, which shuddered twice, then ceased
its powerful labors. In the sudden stillness that followed,
he at length heard the call of a seagull, and then another.
He always felt happier at the seashore.

Three male servants materialized beside the car. Without a word, one of them unbuckled the straps holding the
luggage at the rear and hefted their suitcases while another
man opened the door for Sloane and the third fellow—the
butler, from the look of him—performed the same service
for Bedford. Then he led them all into the house.

"If you would kindly wait in here," he said, indicating
a wood-paneled room off the foyer. "It is early, and I do
not believe the countess has arisen."

Bedford and Sloane obeyed. The chamber was dimly
lit, with a narrow, shadowed window. There were a few
massive pieces of wood and leather furniture. The pictures on the wall were all family portraits, including an
outsized one of the original Commodore.

"Where is the art?" said Sloane, glancing about the
walls. "At least your Mr. Morgan had art. Henry Clay

Frick has art. Carnegie and Mellon have art. These . . ."
She shook her head.

"I thought I saw a picture or two out in the corridor."

"Sailing ships or something. I mean *art*!"

Bedford looked to his watch. "It's nine-forty," he said.
"And the countess 'has not arisen.' "

Bedford leaned forward to catch her eye. "I thought
you wanted to come here."

"Actually, I wanted you to come here."

"And why is that?"

"Because I think you're still a bit of a snob, Bedford
Green, and I thought a weekend here might cure you
of it."

"But you came along, too."

"I thought it might be amusing, but now I'm feeling
decidedly uncomfortable. This grotesquely huge house.
Gates so high you'd think they came from Versailles."

Her head turned quickly toward the doorway, where
the butler was standing.

"The countess will receive you at eleven o'clock in the
library," the man said. "In the meantime, allow me to
show you to your rooms."

"Where is Gertrude?" Sloane asked as they filed out.

"Mrs. Whitney is not here," said the butler, and he said
nothing more.

They proceeded down a normal-sized hall into a vast
interior expanse that might better have belonged in an
Italian palace. Actually, an Italian palace might have fit
into it. The ornate ceiling was at least fifty feet high. The
"room" was a good fifty feet in all its dimensions.

A red-carpeted grand staircase led from this Great
Hall, as the butler called it, through an arch up to the second level, which was rimmed by a marble railing and was
open to the floor below on all four sides. The vaulted
ceiling was gilded and encrusted with decorative art in
elaborate neoclassical patterns. If there was an inch of

space in this house that hadn't had money lavished on it, Bedford assumed it was in the servants' quarters, but they, too, were probably well marbled.

The butler took them first to Sloane's room, which was mauve and pink, and then went on to Bedford's, which fittingly enough was green, and had a view of the side lawn.

"There's a bath adjoining," the servant said. "There are taps for either fresh or salt water, as it pleases you. Both hot and cold. Unless you'd prefer that we draw it for you."

"No thanks," said Bedford with a grin. "That's one thing I'm very good at—drawing baths."

"As you wish, sir. The countess will be in the library at eleven o'clock."

He spoke as if repeating a command, which Bedford supposed he was. When the man had gone, Bedford sat down on the edge of the bed and took in the view from the window, which had been opened to the warm summer air. Through the trees, he could see a house neighboring the Breakers, though it seemed a mile away. He wondered if the mention of the bath had also been in the way of instruction. If so, he would ignore it. He had already bathed that morning. If they wished to think him a tramp or a bohemian for failing to do so an hour and a half later, he was of no mind to care.

It wasn't long before he began to feel imprisoned, just sitting there. He yearned to see the sea, and be near it. Leaving his bag unpacked, he opened the door and, feeling something of an interloper, walked quietly down to the balcony overlooking the Great Hall. As he had not noticed before, there were a number of glass doors off to the left. Opening one, he passed into an upstairs Italian loggia filled with wicker furniture and potted plants. It had marble floors and granite arches along its seaward side that were open to the air. Going to a stone railing beneath one, he looked down at a wide, open terrace below. Beyond it was a long, rolling, perfect lawn descending a gentle slope to the sea—or at least the arm of it known as Rhode Island Sound.

There was a full, cooling breeze here, as there had been on the bay. He took in a deep, happy breath, then looked to either side, surprised to see, two arches distant, his friend Sloane Smith.

"Taking the sea air or did you just feel trapped in your room?" he asked.

"Both," she said. "There's no art in there, either."

He gestured toward the gorgeous lawn. "Would you like to go for a barefoot amble?"

"Yes, I would, but I'm not sure they'd approve."

"Well, let's keep our shoes on, then—for now."

Creeping like burglars, they descended the grand staircase and, with some doing, found their way to the doors leading through the large downstairs loggia and thence onto the terrace. Bedford was surprised that no one was using it on such a lovely day, then noticed a young man reclining on a chaise longue at the other end of it, reading a book. Of a sudden, he looked up, peering around over the back of the chaise like a small boy annoyed to have been caught doing something he shouldn't.

"Bedford Green," said Bedford, taking a step nearer. "We're guests of—"

"The Vanderbilts, no doubt."

"Yes. Are you a guest, too?" Sloane asked.

"No, I'm afraid I'm one of those Vanderbilts." Though boyish, he seemed old enough to have been in the war. There was something about him that suggested he had. "I'm Neil," he said, rising. He was dressed in gray flannels, white shirt, and white tennis sweater. "Neil Vanderbilt."

They all shook hands and the young man's annoyance

vanished. He smiled at Sloane, a little roguishly. "I must know you from somewhere."

"I don't think so. I'm just a poor girl from Chicago."

They all stood there then, awkwardly.

"We were about to take a walk down to the water," Bedford said.

"Yes," said the man, his eyes still on Sloane. "Please do."

He returned to his chair as Bedford nudged Sloane away.

"You're a rich girl from Chicago," he said when they were out of earshot. "Why do you say these things?"

"Not rich by their standards."

"Who cares? Let's enjoy the day."

"There may actually be hope," she said. "Did you see what he was reading?"

"No."

"*Three Soldiers*. John Dos Passos' book."

"That settles it."

"Settles what?"

"He was in the war."

THERE was a long hedge bordering the foot of the lawn and a path around one end that led down to the rocky little beach. Two carved granite benches had been set there to either side of a small outdoor table.

"I'll bet they go skinny-dipping down here," Bedford said.

"I'll bet they don't, but one could."

"You want to?"

"Bedford, please."

"Just a joke. But I daresay Edna St. Vincent Millay would."

"She'd go skinny-dipping all right, but she wouldn't go in the water."

It was time to change the subject. Bedford seated himself on one of the benches.

"That headland you see across the Sound—that's Easton Point. On the other side of that is Sachuest Bay and what they call Second Beach. Do you know what I did there one night?"

"Went skinny-dipping," said Sloane, seating herself on the other bench.

"Yes. But that was another occasion. This was five years ago. A man I knew from the war, an Irishman, named Liam O'Bannion. He had an ocean-going yacht and took me out on it. We ended up in Sachuest Bay."

"You see. You're one of those yachtsman after all."

"Liam wasn't a swell. He'd become a criminal. His yacht was full of scotch whiskey and he'd invited me aboard because he couldn't get anyone else he could trust that night who knew the waters. He had three trucks waiting, right there on Second Beach."

"You didn't tell the police?"

"Sloane, if I wished to commit suicide, there are pleasanter ways of doing it than ratting on Liam O'Bannion. As a matter of fact, I helped him unload it—so we could be away from there all the quicker."

She lifted her head, as though to better see how it might have happened. Then she looked down.

"Some of your friends scare me, Bedford."

"Me, too. Only Liam O'Bannion is not my friend."

"But you said the war . . ."

"You make enemies as well as friends."

"Then why did you get on his boat?"

"He gave me little choice. He never does." Bedford pulled out his watch. "It's nearly eleven." He brushed another bit of smudge from his white duck trousers. "I wonder if I'm appropriately dressed."

"Bedford, you're the only man in Greenwich Village who always looks like he's about to have tea with the Vanderbilts. You're inappropriately dressed there—not here."

He got to his feet. "You look perfect."

"However I look, I'd rather be back on Grove Street."

"Give it a chance. Remember, it's our good friend Gertrude. And we're supposed to be helping her."

The sun was warm, and they walked slowly back up the undulating lawn, which seemed soft enough to lie down on. Bedford thought that a far better way to spend the beautiful day than whatever their hosts had planned for them. He and Sloane could recline in the sun and gaze upon the sea, perhaps holding hands.

It was a short-lived fantasy. The butler was waiting on the terrace.

"The countess is waiting for you in the library," he said, looking at his watch, though Bedford was certain he already knew the time to the very second.

"Thank you," he said.

The room was also high and oversized, though it seemed friendlier than most of the others because it was lined with well-filled bookshelves. The books themselves were expensively bound and all looked the same, as though the owner had purchased them as one enormous set, which perhaps he had.

Bedford glanced up at the ceiling as they entered, noting that it was indeed covered with gold leaf.

The Countess Szechenyi, Gertrude's sister Gladys, was seated in a chair set close to the tall, white marble fireplace, as though for warmth, though it was summer and no fire was on the hearth. She kept looking at it, as though there was something fascinating in the bas relief carvings she hadn't noticed before, until the butler finally spoke.

"Your guests, madam," he said.

She rose, turning slowly with great dignity, a queen receiving courtiers. Then at once her eyes flared and her jaw dropped a little.

"You're not Dr. Horvath!" she said. She looked from Bedford to Sloane, and then back again. "Who are you? What are you doing in my house?"

CHAPTER 5

BEDFORD drove out through the Breakers' gates as slowly as he had entered, a small, defiant gesture that belied his raging impulse to flee from the place as swiftly as possible.

"That was about as mortifying an experience as I've ever been through with you," said Sloane. "And there have been plenty."

"I'm sorry," he said. "This certainly was all my fault. When Gertrude said her place at Newport, I just assumed she meant the Breakers. I had no idea she and Harry had a house of their own. You could fit every Vanderbilt I ever heard of in that 'Great Hall' at the Breakers."

"She didn't give you an address?"

"I suppose, in Newport, Vanderbilts don't need addresses."

"But you know where to go now?"

"Yes. Over to Bellevue and then down a couple of blocks. Just as the butler instructed."

"Too, too amusing that the countess didn't recognize your name, even though you were such a big whiz New York society columnist. If I weren't so glum, I'd laugh."

"Countesses probably don't read the *New York Day*."

"Who do you suppose that Dr. Horvath is that they mistook you for?"

"No idea."

"Isn't that a Hungarian name?"

"I believe it is. But as the countess's husband is Hungarian, that shouldn't be a surprise."

"A Hungarian doctor, traveling with a young, attractive, female assistant, to whom he isn't married."

Bedford chuffed the big Packard to a halt at Bellevue, waiting as a high-wheeled truck filled with produce rumbled and rattled by.

"How do you know she's young and attractive, Detective Smith?" he said, turning into the tree-lined avenue. "And why not married?"

"The butler didn't bat an eye when he saw me—and if I may be immodest, I am young and attractive. And they gave us separate rooms without even asking."

She folded her arms, looking disdainfully at the high walls of an estate as they rolled by.

T**HE** summer home of Gertrude Vanderbilt Whitney was much less ostentatious than the family's great pile of stone up the shore. Pale gray in color with white trim and peppermint-striped awnings, Gertrude's house was only two stories, though it had a steeple-like central tower that reached to nearly four. There were flowering shrubs everywhere, with creeping vines covering twin trellises on the front porch. It was definitely a porch, not a veranda, though it wrapped around the side of the house.

"Are we calling on Gertrude, or Willa Cather?" Sloane said. "This place would look fine in Dubuque."

"You were concerned about *my* snobbery?" Bedford said, halting the car and turning off the engine.

He heard his name called, and saw Mrs. Whitney hurrying toward them from the porch. She was dressed in pants and a light summer blouse—a rather daringly informal ensemble for Edith Wharton land.

"You darling people," she said. "I feared you'd been in a motor crash."

Bedford explained the reason for their delay, apologizing for the faux pas. Gertrude simply laughed.

"You must have given Gladys a fright," she said. "She's always been a bit nervous about strangers getting into that big house. But don't worry. We'll put things right later. Now come in, come in."

They were shown to rooms less commodious but far more comfy and inviting than those at the Breakers—each with an ample view of water. Gertrude gave them time to wash and change, then served lunch on a small terrace facing the ocean. She chattered happily about the weather, the summer season in Newport, a rumor that the recently late President Harding may have been murdered by his wife, and the artist Edward Hopper, whose work continued to enthrall her. But nothing about ladies named Zala, or a need for a gun.

"Some say Hopper's paintings are all about death," Gertrude said, lighting a cigarette. "This impending sense of it, even in his landscapes. But I disagree. It's simply a mystery. We don't know what's impending, what's lurking. Something is, but we don't know what. That's the fascination of his pictures. I just love them."

"Do you think he'll be exhibited?" Sloane asked.

"Of course. I'll do it myself." She pushed back her chair. "Now, I have to run into town for a bit. You two make yourself at home. Use my beach. Whatever you want."

Bedford stood up, as Gertrude wanted to rise. "Is there anything you wish us to do?" he asked.

"Do? Enjoy yourselves. We'll dine here tonight. You can meet my son, Neil."

"We just did," said Sloane.

"Where?"

"At the Breakers?"

"Oh, that must have been the other Neil—the General's son. He likes to stay there, though his parents don't. Tonight's Neil is mine. Tomorrow, we're to go sailing with the General. In the afternoon."

"He's a Neil, too, isn't he?" said Sloane. "What do you call them all when you're all together?"

"We call them Neil," said Gertrude, laughing. "Except for the General, who's called Neily. Anyway, the boys all know who they are. Tomorrow night is the big party at the Breakers—a dance party. You should like that, Sloane. I do enjoy watching you dance. They've hired a band from New York. A jazz band. I believe it has some colored musicians."

Sloane smiled sweetly.

"So," said Gertrude. "I must be off."

"Didn't you want to talk to me about something?" Bedford asked.

"Oh yes, Bedford. About lots and lots of things. And I'm sure we'll have lots of time to do that this weekend."

She patted his shoulder, then hurried into the house. A moment later, a butler and maid appeared and began clearing the table. When the task was completed, the butler paused and asked if they wanted refreshment.

"Do you mean lemonade or a cocktail?" Sloane asked.

"Whatever you wish, miss," he said.

"I'll have lemonade with some gin in it," Sloane said.

"Me, too," said Bedford.

"Lots of gin," said Sloane.

When they had finished their drinks, Sloane leaned forward, slipped off her shoes, rolled her stockings down over her knees, then pulled them off, one after the other.

"Where are you going?" Bedford asked as she stood up.

"For a walk," Sloane said. "On the lawn."

GERTRUDE'S husband, Harry, whom Bedford had only met twice, had remained in New York, his absence explained as having something to do with horses. There were consequently only the four of them at dinner, with the conversation dominated by Mrs. Whitney and her son, a man of serious mien in his middle twenties.

Like Bedford, he had been a flyer in the war and Gertrude was very proud of the fact that he'd been awarded the Distinguished Flying Cross. Like most combat veterans, he was reluctant to talk about his war experience, which included becoming the Army Air Service's chief instructor of advanced combat tactics at a very young age. But he seemed uncomfortably keen on learning more about Bedford's military service—though he already seemed to know quite a bit about it.

"I've heard of you, Captain Green," he said. "You're the Yank who insisted on flying with the Brits."

"I flew with the French as well," Bedford said. "Before the Brits."

"Right. No one's calling you timid. You were in the thick of it before we got into the war. Grant you that. But when we did get in, you switched to the British. Why not fight for your own country? We could have used you."

Sloane hated talk of the war but now made an exception.

"Bedford shot down three German planes," she said peremptorily, as though that sufficed to settle the matter.

"Right," said the young Whitney. "But they went down as French and British kills."

"There was a pilot in my squadron named Liam O'Bannion," Bedford said. "His cousin was killed by the British Army in the 1916 Dublin Easter rebellion. He shot down eleven German aircraft. You might better ask him why he flew for the British."

The discourse had ceased to be mere conversation. Neil Whitney said nothing more. No one did, for more than a minute. Bedford sensed Gertrude's eyes coldly upon him, as though considering whether she had made a mistake with her invitation.

"When I was with the French," Bedford began, "there was another American pilot in the unit who was colored. Eugene Bullard. The French called him 'the Black Swallow of Death.' "

"A *colored* pilot? In combat?"

"He had a couple of kills. He was a first-rate pilot. When the U.S. joined the war, the American pilots in our *escadrille* transferred to an American squadron, but they wouldn't take Eugene, because he was a black man. This was ridiculous. A veteran pilot like Eugene was worth a hundred inexperienced white ones. It made me angry, and I switched to the Royal Flying Corps, with the help of friends. With their continuing help, I was able to stay there."

"And were there colored pilots in your British outfit?" Neil Whitney asked.

"No. There weren't. But the U.S. Army should have taken Gene."

"I can see where all that must have been awkward for you," said Gertrude quickly. "Now, what would everyone like to do this evening? I have some castings of some new sculptures in my little studio here. Would you like to see them?"

"Very much," said Bedford. "But shouldn't we talk about this countess of yours?"

Neil Whitney gave him an astonished look.

"Bedford, I don't suppose my sister Gladys would very much want to be talked about," Gertrude said.

Bedford flushed. "I didn't mean Mrs. Szechenyi. I was referring to . . ."

Gertrude's face remained blank. Sloane was not helping.

"I believe you had some concerns about a Countess Zala," Bedford said. "A Hungarian lady."

Mrs. Whitney fidgeted in her chair, her hands fluttering a moment. "Oh, that? Yes, I had a curiosity about someone, and thought that you, being a man of so many parts—but now all my questions have been answered. I invited you two out here to have fun, Bedford. So let's do that and not worry about anything else."

Her son, however, still had aviation on his mind.

"Air transport, Green," he said. "It's the future."

"How do you mean?"

"Airplanes. Big planes. Like those Hun Gotha bombers. They'll carry people, just like trains do. Someday they'll replace trains. Who knows? One day they'll replace ships. Seaplanes, Green. Think of that."

Bedford thought of that. "I suppose you're right. But not anytime soon."

"There you're wrong. Deuced wrong. In a year or two we'll have some sort of transport service in the air. And we're going to need pilots. Good pilots."

He was talking not in generalities but specifics. The "we" included himself.

"Are you offering me a position?" Bedford said.

The other man grinned. "Sure."

"Bedford owns an art gallery, Neil," his mother said somewhat sharply, as though her son had suggested something unseemly. "He's very happy doing that."

Neil Whitney now frowned, as though hearing lunacy.

"Who is Dr. Horvath?" Sloane asked Gertrude.

"Who is who?"

"The doctor Bedford was mistaken for at the Breakers," said Sloane. "Is someone ill?"

"Ill? Why no. Dr. Horvath isn't a physician. He's a professor of some sort. History, I think. A friend of my sister and her husband. A recent friend."

"Hungarian?"

"Yes. I believe so. Why do you ask?"

SLOANE came into Bedford's room as he was preparing for bed, knocking before entering but not waiting for a response. She dropped into a chair by the window and looked out it for a long moment, as though there was something there beside darkness.

"I want to go home," she said finally.

Bedford had been unbuttoning his shirt, but stopped. He seated himself on the edge of the bed, smiling pleasantly, wishing he had his shoes on. Walking about in socks was ill-mannered, his grandfather had always said—the same grandfather who had instructed him that a gentleman never went about in public without his jacket.

"As you wish. Are you sure I'm cured of my snobbery?"

"I don't know if you're cured, but they aren't."

"Don't you want to find out about this mysterious countess?"

"Countesses are beginning to irritate me."

"Perhaps tomorrow's party will revive your spirits."

She rose wearily, and started toward the door. "An impossibility. Good night, Bedford."

CHAPTER 6

BEDFORD'S notion of sailing was beating close-hauled into a twenty-five knot wind with water hissing over the rail in a boat small enough to require one's weight hiked well over the windward side to keep the craft from capsizing.

The Vanderbilts appeared to prefer floating mansions. The General's sailing yacht *Ilderim* was nearly a hundred feet long at the bowsprit, a seagoing, sloop-rigged vessel large enough for tea dancing on the aft deck. The gentleman seemed a very competent skipper, taking the helm as they passed out of Narragansett Bay and rounded Brenton Point into ocean waters used for the America's Cup races. His crew responded in lively fashion to his politely rendered commands, setting the sails with perfect trim for the quartering breeze.

The General appeared to be immensely proud of his boat, which was as neat, polished, and splendidly rigged as any Bedford had ever encountered and a most agreeable vessel to sail from the look of the way she handled. The General said it had originally belonged to his brother

Willie, who had died the year he'd acquired it as a twenty-first birthday present, leaving it to "Neily."

Tall and thin, with a manicured Vandyke beard and moustache that seemed a mate to those sported by England's King George and the late Czar Nicholas, the General had the same large eyes and dark brows as his sisters. Straight as a mast whether standing or seated, he seemed well suited to his military title, but when he smiled—a careful, cheek-crinkling grin—he put Bedford in mind of a master jewel thief.

"First-rate afternoon," said the General.

That it was, though the wind continued light, with occasional puffs and gusts. Unlike the smudgy haze that shrouded midsummer New York, the Rhode Island sky was clean and bright. The great houses on the cliffs and bluffs of the Newport peninsula stood out clearly—the windows of some glittering in the sun as they passed by.

"Do you come out here often?" Bedford asked, looking up the towering mainmast. The sails on the *Ilderim* probably cost as much as Bedford was going to earn from his gallery that year.

"Not as often as I'd like." A shadow of discomfort came over the General's face. "Mr. Green, aren't you the same gentleman who writes a column for the *New York Day*?"

Bedford hesitated. "Used to do. Now I deal in art."

"I believe you were most kind to my wife, in your writings," the General said. "She has remarked upon it, for that was, shall we say, unusual."

Bedford had written of the flamboyant society lady as though she were an admirable theatrical personage like Claire Pell. He'd had no idea how these columns had been received by their subject.

"I'm surprised you would read a paper like the *New York Day*, sir."

"Actually, I haven't. But Grace has mentioned some of the things you wrote."

"Well, she's made a considerable contribution to the life of the city," Bedford said cautiously. "I just took note of that."

"As I say, Mr. Green. It's appreciated. Newspapers are seldom so well mannered."

The General's wife was not aboard the yacht, but Bedford expected she'd be noticeably present at the evening's frolic.

They sailed on silently for a few minutes. There were other boats out on the water—most of them as large.

It seemed a good opportunity.

"Are you by any chance acquainted with a Countess Zala?" Bedford said.

The General blinked, looking a bit startled, then turned to adjust the helm, as though they were on specific course, and not just cruising about.

"Why do you ask?" he said finally.

Bedford had expected him to say he'd never heard of her.

"Someone in the city was asking about her," Bedford said, not revealing that he meant himself. "In connection with Newport."

"Oh."

"Does she have a house here?"

"I believe there is some such woman living up the bay in Bristol," the General said.

"Will she be at the party this evening?"

The General's eyes were now fixed forward, at the other passengers gathered near the main cabin. "No."

With that, he changed the subject to America's Cup racing.

After a few minutes, Bedford excused himself and joined the rest of the passengers, seating himself next to an unhappy-looking Sloane.

"Enjoying the sea air?" he asked.

"This is such a pointless amusement," she said, waving dismissively at the yacht and all that surrounded it.

They were apart from the others—and, Bedford hoped, out of earshot.

"Pointless, but pleasant," Bedford said quietly. "Perhaps you'd have more fun with my kind of sailing."

"I'd get all wet."

"You must try it sometime."

"Not this bloody weekend."

"You'll cheer up tonight. A jazz band."

"I'm going to get blotto."

Bedford patted her knee. "Maybe I'll join you."

Young Neil, the General's son, was sitting against the rail on the other side of the yacht, still reading. His eyes caught Bedford's and he nodded, then returned to his book.

Close to the companionway leading down to the *Ilderim*'s main salon was a very striking dark-haired young woman in white skirt and navy blouse who could not have been more than twenty. She glanced away when Bedford looked at her but he had noticed her watching them.

She'd introduced herself simply as Gertrude's sister-in-law but Bedford knew more precisely who she was, recognizing her not for herself but for her exact resemblance to her twin sister, Thelma, whom Bedford had encountered at a number of Upper East Side parties during his social reporting days.

Thelma and Gloria, the glorious Morgan girls, as bound for spectacular marriages as streaking meteorites for the earth. Thelma had got herself a British aristocrat; Gloria, a Vanderbilt.

"She keeps looking at me," Sloane said.

"Maybe she's afraid you're competition," Bedford said. "That's Gloria Morgan. She married Reggie Vanderbilt two years ago. He was forty-two and she but a maid of eighteen. Now she's by way of being a widow."

"A man as rich as that had to wait until forty-two to get married?"

"He was married before—to a very beautiful woman named Cathleen Neilson. They divorced and she remarried, to a Newport man. Colford's the name, I think."

"Wasn't Reggie the brother Gertrude said drank too much?"

"Hootch and horses. That was Reggie."

"And fillies," said Sloane. She seemed annoyed. "That Gloria is staring at me again."

"If you go sit by the General, she won't bother you."

"No thanks. I'll stick with you. But only because you're my ticket out of here."

"We should have some time before we have to get ready for this evening," Bedford said to Sloane. "Would you care to accompany me on a little drive up to Bristol?"

"Is that on the way out of here?"

"Not really. It's a small port on the eastern shore of the bay—about an hour away."

"You just don't want me to get blotto."

She smiled at him, then noticed that young Neil had his eyes on her as well, with almost rude directness. Her smile broadened to almost comic proportions. She waved vigorously. Then she leaned close to Bedford and kissed him hard on the mouth. She'd had more gin, and blotto seemed not far distant.

THE eastern road up the eastern side of Narragansett Bay went to Providence and was paved. Still, the Packard managed to kick up dust, compelling Sloane to scrunch down behind the motorcar's windshield.

"How do you propose to find this countess?" she asked.

"There can't be many in such a little town."

"I don't know. Rhode Island seems to be knee deep in them."

He took note of one of the gauges on the Packard's dashboard.

"We'll start at this filling station," he said.

THE attendant, a youth who wore a woolen cap despite the heat, was of no help. Neither was an older woman they stopped along the sidewalk of the town's main street, or two men who were varnishing a hauled-up sailboat at a waterfront boatyard a block to the west. The grocer knew of no one named Zala. Neither did the postmaster.

Bedford doubted that the General was a devious man who would deliberately mislead him.

They were standing on the brick sidewalk next to the Packard, which was occasioning stares from a few passing motorists.

"I think we have exhausted the possibilities of this municipality," Sloane said.

He looked down the street. "Let's try one more place."

There was a bookstore in the middle of the town, an establishment where people might be better informed and more prone to conversation. The proprietor, a studious sort of fellow with a remarkably full brown beard and old-fashioned small round spectacles, seemed wary of Bedford and his questions at first, claiming the name "Zala" was in no way familiar to him. But as Bedford described the lady in question at greater length—as young, dark-haired, very pretty, perhaps neurotic, and Hungarian—he caught a glint of recognition in the man's eyes.

"So you know her," Bedford said.

"No. Not even sure if it's who you mean. But there's a woman up the shore a ways. A real beauty, but crazy as a loon. Got some money, that's for sure. But she doesn't spend it in Bristol."

"Do you know her name?"

"No, sir."

"Is she Hungarian?"

"Something like that."

"How do I get there?"

"Take the Providence road about a mile north of town. You'll come to a sign saying 'Maxwell's Boats.' Take that road left, and just before you get to the boatyard, there's a dirt lane to the right that goes along the shore. Old gray house there with a little beach."

"Thank you." Bedford decided he ought to reward the man with a purchase that Sloane might like. He chose Edna Ferber's *So Big*.

"THANK you," Sloane said. "That's very sweet of you. But unfortunately, I've read it."

He sighed. "Gertrude has some Edith Wharton. I know you haven't read any of that."

"I'm going to get blotto, remember?"

"Mrs. Wharton reads better that way." He started the Packard.

THE little shore road was more a gravel path than anything, but the heavy Packard managed it without trouble, though it unfortunately dirtied itself splashing through several muddy puddles. Bedford was going to have to stop somewhere and restore the magnificent automobile's appearance before returning it to Tatty.

The gray house was not hard to find, for there was no other near it. Bedford parked on a scrubby sort of lawn and got out, closing the car door quietly. Sloane remained where she was, looking as though she might go to sleep.

Bedford rapped twice on the wooden frame of the screen door. When there was no response, he peered inside, noting a lot of wicker furniture but little else to indicate active human habitation. He called out "Hello" twice, and then the name of Countess Zala. Neither produced a reply.

Repressing an impulse to open the door and step inside, Bedford walked around one side of the house, finding some bushes, a patch of lawn, and the rocky little beach. He stood at its edge, watching a large sloop with dirty sails work its way up the brilliant blue waters of the bay. Then, turning to go back to the car, he noticed just beyond the bushes a sprawled human form.

Moving closer, he saw it was a barefoot young man, lying on his back in a sleeveless undershirt and dungarees. For a moment, Bedford feared he might be dead, then heard a snort and the rattling beginnings of a snore.

He walked up to the man carefully, standing by his head. He was an unusually handsome fellow, but dirty, disheveled, and unshaven.

"Excuse me," Bedford said. "Could you tell me if this is the residence of Countess Zala?"

The man's eyes opened, then quickly shut, then slowly opened once more. He seemed unable to focus—or speak. All that came out of his mouth were burbles and grunts. Sniffing, Bedford could smell the cheap, bootleg whiskey.

"Sir!" said Bedford loudly. "Can you hear me?"

The man said something unintelligible. Leaning closer, Bedford realized it was profanity, uttered in mumbles. He wondered what other substances the young man had consumed.

He heard his name being called.

"Sorry," he said, returning to Sloane.

"Did you find her?" she said.

"I think this must be the wrong house," he said.

CHAPTER 7

SLOANE made good on her promise, downing two more gins before dinner and two glasses of wine during the course of the meal, which was taken on the rear terrace of Gertrude's house. No one seemed to pay much mind to her indulgence, though Bedford was rattled by her frequent and overloud laughter. Sloane was a woman who smiled when amused, but was not given to hilarity. He sensed a bumpy evening, commencing soon.

"We should be going," said Gertrude. She looked to her son, whose attention was fixed upon Sloane. "Neil, would you like to drive?"

The younger man nodded, without shifting his gaze. Sloane appeared not to notice him. Her eyes on the darkening sea, seeing something else—or nothing at all.

"Sloane," Bedford said. "We're going to the party now."

"The party," she repeated. "Oh goody."

Bedford rose and reached to take her hand, but the gesture was declined.

THE British tropical custom of wearing white dinner jackets against the heat had not quite taken hold in Newport, but Bedford wore his happily, for it had been a gift from Tatty. Gertrude's son was dressed more traditionally in black tuxedo. He seemed to view Bedford as a curiosity.

Gertrude was showing more flair, wearing an extremely expensive summery silk party dress that came down almost to her ankles. Sloane's white frock was less costly and more shimmering, and reached only to her knees, if that. Her only jewelry was conspicuous—an emerald and gold necklace Bedford had never seen before, the color close to matching the gray-green of her eyes. Bedford worried now that in her present state—or a worse one to come—she might lose the thing.

She was still seated, though the others were standing.

"Time to move on, dear," Gertrude said.

Sloane was looking a bit fuzzy. "Would they notice if we didn't come? It is so much more pleasant just sitting here with you, Gertrude."

"Oh my yes, Gladys would notice," Gertrude replied. "She is styling this a *modern* evening, what with jazz music and all. She's gone to some effort."

"Oh dear." Sloane got shakily to her feet.

Bedford moved quickly to her side again, firmly putting a hand to her elbow. Then off they went.

THE dance orchestra could be heard from the end of the Breakers' drive, which was crowded with automobiles of every expensive kind. The music actually was jazz, amazingly—not the uninhibited sort played at Harlem's Cotton Club, but rather sedate and more suitable for the fox trot. Bedford thought he recognized the orchestra's style as that of a New York hotel band of his acquaintance, but that group wasn't noted for clientele this high up the social ladder.

Pulling up behind a peach-colored Hispano-Suiza roadster, Neil quickly hopped out and went to Gertrude's side of the car, snapping open the door. Sloane stumbled getting out, but managed to regain her balance, moving on ahead of Bedford.

They were greeted in the Great Hall by the countess and her envoy husband. She was far friendlier to Bedford and Sloane than she'd been in their first encounter, calling Bedford by his first name and inquiring after his general happiness in his time thus far at Newport. The count, however—so stiffly erect it seemed a slight push would make him topple backward—was unpleasantly curt, responding to introductions with only a quick nod and an even briefer handshake.

Bedford moved on into the party, searching the crowd of guests for familiar faces. He found only Gloria Morgan Vanderbilt, who was with a woman Bedford recognized as her equally beautiful, flamboyant, and socially ambitious twin sister Thelma. They were dancing together, and laughing.

Turning to rejoin Sloane, he found she had gone some distance and was in the company of a waiter, who was unfortunately bearing champagne on a tray. He watched her drink one glass quickly and then take another.

Looking away, he caught sight of the tall figure of the General, who was standing near one of the huge doors that opened onto the lower loggia and the wide terrace beyond. The gentleman noticed him and gave a polite, friendly wave.

"Did you enjoy the sailing this afternoon?" he asked as Bedford approached.

"Very much so," said Bedford politely.

"I expect you might prefer a bit more wind," the General said.

"Yes, as I presume would you."

The General took that as a compliment. "Perhaps we can do better tomorrow."

Bedford had hoped to return to New York the next day. He watched the dancers a moment without speaking, then said, "I went to Bristol this afternoon."

"Whatever for?" The General spoke the words as though humorously.

"To look for this Countess Zala."

"And why is that, Mr. Green?"

Bedford could play tennis with words, too. "I wish I knew."

"Did you find her?"

"Yes—which is to say, I was directed to what I was told was her residence."

"And was she there?"

"No."

"Well, then."

"But it was curious."

"Her residence was curious?"

"Yes. Not the sort of house in which you'd expect to find a countess."

The General smiled, lifting his eyes to the glittering in-laid ceiling. "Not like this."

"Not at all."

"Well, these are hard times for aristocracy, are they not? Most especially the Eastern European sort."

"They seem to be particularly hard for this countess."

"If she is a countess." The General was looking past him. "There's Grace. She'd never forgive me if I didn't in-troduce you."

"I've met your wife, General—in New York. Several times, actually."

"Well, I'm sure she'll be delighted to see you again. Come along, then."

He took Bedford by the arm and ushered him rather determinedly out onto the terrace. Sloane was not far away, dancing with the young Neil Vanderbilt who was the General's son. He appeared remarkably unhappy for someone with the most beautiful woman in Greenwich Village in his arms. For her part, Sloane merely looked blotto. She started to wave at Bedford, but before he could respond, he found himself before the inimitable Grace Wilson Vanderbilt.

Bedford could think of nothing better to do than bow. In response, she blinked and smiled, tentatively, apparently not recognizing him.

"This is Bedford Green, Grace," said the General. "The gentleman from the newspaper. Bedford, my wife, Grace—an admirer of your work."

Her jeweled hand shot out, grasping Bedford's.

"Yes, I know you!" she said. "I've so enjoyed your coverage of the social scene."

"I'm afraid I've abandoned the social scene—and newspapers. I sell paintings for a living now. I own a gallery."

"He's a neighbor of Gertrude's in New York," said the General, as though that might make Bedford more socially acceptable.

"Well, we shall have to buy one." She turned to her husband. "Musn't we, Neily?"

The General nodded pleasantly, but without enthusiasm. There was a wariness in his eyes Bedford hadn't noticed before.

"Pity you're no longer writing your column," said his wife. "We have all Newport here this evening."

"I'm sure the local paper will take appropriate note."

"Oh no, Mr. Green. They're not invited." She smiled at her husband. "Shall we dance, Neily?"

The General stepped forward. "Do excuse us, Mr. Green."

Bedford watched them awhile, then searched once more for Sloane, without success.

A moment later, Gloria Morgan Vanderbilt was at Bedford's side.

"Bedford Green," she said.

"Yes."

"You've written about me."

"I hope not displeasingly."

"Dance with me."

"Yes, ma'am."

Taking his hand, she led him out onto the dance floor.

"Do you mind?" she asked.

"Mind, Mrs. Vanderbilt?"

"Dancing with me. You seem disturbed." She had a slight accent. Bedford recalled that she was born in Belgium and had spent much of her childhood abroad.

"Not at all."

She was an exquisite dancer but, abruptly pulling him close, caused him to stumble slightly. Recovering, he noticed she was looking intently over his shoulder. He made two quarter turns, until he could see the object of her attention.

It was an older man with a moustache, who was now dancing with her sister Thelma.

"I don't know him," Bedford said.

"He's a resident drunk. He was one of my husband's supposedly amusing companions."

"That sort of thing seems to be all the rage tonight."

"Yes. And I'm going to get squiffy, too. Would you like to join me? You and your friend?"

"She's already squiffy, I'm afraid."

"Let's find her."

The music seemed louder now, and the evening warmer.

"Perhaps later."

"Later won't do."

Without waiting for the number to end, she slipped from his grasp and moved off toward one of the waiters. Bedford took the opportunity to return to the interior of the house, where there was less a press of people. In the Great Hall, some of them had draped themselves on the furniture as though models posing for a magazine advertisement.

Bedford strolled past them. Deciding to seek an even quieter retreat, he headed for the library, expecting to find it vacant. But Gertrude's son, the Neil who'd been a flyer in the war, appeared in the doorway as Bedford approached.

"Enjoying yourself?" he asked as he moved past.

"Sure," said Bedford.

Within the chamber was only one man—stout, dark-haired, well-dressed, with a sharply pointed beard. He was actually reading one of the books, adjusting his pince nez as he did so. Bedford received only a glance from him as he entered.

Bedford seated himself in the same chair where the Countess Szechenyi had received him the day before. The bearded man ignored him, turning a page of the book.

"A nice evening," Bedford said.

"Yes. Very pleasant." Another page.

"Are you enjoying the dancing?"

"I do not dance."

He had a pronounced accent.

"Are you by any chance acquainted with a Countess Zala?" Bedford asked on impulse.

The other's head slowly rose, then halted, as though immobilized by thought. "Zala? No, there is no Countess Zala here tonight." He returned to his book.

Bedford could think of nothing more to say. The other continued to ignore him, then of a sudden closed the book, set it on the nearest table, and walked out the door. Waiting a long moment to make certain the fellow was gone, Bedford went to the table and picked up the volume, surprised to discover it was Turgenev's *First Love*—a remarkably romantic work to be found in the library of the railroad-building Vanderbilts.

Bedford returned it to the shelf and then stood uneasily a moment, uncertain whether he wanted to go back to the dancing area, where he feared he'd find Sloane in an embarrassing state. He seated himself in the chair again, pondering yet another Vanderbilt family portrait on the wall, when he was rejoined by the portly man with the sharp, well-trimmed beard.

"You're the art dealer," the man said.

"One of them," said Bedford facetiously.

"Yes. You took my room here, I believe through inadvertence. You're Gertrude Whitney's guests."

"Then you must be Dr. Horvath."

"Professor Horvath," the man corrected. "Imre Horvath." He gave a quick bow of his head.

"I'm sorry," Bedford said. "I hope we didn't cause you any inconvenience. I hadn't realized this house belonged to Gladys Szechenyi."

Horvath lowered himself heavily into the nearest chair, leaning forward, so he could be heard without speaking loudly.

"It's not her house," he said. "The Breakers belongs to the mother, Alice Vanderbilt. Countess Szechenyi's brother, the General, does not like to stay here and Mrs. Whitney has her own place, so the countess has become the chatelaine."

"Are you French?" Bedford asked, certain he was not.

"In no way."

"Hungarian, then."

"Yes. Of course. Imre Horvath. And you?"

"Bedford Green. American."

"Are you here to sell paintings? They only like paintings of themselves—and boats—except, of course, for Mrs. Whitney."

"No," Bedford said. "I'm here because I'm looking for someone. A Countess Zala."

He looked again for a sign of recognition in the professor's eyes, but there was only the blankest of stares.

"Zala."

"Yes. I'm wondering where she is."

The professor sat back, more stiff than relaxed. He tilted his head, eyes traveling over the carved, curved cornice above down to the Cippolino marble of the huge fireplace hood. "What do you think of this house?"

Bedford sought an honest answer. "It's very expensive."

"It is too big." Horvath slapped his knees, then rose. "It is much too big."

He started from the room, but Bedford quickly got to his feet to move beside him.

"Do you know the countess, then, sir?"

"Madame Szechenyi? Of course."

"No. The Countess Zala."

"It occurs to me there is a woman who might possibly be the one you seek. What do you want with her?"

"I'm not certain. I was expecting to be introduced to her this weekend."

"Here?"

"Possibly."

"The woman I refer to was supposed to accompany me here from New York, but she was not at Grand Central Terminal, as had been arranged. Upon arriving here, I discover she is not invited, though a room had been prepared for her."

Hovarth began moving toward the door again.

"Are you here as a guest of the count?" Bedford asked.

The other man halted. The band was playing more loudly now, a singer's lovely voice mingled with the saxophones.

"Mr. Green," said Horvath very formally. "I am a guest as you are a guest."

And with that, he turned his back and walked on, disappearing into the corridor and the Great Hall beyond.

Bedford saw a waiter with champagne, and asked for a glass. As he sipped the wine, he listened more intently to the music, then abruptly set down his drink and returned to the lower loggia.

The band was at the other end, but playing on a raised platform. Despite all the dancers between them, Bedford could see the singer clearly. He waved to her, raising his hand high, but she showed no sign of recognition. By the time he'd maneuvered himself through the crowd, she'd finished her number. She turned away to drink hurriedly from a glass one of the musicians handed her, then stepped to the front again. Only then did Claire Pell take note of Bedford.

"Hello."

"Hello."

She seemed pleased, and somewhat relieved to see him—as though he were a person late for some rendezvous. Then of a sudden her face colored and she turned away. Bedford looked to see the butler staring at her.

The orchestra had begun to play "My Man," a hit song two summers before but one not conducive to the tempo of dance. Most of the couples stopped their turns and stood listening to the music.

She ignored him while she sang. He had to remain there through two more numbers before she relented, stepping daintily off the platform.

"Well, here you are," she observed, "just as you said."

"And here you are," he responded. "Just as you didn't say."

"I can't talk to you now," she said. "I'm working."

"No you're not. You just finished your set."

The band leader gave Bedford a quick dark look.

"Please," Bedford said. "Have a drink with me. Champagne. In the garden."

She hesitated, then reluctantly hopped off the little stage, as though resigned to a miserable fate. Bedford tried to help her, but she pushed on ahead of him, moving through the dancers to the outer edge of the terrace. As she didn't know where to go next, she halted, waiting as he gathered up two glasses of champagne.

"This way," he said, preceding her off the terrace and onto a path leading around to the south side of the mansion between manicured flower beds. The sea breeze was unimpeded here, cooling skin and, he hoped, tempers.

Claire took a large gulp of the wine, then tossed her head back, her blonde hair bright in the light of the rising moon.

"These people," she said. "Your friends."

"What's wrong?" he asked.

"We were told we were invited for dinner," she said. "They fed us in the kitchen! The kitchen!"

"I'm sorry. If I had known, I'd have had you eat with us—at Gertrude's."

"They didn't even speak to us. That servant dealt with us. And he hovered around like we might steal something. They're putting us up in some ratty old inn in town. When are they going to stop treating people in show business like tramps?"

In New York, Claire was the Queen of Broadway—depending on the show. At all events, a princess. When she and Bedford walked into the Café Très Vite, their favorite bistro on Forty-sixth Street, waiters rushed to attend to her. Her reception here was doubtless quite vexing.

"Gertrude's my friend," he said. "The others aren't. You know their type. They even try to snub each other. Why did you take this job?"

"Because my show is closing, and the money's good."

"Your understudy's on tonight?"

"Yes. I thought I'd give her a shot before it's over. She has the matinee tomorrow as well—if the show lasts that long. Freddy said something about my going on the road with him. Cleveland, Chicago. Maybe Los Angeles. I don't mind singing with a band. I just hate to *have* to sing with a band."

He stepped forward, and put his hand on her shoulder. She stiffened.

"There'll be another show, surely."

"Not till October—if I get the part."

"If you go to Los Angeles, there's Hollywood. I keep telling you you're a natural for the films. You could get a place like this for yourself someday—and have a lot of fun not inviting them."

As if on cue, Sloane came stumbling upon them, wine-glass in hand, its contents miraculously unspilled.

Her eyes alighted on Claire uncertainly.

"Miss Pell," she said. "I thought you were on stage, singing."

Claire had no reply.

"The most awful man has been pursuing me, much as though I were a runway pet," Sloane continued. She sipped, stepping forward to put a hand on Bedford's shoulder for balance.

"Which one is that?" Claire asked. "There's a house full of them. And it's a big house."

"I do not know and I do not intend to know. I am not going back in there." Sloane made a sweeping gesture toward the house, this time sloshing quite a bit of wine out of her glass. She looked at it, drank the tiny bit of champagne that was left, then set the glass down daintily in a flower bed, rising unsteadily.

Bedford stepped forward to put his arm around her waist. "I never knew you had such a drinking problem," he said.

"I have a drinking problem," she said. "Someone has ripped my frock."

She turned to her left shoulder, where the strap was dangling.

"I hate it here," Claire said. "I'm going to finish my next set, go back to the inn, and then go home."

"I'll drive you," Bedford said.

"No, no. You have your hands full, as one can plainly see."

She hurried back up the path to the terrace, as though the milling swarm there offered sanctuary.

"Oh dear," said Sloane, with a sudden cold seriousness. "I've come between you and Claire."

"You've come between yourself and your senses. Perhaps we should take a walk."

"Yes," said Sloane. "A walk. What is it that your friend Tatty Chase says? 'Dee-lighted.' I'm dee-lighted." She stuck her hand in the crook of his arm and propelled them both forward into a lurch toward the lawn.

"What happened to your beau?" Bedford asked.

"Which?"

"The Neil who's the son of the General."

"He's hardly my beau. He's in a fit of pique because his parents wouldn't let him bring some girlfriend to the party. They disapprove. Which is funny, because the Vanderbilts used to disapprove of his mother."

"Which girlfriend?"

"I don't know. Apparently, he has many."

"But not you?"

"No. Definitely no."

"It grows curiouser about this countess," he said.

"The only one who's curiouser is you. The Vanderbilts don't seem to have any interest in her at all. I can't understand what Gertrude was so distraught about. It's strange."

"Yes it is."

"Did you know that the first Cornelius Vanderbilt had a fortune of more than one hundred and five million when he died?" Sloane said. "Can you imagine that? One person, having that much? And that was fifty years ago!"

"J. P. Morgan had more."

"Not back then, he didn't. Imagine what these Vanderbilts have now."

She turned around. They were quite a way down the slope of the lawn and had a fulsome view of the great house and its grounds. All of its numerous windows were illuminated, and in the moonlight, it had a fairy-tale aspect. The music seemed sweeter at the distance.

"It all looks so gay and marvelous," Sloane said. "Yet think how miserable they must be."

"I can take you down to Hester Street and show you people a trifle more miserable."

"The point is, the rich needn't be miserable, but they are."

"How is that?"

"All they do is get drunk and have affairs and play with their toys. They don't do anything with their lives."

"I suppose they think amassing fortunes is doing something."

"And how many Vanderbilts even do that now?"

He might have brought up Gertrude's son, or for that matter, Gertrude, who was considered one of the finer sculptors in the country. But he realized Sloane was falling back on Greenwich Village habits. This was the sort of conversation they might have in Chumley's—at three in the morning.

"Let's go down to the water," he said.

"Dee-lighted," she said. She took his hand, swinging both their arms in a wide arc as they progressed to the bottom of the lawn. The breeze had shifted to the west, and the sound beyond the hedge was of water washing gently against the bank.

"Look at all those lights out on the water," she said. "So many boats."

"It's a nice night and a popular harbor."

"You said your friend O'Bannion runs rum through here?"

"He used to, at any rate. Probably still does. But over on the other side of the sound."

Sloane took a deep breath and let it out slowly.

"Mmm, that's better," she said. She paused a moment. "I want to go wading."

"All right."

They followed the path around the hedge they had taken that afternoon down to the narrow beach. Sloane used his shoulder to steady herself as she removed her shoes and stockings. She stepped to the edge and put in her foot.

"It's warm," she said.

"It's August," he said.

"I've just had a brilliant idea," she said, and moved away from him toward one of the benches.

In a moment, she had her dress off.

"Skinny-dipping?" he asked.

"Yes. Of course. Now, look away, Bedford. As I've told you many times, I'm not about to embark on an affair with you."

He did as bidden. Hearing her enter the water, he turned finally and saw her pale white back in the moonlight. Then she lowered her head and plunged beneath the surface. When she came up again, shaking the water from her head, she seemed much less blotto.

"You, too, Mr. Green," she commanded.

"That's probably not wise."

"Oh yes. Very wise. It's wonderful."

"Very well."

He was in the water within a minute, then swam to where she was. It was deep, and he could not touch bottom.

She tilted back her head, looking at the moon and stars. "Now, at last, I am happy."

He could hear the band music clearly, and people's voices. It was difficult to tell how near they might be.

"Perhaps we shouldn't linger too long here," he said.

"Bedford Green, heroic aviator, killer of Germans, winner of medals—and you're afraid you might be caught *swimming*?"

"Just having a care for your reputation, madam."

"Mademoiselle," she corrected. "And tonight, not a fig for reputation." She took two strokes and came nearer. "Kiss me, Bedford."

"We'll go under."

"I don't care. Kiss me."

"Then can we go in?"

"Are you afraid I'm going to embarrass you? Or is it that Claire might see us?"

"I don't know what I'm afraid of."

She came a stroke nearer—very near indeed. He put his right arm around her, using his left to help tread water, then leaned forward till their lips came together. She put both arms around his neck, and kissed him harder.

As he feared, they went underwater—not far—toes touching the sandy muck. Then a little kick, and they were on the surface again.

"Mmmmmm," she said. "This party may have possibilities after all."

"Perhaps I should have gotten blotto, too."

She made a splash.

"Stop that," she said.

"Stop what?"

"Stop being fresh."

"Sloane, I'm not doing anything."

"Yes you are. You put your hand where a gentleman shouldn't—at least, not at this stage of our relationship."

"I haven't done that, Sloane."

"Yes you have. And your fingers are cold."

"No they're not." He put both hands on her shoulders.

She looked from one to the other, then backed up a little and reached behind her. Turning around to look, she screamed, shoving herself away with a great whoosh of water.

"Sloane? What's wrong?"

She was staring at a glimmer of moonlight, as though it had been about to devour her. But it was not simply a reflection. Bedford swam near and studied the form, touching something cold and slippery that seemed both hard and soft at the same time. He pulled gently. A human hand came up from the water, fingers spread. And then an arm. And then a human head—a dark-haired woman with pale white skin and eyes wide open.

Sloane screamed.

CHAPTER 8

SLOANE swam and waded to the shore and frantically began to dress, as if in preparation for a mad flight from the scene. Bedford grimly pulled the unfortunate young woman they'd found onto the rocky beach and placed her carefully on her back. Then he quickly put on as many clothes as he could manage before the first of the guests who'd heard Sloane's scream came around the hedge.

"What's wrong?" said a young man, his eyes on Sloane, who was putting bare feet into evening slippers.

Bedford drew the youth's attention to the body. "We found her just offshore. I'm afraid she's dead."

A woman looked over the young man's shoulder, then dashed off, crying: "A drowning! Someone's drowned."

"Get a lantern from the terrace," Bedford said to the youth.

"What?"

"Please. A lantern."

Bedford knelt beside the naked corpse. In the moonlight, he could see a large ring on one of her hands, and a dark necklace around her neck. Peering more closely, he saw that it was not jewelry at all, but a thin rope or cord.

He carefully pulled it free of the flesh, finding the material oddly soft—perhaps velvet. Not wanting to lose it, he stuffed it into a pants pocket. Then he stood up, a little dizzy.

People were crowded all around now—chattering excitedly—the boredom of another pointless summer party broken by this grimly thrilling diversion.

The young man was back with a lantern. He held it low over the dead woman's face.

"Who is it?" someone asked.

"Don't know."

"Hard to tell."

"Poor thing."

"Rocks out there. Dangerous."

People began to move aside to make way for the tall, commanding figure of the General. He stood at the dead woman's feet looking like a military field officer examining casualties, nothing betrayed by his expression.

"Is this a drowning, then?" he asked.

"I don't think so," Bedford said.

The General took in Bedford's damp and disheveled appearance.

"Did you try to rescue her?" he asked.

"We went for a swim and, uh, encountered her. I pulled her in."

"The police must be sent for." He turned to the onlookers, finding his nephew, Gertrude's son Neil. "Would you be so kind?"

"Yes, Uncle. Of course." He moved off for the house as though asked to fetch a woman's forgotten wrap.

Bedford picked up his jacket, started to put it on, then removed it and draped it over the dead woman's torso instead, unfortunately having to leave her face uncovered. Her expression was one of anxiousness and alarm, as though she had just discovered some terrible, horrible secret.

Sloane had vanished, perhaps following Neil Whitney back up the lawn. Bedford was torn between going after her and remaining with the dead woman.

"Perhaps we should clear the area," Bedford said to the General.

"Indeed. Ghastly business." He turned, the commander facing his troops. "Ladies and gentlemen. If you'd return to the terrace now, I would be most appreciative. We'll attend to matters here. Please, please return to the house."

The General advanced upon them, and they backed away, turning like herded sheep and moving in twos or threes back up the sloping lawn. Neil Whitney appeared coming through them, bearing another lantern.

"The police have been called, Uncle. They'll be here presently."

"Did you inform Count Szechenyi?" the General asked.

"Yes. He seemed quite indignant."

"Is he coming down here?"

"I do not think so."

Bedford knelt by the body once more, taking advantage of the increase in light. Lifting his jacket carefully, he noted a bruise on the woman's left hip and a jagged scrape along her right shin. Holding up her hands, one by one, he found nothing amiss with the right but abrasions on the knuckles of her left and bruises on the forearm.

"What are you doing?" the General asked sternly.

"Trying to determine how she might have died." He examined her face, finding an abrasion and a bruise on her right cheek.

"That's damned obvious, isn't it? The poor woman drowned."

"She has some cuts and bruises."

"That can happen falling off a boat. It can happen on a boat without falling off it."

"Not much wind today. Less tonight."

"Mr. Green, this is really none of our business. Leave it to the police—when they come and take her away."

"It's just very curious."

"You found her in the water. It has nothing to do with this house. If you hadn't taken note of her, she might have drifted down to the house next door, or all the way down to Sheep Point."

"But I did take note of her, sir. I discovered the body. I'm going to be asked questions."

"Yes, I suppose you are. Damned nuisance."

The band, weirdly, began to play "I'm Just Wild About Harry." Then, abruptly, almost in midnote, it stopped.

"General, if you please," said Bedford. "Could you come take a look?"

"Please. Didn't we see enough of this sort of thing in the war?"

Bedford had seen a dead woman in the war—a Belgian, young, but a mother, she and her infant killed by a British shell that had missed its intended mark. At the time he thought it murder, but no mystery.

"If you would, sir," he said.

The General moved nearer, leaning down to look where Bedford indicated.

"I see a bruise—perhaps a cut. Nothing that might prove fatal."

"Do you recognize her?"

"No. I don't think so."

"She's not the Countess Zala?"

"Sorry. I've not laid eyes on that woman."

"You haven't? You told me she lives in Bristol."

"That's what I was told. I never met her. Perhaps you might inquire of Count Szechenyi."

"At the moment, he's not here."

"No, he's not. Please, Green. Let us leave this to the police."

Bedford stood up wearily, then went to the bench and

sat down. The General joined him. The dead woman lay with her head tilted back slightly, and she seemed to be looking at them with her frightened eyes. Bedford turned away from her.

"Would you like something to drink—something stronger than champagne?" the General asked.

"The police are coming, sir. Shouldn't you be putting your spiritous liquors out of view."

"They won't bother us about that," the General said. "They are, shall we say, understanding." He looked to a servant who had posted himself at the edge of the hedge.

"Quigley," said the General, "would you be so kind as to have someone fetch us a bottle of scotch whiskey and two glasses?"

"Certainly, sir."

THE police arrived in two cars, one full of uniformed police officers, the other carrying two detectives—the large contingent doubtless a consequence of the importance of the Vanderbilt name.

Relieved of their morbid duty keeping watch over the dead woman by two burly uniformed cops who had brought what looked to be an army surplus field stretcher, the General and Bedford walked back up the lawn, whiskies in hand. Bedford had retrieved his dinner jacket, but was reluctant to put it on.

"I suppose you'll be going back tomorrow—what with all this awful business?" the General asked.

"Probably. I'm sure my friend Miss Sloane would like to return."

"Yes. She seemed quite shaken."

The General paused to take a sip of his drink. Bedford did the same. The policemen had wasted no time with the body and were bringing it along in a rapid trudge, the woman's arm dangling from beneath a blanket. They were veering away to the side of the house, heading for the drive and a vehicle in which to transport the woman to whatever place in Newport received such lamentable cargo.

In New York City, bodies were not removed until homicide detectives had thoroughly examined them and their circumstance. The two at the Breakers seemed more interested in what witnesses had to say.

They were waiting for him in the kitchen. The band members were there, too, though Claire was not in evidence.

Sloane sat sullenly in a corner, her clothing still in much disarray. Bedford went to her first.

"Did they talk to you?" he said quietly.

She seemed too weary even to lift her eyes to him.

"Yes. A little."

"What did you tell them?"

"Just that she was floating there, right off the beach."

Bedford nodded, then gave her hair a comforting stroke.

"Mr. Green?"

Responding, he went to the table in the center of the room where the two detectives had seated themselves. Both were wearing cheap woolen suits, despite the warm summer weather.

"Your lady friend . . ."

"You mean, Miss Smith," Bedford corrected.

"Yeah. She says you found the body out in the water."

"Very near the shore, actually."

"You see anyone else?"

"No."

"No boat?"

"A lot of boats. None of them all that near."

"You heard nothing? No splash or anything?"

The other detective did not speak, but was taking notes.

"No. I think she'd been in the water for a while."

"Why's that?"

"Because I didn't hear anything. The winds are calm. It would take her a bit to drift in—unless she was killed nearby."

Both detectives leaned back. "What makes you think she was killed?" the talkative one asked.

Bedford reached into his pants pocket, pulling out the velvet cord. It had dried a little, and was a crimson color. He set it carefully on the table.

"This was wound around her neck."

"Why'd you take it off?"

"I didn't know what it was. And then I didn't want it to go astray."

The talkative one picked up the cord and examined it. "She could've gotten fouled with this in the water."

"I suppose that's a possibility."

"What were you doing there?"

"I'm a guest at the party. I was, anyway—while there was a party."

"Are you staying at a hotel?"

"No. With Mrs. Whitney. At Whitney Cottage. It's next to a house called Rosecliff."

"We know that." He shut his notebook, then reopened it. "Can you identify the victim?"

"No. Why do you think I could?"

"Just asking."

"But if I were you," Bedford said, "I'd inquire after the whereabouts of a woman known as Countess Zala, up in Bristol."

"A countess in Bristol?"

"Yes."

"You think this woman is her?"

"I don't know. I think it's a possibility."

Sloane looked as though she might at any moment slide onto the floor.

"What do you know about this countess?" the detective said.

"Very little. I think the Vanderbilts know more."

"Why's that?"

"Something about Hungarians. Count Szechenyi is Hungarian, and so, I believe, is this Countess Zala."

"You think there's a connection?"

Bedford shrugged. The two detectives looked at each other, and then the one with the notebook shut it.

"Okay, Mr. Green. You're free to go."

THERE were cars aplenty to take them back to Whitney Cottage, but Sloane, despite her obvious fatigue, insisted they walk. She had taken off her shoes and was walking barefoot on the grass at the side of the road.

"This was the worst party I've ever been to," she said.

"I'm sorry."

"It's not your fault. It's mine—for passing on Gertrude's ramblings about that countess."

"Which she has yet to pass on to me."

"I know. I don't care. I just want to go home."

"I don't think I'm quite up to driving back tonight."

"No. But first thing in the morning."

"All right."

"Promise?"

"Promise."

CHAPTER 9

GERTRUDE was surprisingly cheerful at breakfast, talking about the party as though it had concluded happily, asking how Bedford and Sloane had enjoyed the orchestra and singer.

"I always enjoy Claire Pell," Bedford said circumspectly.

"Yes, I forget. She's your friend," said Gertrude. She stirred her coffee. "It's rare for us here to have that kind of entertainment."

"What kind of entertainment is that?" Bedford asked.

"Why, Broadway stars, of course."

"How is it she was invited to perform here?" Bedford asked.

"I don't know," said Gertrude, nodding to a butler to pour more coffee. "Gladys arranged it. Or the count. Surely you don't mind?"

"Not at all. I'm just sorry the evening ended so badly for her."

"For all of us, my dear. For all of us."

Sloane stared at her food, finally taking a bite.

"Do you know where they're staying?" Bedford asked. "The orchestra? And Claire?"

"Oh, I'm sure they've left for New York by now. That was their intention."

Bedford wanted to ask if Claire had left word for him, but did not.

"We're leaving also," Sloane announced.

"Yes," Gertrude said with a quiet sigh. "It's so sad. But we all must get on with things." She turned to Bedford. "The police telephoned. They're decided last night's unfortunate incident was a drowning. You won't be detained."

"A drowning?"

Gertrude put her napkin daintily to her lips. "Yes. That poor woman."

Bedford said nothing, letting silence gather. Gertrude fooled with her napkin. Sloane turned to look out the window at the sea.

"Have they identified her?" Bedford asked.

"I don't think so. They didn't say."

Bedford finished his coffee. "Well, then, I suppose we should get under way. Thank you so much for having us, Gertrude."

"I'm so glad you finally were able to join us in Newport. I'm just so sorry . . ."

"I'll fetch our bags."

"You needn't bother, dear. That's already been done."

GERTRUDE came outside with them and stood by the car as Bedford loaded the luggage. Her son, Neil, was apparently still asleep—or elsewhere. Bedford didn't ask.

He held the door for Sloane, then came back to his side of the car and climbed behind the wheel. He hesitated before activating the starter. It was a big, wonderful automobile but the drive to New York would be long and hard.

Smiling at Gertrude, he finally turned the switch. The engine coughed, caught, and then roared. Easing back on the gas, he bit down on his lip, then reached and switched off the motor.

"Gertrude, at the risk of seeming impolite, I'd like to clear the air about something."

"Clear the air?"

"You told Sloane that one of the reasons you were interested in having me out here was that you were worried about a Hungarian woman called the Countess Zala and wanted my help in finding something out about her. You specified my help, though your sister's husband is the Hungarian minister to the United States and a count himself."

Sloane gave Gertrude a baleful eye. "Forgive me. I did tell Bedford that."

"Perhaps you misunderstood," said Gertrude, flustered. "I think I said he might meet the Countess Zala here."

"But I didn't meet her," Bedford interjected. "Or did I? Was she the woman who washed up on the beach?"

"The Countess Zala did not attend the party."

"Was she the woman on the beach?"

"I don't know. I didn't look."

Bedford gripped the wheel tightly, holding his temper. "Gertrude, do you know this woman, or not?"

"Which woman?"

"Either. Both."

His exasperation had communicated itself.

"I've not met the Countess Zala. I only know she's someone young Neil—the General's son—knows from New York. They apparently became quite friendly, and the family was interested to learn something about her."

"As interested as your mother was in the General's wife before he married her?"

Gertrude stiffly ignored this, but continued.

"Count Szechenyi tried to find out about her but was unsuccessful. Someone suggested hiring a private investigator, but the General, of course, refused. That sort of thing—it isn't done."

"If your family felt so strongly about her, why was she invited to last night's party?"

"She wasn't. Gladys was firm about that. But young Neil insisted she come no matter what. They had a bit of a row, I'm afraid."

"I talked to a Dr. Horvath. He said he was to have met the countess at Grand Central and accompanied her here. Your sister prepared rooms for them, as you may recall."

"Bedford, this is getting tiresome."

"Where did your nephew go last night? To look for her?"

Sloane began tapping her foot impatiently.

"I don't know where he might have gone. He was displeased, I believe. I've not spoken with him since. And that's all there is to that."

"Very well."

"I'm terribly sorry if you were importuned." Gertrude politeness was strained. "I hadn't realized Sloane had discussed this matter with you. She needn't have."

"So terribly, terribly, terribly sorry, Gertrude," said Sloane angrily. "We were both only trying to help."

"Yes, dear. I'm sure you were. But now there's no need."

Bedford restarted the engine. "Goodbye, then. All's well that ends well." He meant that as sarcasm, but Gertrude took it as a pleasantry.

She stepped back, and waved. Bedford did the same, then backed the Packard around, moving sedately down the drive.

"All hasn't ended particularly well," Sloane said bitterly.

"I know."

He turned right up Bellevue Avenue, then left along Memorial Boulevard, and north again on Thames, following the waterfront. Narragansett Bay glittered to their left between the many boat masts, halyards, and shrouds.

"You've gone past the ferry," Sloane said at length.

"I know. I have a great favor to ask of you, Sloane."

"No. I'll not stay here another day. Or hour."

"What I'm asking is whether you'd mind going back by train."

Sloane blinked, then looked at him mockingly. "Would I mind relaxing in the comfort of a first-class railroad compartment—that you are going to pay for—rather than bump along with wind and dust in my face for two hundred miles?"

"That is the question, yes."

"The choo-choo, if you please."

"Done."

"You're going to stay a little longer? Why?"

"Because all hasn't ended well. In fact, I'm not sure it's ended at all."

She studied him. "Are you quite all right, Bedford?"

He took her hand. "I'm fine. Just need to relieve my curiosity."

"Oh dear. Disaster looms."

"It's slow at the gallery. Keep whatever hours you wish. I won't be too long."

She squeezed his hand. "You've helped me when I needed it, Bedford, but I just can't stay."

"I understand."

"When I get back, I'm going straight to Chumley's and throw myself at the first unwashed verse libre poet I can find. With luck, he may even be a Bolshevik."

"I won't be long."

T##E gray house looked much as it had the previous day, except for a ramshackle Ford Model T Speedster parked at the front and the lack of a sleeping drunk on the lawn. Bedford parked the Packard behind the other car and then sat a moment, pondering the approach he would take. There was really only one.

He walked to the screen door, and rapped twice. When there was no answer, he opened it and took one step inside.

"Hello!" he said, loudly enough to wake anyone who might be sleeping.

Before him was a long room with a dusty look to it. A man appeared in the doorway at the end, the same who'd been on the lawn the previous afternoon. He was erect, but did not seem much more alert.

"Who're you?" he said. His speech was so thick and slurred it seemed another language.

"Sorry," said Bedford. "I knocked, but no one answered."

"That doesn't mean you can just walk in here. Get the hell out."

"I've come about the woman who lives here." He thought on this. "The woman who owns this house."

"She ain't home. Now get out."

His voice threatened, but he made no move toward Bedford. Rather, he vanished from the doorway.

"I fear she may be dead," Bedford said, raising his voice. "There's been a drowning. I need you to look at the body—to make identification, if possible."

The youth reappeared, wide-eyed and slack jawed. "Dead? What happened?"

"Her body washed up by the Breakers—down in Rhode Island Sound."

"She didn't come home last night."

"Yes. I know. I'm terribly sorry, but . . ."

"Where do you want me to go?"

"To the Newport police station."

"Are you a policeman?"

The youth was standing very near now. He wore no shoes and had muddy feet. His dungarees were stained with boat gunk and there were similar smears on his undershirt. He wore no other shirt, and he seemed not to have shaved since Bedford had first looked upon him. There was no guessing when he'd last bathed.

"I'm afraid I'm the one who discovered the body."

"Are you a Vanderbilt?"

"No. A friend."

"Do you know Neil Vanderbilt?"

Bedford smiled. "There seem to be several of them."

"He's a young guy."

Bedford stepped back to the screen door. He wondered if he should try to make the youth clean himself up, but that was probably asking entirely too much in the circumstance.

"Could you put on some shoes and a shirt?" he said. "The police would doubtless appreciate it."

The other looked down at his feet, then around the room. "Do you want a drink?"

"No thank you."

"You know, I think I'm out of liquor. She was going to bring some home, but she never showed up."

"Please, sir. Let's go. Perhaps, after we're done with this unfortunate business, I can acquire some more refreshment for you."

"I got the shakes."

"This won't take long."

"You'll get me more?"

"As much as you want."

The other's eyes brightened. "Be right with you."

He shuffled down the hall and into another room, wiping his mouth with the back of his hand. Bedford seized the opportunity to make a quick perusal of the living room, looking for a photograph, but there was none.

Hearing the young man go into the bathroom, he moved on into the kitchen, wishing he hadn't. He could not imagine anyone acquainted with the Vanderbilts in even the slightest way living like this.

The smells from the sink and the garbage can were

more than he could bear. They put him in mind of a week he had once spent in the trenches near Ypres. He went outside and waited in the car.

T HE youth seemed perfectly accepting of all aspects of his situation. He made no conversation on the drive down to the Newport police station, but answered questions when asked. He told Bedford his name was Joe Christopher.

"Are you from around here?"

"No."

"Where did you meet her?"

"Who?"

"The Countess Zala?"

The young man made a face, glancing at Bedford as though he'd had all his screws loosened.

"In a bar—in Providence."

"Odd place to meet a countess."

"I didn't think she was a countess."

"Where were you last night?"

"I fell asleep. Early. Had a bit to drink beforehand."

Bedford thought of mentioning their encounter on the grass outside the Bristol house, but thought better of it.

A DESK sergeant at the main police station directed them to the morgue, which was nearby. A yawning attendant received them, not warmly.

Bedford made his request, saying the young man would identify the victim.

"Okay," said the attendant, pulling out a sort of ledger book. "What's her name?"

He looked at Bedford, who turned to the young man.

"Her name," he said.

The youth shrugged. "Maggie."

"Maggie what?" Bedford demanded.

He shrugged again. "She told me, but I forgot."

"You were living with her!"

"Not for long."

The morgue attendant began drumming with his fingers. "You gotta tell me her name."

Bedford started to lose his temper, then caught himself. "There's some confusion here," he said. "Once we make a positive identification, we can sort it out. She's a drowning victim, brought in late last night. A young, attractive woman, with long dark hair—and a ring on her finger. She was found in the water over by Mansion Row."

The attendant consulted his book. As Bedford suspected, there were few new entries.

"Margaret Howard," the man said, stopping his finger at a name.

"Howard?" said Bedford.

"Margaret Howard," the attendant said. "Has to be the one. Nobody else come in last night."

Bedford stared down at the counter top for a moment.

"May we see her? You'll need an identification."

"We already got one."

"What?"

"She's been identified. Earlier this morning. Margaret Howard."

"Who identified her?"

"Her husband. Paul Howard, of Bronxville, New York."

"Bronxville?"

"He's taken the remains."

CHAPTER 10

T H E house," Bedford said. "Is it yours, or hers?"

The youth now seemed ready to kill—or even die—for a drink. The bootlegger he'd directed Bedford to was in East Providence.

The Packard headed there at a high rate of speed, churning up considerable dust.

"It's hers," the young man said finally. "Her husband gave it to her. Gave her anything she wanted."

He was perspiring heavily despite the rush of air.

"And what do you do, Joe?"

"Do?"

"Occupation. Work. I, for example, am an unsuccessful art dealer."

The youth gestured at the Packard's dashboard. "You do all right."

"I borrowed this," Bedford said. He glanced pointedly at the other's wretched clothing.

"I'm a student," said Christopher finally.

"Where?"

"In New York."

"No, I mean, what college?"

"I'm not in a college now, but I was."

Christopher rested his chin on his updrawn knees, saying nothing more, his interest obviously concentrated on their arrival at the bootlegger's.

B EDFORD bought him an entire case of whiskey, asking if that would suffice. Assured that it would, he left the youth at the gray house to his mourning, if that was what he intended, then sped back to Newport again, taking Valley Road on the east of town directly to Memorial Boulevard, and thence swiftly to the Breakers.

Both entrance gates were closed. He parked the Packard to the side of one and was about to push an electric button set on a panel to the side, when he noticed a smaller gate along the fence by a footpath. It was unlocked. Following the path through a thickness of trees, he emerged at the large gravel courtyard. He hesitated, wondering if he should go directly down to the beach, then thought better.

The same annoying butler answered the door, viewing Bedford with even more disdain than before.

"Countess Szechenyi is not at home, Mr. Green," he said.

"I wouldn't want to bother her in any case," Bedford replied. "I fear I dropped some things on the beach last night when I—when we were bringing that poor woman ashore. I wonder if you'd mind if I looked."

The man did indeed seem to mind. "Just to the beach, then?"

"Yes. I'm sure it wasn't in the house."

He would have liked to look around in there but knew he'd be asking far too much.

"Very well. I will accompany you."

As though Bedford was going to steal some pebbles.

There were a number of items lying around the

benches, including an expensive Mark Cross fountain pen Tatty had given him. He pocketed that first; then the small assortment of other objects at hand.

"I fear my friend Sloane spilled her handbag as well," Bedford said. "We really were in a state."

The butler nodded, now looking a bit bored.

Bedford was about to leave, but noticed a bit of flotsam in the water just at the shoreline. It was mostly old vegetation, but in its midst was a piece of red cloth. Squeezing the water out of it, he stuck it in his pocket with the rest.

Bedford wasn't certain as to whom the various things belonged. That could be sorted out later, though he suspected some of the objects might have been mislaid there long before the party and its unfortunate conclusion.

"Thank you," he said, turning toward the path that led back up around the hedge.

"Will you be visiting us again, Mr. Green?" asked the butler as they crossed the lawn, his tone indicating it was not the most welcome of ideas.

"Not anytime soon, I should think."

"Well then, good day, sir."

GERTRUDE'S "cottage" was nearby, but Bedford wanted more to speak with the General. Not knowing which was the man's house, he elected instead to drive to the waterfront and the yacht moorings.

The *Ilderim* was in her slip, brightwork gleaming in the sun. No one was on deck, though a gangway had been run out to the dock. Bedford stood at its foot for a long moment, then went aboard, heading aft. He encountered a crewman—a steward—coming up the stairs from the main salon. The man seemed startled by Bedford's presence.

"Sir?" he asked.

"I'm looking for the General. I was a guest of his on board here yesterday."

The man set down the large canvas bag he was carrying. "He's not sailing today. You'd best try his house."

"And where is that?"

"You don't know?"

"I've been staying at Gertrude Vanderbilt's house."

"And she can't tell you where the General's is?"

It occurred to Bedford that the Vanderbilts probably would not appreciate such impertinence directed at one of their guests.

"I've come aboard," Bedford said, putting starch in his voice, "to find something I believe I must have dropped here yesterday."

"And what is that?"

"A Mark Cross pen," said Bedford, failing to add that the pen was already in his pocket.

"We haven't seen it."

"Doubtless not," said Bedford, even more archly. "I propose to look for it."

"But the General's not here."

"I'm sure the Vanderbilts will approve. I am quite sure they will not approve when I tell them you refused to let me look for my possession."

With a grudging scowl, the man moved aside.

Bedford had gone below decks only once during their afternoon's sail and then only to use the water closet and procure fresh drinks for Sloane and himself in the yacht's grand salon. It was there that he halted, sensible to the presence of the steward. Looking about various pieces of furniture, he took note of how bare the room was—walls and portholes included.

"Where are the curtains?" he asked.

"In the bag on the dock. I'm taking them to be cleaned."

Bedford now recalled that they'd been red—and possibly velvet. He could not remember if they'd had cords attached, but could think of no excuse for looking into the cleaning bag. He got down on his hands and knees, searching under a divan, and then a table. The carpeting was immaculate.

He stood up. "Was she out last night?"

"Who?"

"Not a 'who.' This boat."

"No. And we won't be out for a while. The General told us to clean it up. He's taking his steam yacht to New York."

"To New York?"

"Yes. He and Mrs. Vanderbilt and their son sailed this morning."

There were voices above—doubtless other crewmen returning from some errand.

"Very well," said Bedford. "Thank you." He started for the companionway and the stairs leading on deck.

"What about your pen?"

Bedford pulled it from his blazer pocket with a flourish. "I found it."

STOPPING at the first filling station he could find, he replenished the Packard's gasoline supply and inquired as to the location of the General's Newport abode. The directions he was given were egregiously incorrect, leading him to Marble House, the abode of Vanderbilts he'd not yet met. As it was near Gertrude's, though, he went on to her house, finding his friend's large motorcar parked in her drive and the lady herself in her foyer, beside a large mound of luggage.

She was surprised and not pleased to see Bedford at the door. She invited him in but not to a seat or refreshment.

"Bedford. I thought you and Sloane had left hours ago."

"Sloane did. I've stayed behind to make some inquiries."

"Inquiries about what?" She turned away, as though looking for something.

"The Countess Zala."

An aggravated sigh. "We're about to leave, Bedford."

"So I note. A very short summer."

"We're not shutting up for the season. But after last night's unpleasantness, well, we thought . . ."

"My inquiries have been about precisely that. The police have identified the deceased as a Margaret Howard—a married woman from Bronxville."

"Bronxville." She pronounced the name as though it were some far-off exotic place.

"Her husband has already taken the remains."

"It's very sad."

"How does one get a 'Countess Zala' out of a Margaret Howard?' "

"I don't know that one does."

A servant arrived with two more bags, then waited for further instructions.

"Put all these in the other car when it comes," Gertrude said. "We'll be leaving presently." She looked again at Bedford, quite sharply. "Is there anything else you need?"

"Just a fuller explanation."

Another sigh, then she seated herself in a gilt-backed chair against the wall and bade him to do the same in one opposite.

"Very well." She lighted a cigarette. "There's not much to say, really. This woman apparently became attracted to the General's son, young Neil, and when his parents voiced their disapproval, she made a death threat against us."

"All of you?"

"That was never clear."

"But death?"

"Yes."

"And she's an actual countess?"

"We're not certain. Count Szecheyni said he knows of such a family but has been unable to verify whether this woman was a member of it. That's what we were hoping you could do, but now it doesn't matter, does it? It's all behind us."

"Because of what you said to Sloane, you know, I actually did bring my gun."

"Well, that was very foolish of you, Bedford. I hope it doesn't cause you any trouble."

"Me, too."

She stubbed out her cigarette and rose. "Now, let's forget about the whole thing. We'll get together in New York. We'll have a party and you and Sloane will come and we'll all have a lovely time."

"Unlike the uninvited Countess Zala—who had to crash." He got to his feet as well.

"Please, Bedford. No more of this." She gave him a quick kiss on the cheek, then went to the door and held it open for him. "We'll see you in New York. Safe journey."

Bedford went to the Packard without another word.

THE inn where he booked a room for the night proved to be the same one that had been used by Claire and the band for their stay.

Bedford thought the establishment more quaint than ratty, and was happy to discover his window had a wide view of the waterfront and Narragansett Bay.

Going to the bed, he spread out the items he'd recovered from the beach. The Vanderbilts kept their place immaculate, so he assumed the things had been dropped the night before. The servants who cleaned the beach hadn't got to it yet.

There was a comb, slightly broken; a green button, probably having come from Sloane's party dress; a playing card; a metal matchbox; a large copper coin; and a handkerchief with lipstick on it. He also laid out the piece of red cloth. The coin was of most interest, especially when he held it close.

It was foreign, presumably Hungarian. It also bore a distinguishing mark: a diagonal cross scored across its surface with some small, sharp instrument.

The dead woman had been naked in the water, and it was doubtful she could have been carrying any of these things. The red cloth was another matter. Spreading it out full, he realized it was a hair ribbon—crimson, just like the velvet cord. Fetching that from his suitcase, he put the two side by side. The hair ribbon was satin, but the color was precisely the same.

H̱ E slept for the rest of the afternoon, then dined alone on fried sea scallops and mashed potatoes, afterward going for a walk along the wharves. There was an America's Cup J-Boat tied up at one of them—its awesome, graceful form suggesting royalty among commoners. Bedford came near it, gazing up the mast and imagining the tons of billowing sail she must carry. Such vessels were the ultimate of their type—existing only because the very rich wished them to. That much could be said on behalf of the unequal distribution of wealth, though it wasn't much.

At dusk, he retrieved Tatty's Packard and headed north out of town on the road to Bristol. Stopping at a small restaurant on the main street for apple pie, ice cream, and coffee, he chatted with the waitress for a few minutes, asking finally if she knew anything of the woman who had drowned at the Breakers. The woman said she knew nothing at all, except that the victim was a crazy person with small morals, a great deal of money, and a worthless bum for a boyfriend. The waitress knew nothing of Hungarians or nobility.

Later, turning onto the gravel road, Bedford extinguished the Packard's headlamps and proceeded slowly, guided by faint outlines in the twilight. There were no lights on in the gray house—a sign Bedford had been correct in his assessment that Joe Christopher would have taken immediately to bottle, and would now be in a similar state to that in which he had first encountered the youth the day before.

Bedford took two things with him from the car—an electric lantern whose beam was focused with a lens, and the thirty-two-caliber Savage automatic pistol he had brought with him—as he had thought had been Gertrude Whitney's wish.

The pistol he slipped into a pocket. The lantern he kept off. As he had expected, the screen door was unlatched. He waited before it, listening, hearing only the call of night birds. He knocked, rapping the frame of the door three times. When there was no response after a full minute, he opened the door and spoke the youth's name. No reply was forthcoming.

Formalities concluded, he stepped inside, closing the door quietly behind him. Standing still again, he heard only the sound of a clock ticking. Finally, satisfied, he turned on the lantern. The battery was not at full strength, but there was a sufficient glow.

The house was old, narrow, and conventional in design. Finding nothing of interest in the dining room, and only unpleasantness in the kitchen, he followed the main hall the other way to a messy-looking bathroom and a back bedroom with a partially opened door. Shielding the light from the electric lantern, he peered within.

As Bedford had calculated, Christopher lay sprawled on an unmade bed, eyes closed, mouth open, oblivious to all.

A whiskey bottle was sitting upright on the floor beside him.

"Mr. Christopher?" Bedford said in a normal, conversational tone.

There was no movement—not even the flicker of eyelids. Just strangely quiet sleep.

Stepping backward, Bedford pulled the door to where it had been, then retraced his steps back down the hall to where a flight of stairs led to the second floor. Mounting them with care, his shadow flickering on the wall from the lantern's light, Bedford ascended to a smaller, narrower hallway with three doors—one to a bathroom; one to a tiny, unused bedroom stacked with boxes and piles of clothing; and another to a large and handsomely furnished bedroom with canopied bed and two chests of drawers.

Entering, he moved to the nightstand, where he found one thing he'd been searching for from the beginning—a silver framed photograph of an attractive dark-haired woman standing next to a handsome young man on a wide expanse of grass with trees and a tall house or apartment building in the background. Lifting the lantern and holding the photo close, he studied the image carefully. He had no doubt whatsoever. It was the woman whose body he had pulled from the water.

The young man was the General's son, Neil, dressed in a military uniform.

Setting the picture down, he began going through drawers. He was startled to discover that the one in the nightstand contained a large Wembley military revolver of the sort he had carried as an officer in the war. It was fully loaded. He thought of taking it, then changed his mind, deciding instead to remove the bullets and put them in another drawer where they couldn't readily be obtained.

Turning to the dresser, he found a bound stack of letters under neatly folded lingerie in a top drawer. Atop the other dresser was a book published in a language he took to be

Hungarian. There were other discoveries, but only the letters and the framed photo interested him. He pondered the propriety of taking them, deciding ultimately that, as they were her possessions, and he was in a sense acting on her behalf, it was the right and necessary thing to do.

Gathering them up along with the book, and taking hold of the electric lantern, he departed as expeditiously as he could. Not even a dog barked when he started the Packard.

RETURNING to Newport, he drove past the inn, down the waterfront, and out Wellington Avenue onto the peninsula where the larger estates were located. Motoring, especially at night, helped him focus his thoughts, and he had many to sort through. Clearly, there was little to be gained by lingering in Rhode Island. He would leave in the morning for New York. If he'd been able to remain in town as Gertrude's guest, with the access to all the other family members that provided, continued residence might be more rewarding. But at this point he doubted there were any Vanderbilts left in Newport.

There were more boats out that night, taking advantage of the blissful summer weather. As he neared Brenton Point, headlights appeared behind him. He thought nothing of them, until he noticed that the other automobile was rapidly closing the gap with the Packard. Bedford was driving at a fair clip. He slowed, thinking the other vehicle might be a police car.

It drew rapidly up behind him, then slowed to match his speed, hanging there, even as they went through the two right-angled switchback turns by the Coast Guard station.

Bedford tried speeding up, but accomplished little. The blinding flare of headlamps continued, sliding from side to side as they went around the curves. Once past Brenton Point, tearing along Ocean Drive, he pulled close to the edge of the road to let the other pass, but the driver declined.

Finally, bumping over the wooden bridge that led to Cherry Neck, the other car pulled fully out to the side and then accelerated flat out. As it roared past, the cylinders of its big engine laboring mightily, Bedford tried to get a look at the occupants. But at that instant, the other car slid suddenly sideways.

Bedford had neither time nor space to do anything to save himself. He clutched the wheel tightly, hoping to keep control in the forthcoming collision he could not possibly avert. The other auto then veered away, kicking up dust and gravel as its wheels dug into the opposite shoulder. An instant later, it was swerving toward him again.

He stood on the brakes, but that proved an idiotic mistake. The wheels instantly locked, the Packard slid out to the right, slid left again, then spun around, completely out of control. Still clutching the wheel, Bedford watched helplessly as it ran off the road to the right, careening sideways, throwing up an even greater cloud of dust. An instant later, it struck a large boulder, turned almost on its side, came down with a gravel-scattering thump, and plowed into sand and rock.

When it stopped, it was tilted at a steep angle, steam rushing in a large, hissing cloud from the radiator. The other car, a peach-colored foreign roadster, kept going, and was soon lost in the night.

CHAPTER 11

THE nurse at the hospital was pretty and talkative, cheerily informing Bedford of the extent of his infirmities, of which his pain had already provided him a substantial inventory. Happily, no bones were broken, not even his several sore ribs, and the cut along his right eyebrow not as deep as he'd feared. But his ankle had been badly twisted from when he'd fallen getting out of the Packard and it was still swollen, and his head, shoulder, and right thumb and wrist hurt considerably. The passing hours had brought no abatement.

He'd been brought to the medics by the police, who'd been summoned to the accident scene by a passing motorist. When he'd told his tale of having been run off the road by a peach-colored Hispano-Suiza, the uniformed cop sent for a detective. The man who arrived shortly after sunup was one of the two who'd come to the Breakers the night of the party.

"Have you been drinking, sir?" he asked Bedford.

"No," said Bedford.

"You know that's against the law."

"So the Vanderbilts told me at their party."

The detective smiled. "A peach-colored roadster, you say?"

"Yes. Hispano-Suiza."

"You recognized it as a Hispano-Suiza at night?"

"I recognized it as one I'd seen earlier in my visit—unless you're awash in Hispano-Suizas here in Newport."

"And it ran you off the road?"

Bedford shrugged. "It was erratically driven. Beyond that I cannot say with certainty."

"What?"

"I can't swear that it was a deliberate act."

"Do you know whose car it is?"

Bedford shook his head.

"There is an automobile of that description that belongs to Mrs. Gloria Morgan Vanderbilt."

Bedford thought upon this. "Are you going to talk to her, then?"

"Talk to her? Possibly. But we have no proof of anything. Do you? Any witnesses?"

"I'm not sure."

"Did the other car strike yours? Maybe leave some paint?"

"I don't think so. It just swerved sideways, giving me no choice but to drive off the road."

"Hmmm." The detective closed his notebook. He hadn't written anything.

"Is that all?"

"Yep."

Bedford stood up shakily. "I need to telephone someone."

"Who's that?"

"The lady whose car I wrecked."

It was unable to make a connection to Tatty's New York number from the hospital. Taking a taxi to the inn, he finally got through. The phone was answered by Tatty's Russian maid, Sveta.

"Halloo?"

"Sveta. It's Mr. Green. Is Miss Chase there?"

"Miss Chase? *Nyet*. Not in house."

He recalled that Sveta also spoke French. *"Quand elle retournera?"*

"Halloo?"

"C'est très important. J'ai eu un fracas avec le voiture de Mademoiselle Chase. Le Packard, il est fini."

"What?"

She didn't speak his sort of French, apparently. "Sveta. Listen carefully. Tell Miss Chase there's been an accident. Her Packard is wrecked."

"You wreck Packard?"

"Yes. *Oui. Da.*" He gave Sveta the telephone number of the inn, repeating it twice in both English and French, then hung up, hoping for the best.

Once in his room, he painfully lowered himself into the armchair by the window, mentally assessing the things he next needed to do. Before he could attend to a single one, he fell asleep.

When he awoke, it was still daylight, but barely. His first attempt at rising from the chair sent flashes of pain down his back and leg. The second effort was more successful. Limping, he went to use the bathroom and thought of drawing a bath, but decided to postpone that agony. Instead he would eat.

The room service waiter, an older, unhappy man, took his time. Bedford ordered coffee and a cheese sandwich. As the waiter was leaving, Bedford called him back.

"Is it possible to acquire a bottle of whiskey in this community?"

"Yeah. Sure. For a price."

"And what would that be?"
"A dollar for the whiskey. A fiver for the acquirer."
Bedford made a face. "All right."

HE had put the items he'd taken from the dead woman's house in his luggage, which was still with the Packard in the repair garage. He asked the inn manager to send for it, then lay down on the bed and waited, eventually falling asleep. To his astonishment, the luggage arrived before the food and whiskey. When both were at hand and the bearers tipped and gone, he set about examining the stolen goods as he had the gleanings from the beach the day before.

The silver-framed photograph intrigued him immensely, if only because it provided him with a look at the woman as she had been alive and well—her face infused with vitality and happiness. She was smiling in it, her head tilted to the side, though not toward the young Vanderbilt.

Bedford held the image closer. There was something vaguely but compellingly familiar about the setting, but he could not identify it. Eating his sandwich, he drank half his coffee and then poured some of his bootleg rye into it.

His memory was jarred. He had been on that patch of grass in the photo—in uniform, like young Vanderbilt—while on leave in Paris.

The little greensward was a park not far from the Place de la Bastille, and had been a dueling ground in olden times. The building in the background was a house, and a very grand one. It had been the home of Victor Hugo. Bedford had himself taken an Englishwoman there he had met at a *bal musette*.

The book he'd taken had the simple title *Vigyazat*. Having not the slightest clue as to what it meant, he thumbed through it, deciding it was a novel. There was a penned inscription on the title page, "*Koszonom, Magda.*" The first and only edition of the book, it had been published in 1905 in Budapest.

He poured himself another drink and turned next to the letters, for the first time feeling a touch of shame for such ghoulish snooping. He reminded himself that they would otherwise still be in the possession of the pathetic Joe Christopher.

Several were in Hungarian. These he set aside. The others were in English—one, in a woman's hand, in very bad English. It was in its brief entirety a complaint, about the parsimony of an unnamed man.

There were two others having to do with money, also from a woman, but a different one. The remaining letters were from three different men, all of them amorous, but none of them signed by a "Neil."

Bedford read through them all one more time, then looked again at the ones in Hungarian. Checking at his watch, he made himself as presentable as possible and made his painful way downstairs to the inn's front desk.

"I need to place a long-distance telephone call again," he said.

"New York City?"

"Close."

RETURNING to his room when done, he lay down on his bed again, staring up at the ceiling. Sleep came before he could come to any significant conclusion about anything, save that he wished he could have talked to the woman while she was still alive.

H **E** awakened at dawn, finding the pain of the previous day replaced by an equally inhibiting stiffness. Slowly sitting up and shifting to the edge of the bed, he stretched out his arms and legs as best he could.

Rising seemed hardly worth the effort. He lay back, listening to the sound of gulls and a lifting sea breeze from the window. They brought an odd sort of contentment. To enhance this blissful state, he tried to think of pleasant things, of paintings he loved, of women. Of Sloane. In a moment, he was again asleep.

H **E** awakened next to a sharp rapping on his door. Thinking it must be the room service waiter once more, but unable to recall what he might have ordered, or when, he forced himself to his feet. Perhaps it was the police.

Pulling free the bolt, he turned the knob and opened the door a few inches, then a few inches more.

Pearls and light summer dress; white gloves, white shoes, and a white satin hair ribbon.

"*Mon dieu*, Bedford. Look at you. Are you all right?"

Then Tatty Chase gently pushed past him and entered the room.

H **OW** long did they say it would take to fix it?" she asked.

"I'm sorry," said Bedford, seated uncomfortably beside Tatty in the rear of the Pierce-Arrow as her man Albert drove them along the coast road out on the peninsula. "They weren't sure they could."

"Oh, pishtosh. Packards are indestructible. Anyway, it will be such a hoot when father learns that it wasn't me this time."

"I doubt that 'hoot' is the word he'll use."

"He likes you, Bedford."

"How can that be?"

"It's probably the way you dress—most of the time."

Bedford looked down at his filthy and stained white duck trousers. He had fresh ones in his suitcase, but it hurt too much to remove the ones he had on. He rubbed his chin. He had neglected to shave, among other things. He could not believe he had descended to this state.

"Have you made any progress with your Hungarian woman?" Tatty asked.

"Quite the contrary. She's dead."

"Oh dear."

Tatty pushed a strand of her blond hair back away from her face with her fingers, tucking it back under her white satin hair ribbon. "She was murdered?"

"Her body washed up at the Vanderbilts' house. There was a red velvet cord around her neck."

He pulled it forth. She gave it a glance, and shuddered.

"Gosh," she said.

"The police have ruled it a drowning."

"That sounds remarkably stupid."

"It's remarkably deferential—to the Vanderbilts. Case closed. Accidental death. Tidies everything up, without their having to be involved."

"Are they involved?"

"Wish I knew. I think one of the young men of the clan was romantically involved with the woman."

"Do the police know that?"

"I'm not sure. It doesn't seem to matter."

"Did you tell the police about the cord?"

"Yes. I gave it them. They gave it back to me. They don't care. They've released the body to the woman's husband."

"She had a husband?"

"Lives in Bronxville."

"Bronxville? What countess would live in Bronxville?"

They started around a curve lined with boulders. "This is it coming up. Pull off on the right, Albert—but not like I did."

Albert pulled off smoothly onto the sand, missing all the rocks.

Tatty opened her door. Bedford wanted to help her out of the vehicle but he could barely get himself out of his seat. The more he rested his ankle, the more it hurt when he next tried to use it.

"She came along there like the proverbial bat out of hell, hung on my rear end, and then attempted to pass me, with disastrous effect. I don't know that it was deliberate, but she didn't slow. When I disappeared from the road, she didn't stop to see what happened."

"She?"

"I believe the car belongs to Gloria Morgan Vanderbilt."

"*That* woman."

"So it seems."

"Was she drunk?"

"I've no idea."

"Was she driving?"

"Not certain about that, either."

"Were you drunk?"

"No. But I'd certainly like to be right now."

Tatty walked a ways into the rocks, making an assessment.

"You could have been killed," she said.

"I've had worse aeroplane crashes."

"A nobler cause, Bedford."

Tatty prowled a bit further, retrieving a large, broken headlamp that she had last seen affixed to her beautiful car. Then she stood a moment, looking along the shoreline that curved in sweeps into the distance.

"This is all very upsetting," she said.

"Yes, it is."

She turned and came back toward him, holding the
ruined headlamp as though it were some precious find.

"Poor Bedford," she said, running a finger gently over
the cut above his eye. "If you wanted to go to the beach,
we could have gone to my place in Sagaponack."

"At the moment, I truly wish I had."

She kissed his unshaven cheek, making an odd face
afterward, then gave him a bemused smile. "Come on."

"Where are we going?"

"To call on Mrs. Gloria Morgan Vanderbilt. Then we
must get you clean."

THEY had to make a number of inquiries before learning
the proper address, which was up in Portsmouth, north
of Newport on the road that led to Bristol. Tatty hurried up
the steps beneath the porte cochère and rang the doorbell
several times. By the time Bedford was able to catch up
with her, the door had been opened by a maid with a
French accent.

"Madame Vanderbilt is not at home," she said.

"When is she coming back?" Tatty demanded.

"Not today. She has gone to the house on Long Island."

The accent wasn't French. Bedford recognized it as the
more musical Belgian.

Tatty reached into her purse, extracting a visiting card.
"I am the Countess Iovashenkova. Madame Vanderbilt has
wrecked my automobile. It is being repaired at a garage
here and I will expect her to pay for it. She may telephone
me at this number."

The maid took the card gingerly, looking as if she herself were in serious trouble.

"Thank you," Bedford said.

She gave him a tiny smile, then hastened back inside.

W**HEN** did you become a countess?" Bedford asked.

"Upon the death of my poor mother."

"I never knew."

"Pishtosh. I've told you about the estates we owned before the damned revolution. Do you think they are acquired by mere commoners? Not in Russia. If you doubt me, you are welcome to consult the registry at the Russian Nobility Association."

"I do not doubt you ever."

She patted his knee. "You are noble in your own peculiar way, Bedford."

He stared ahead.

"Are you not feeling well?" she asked.

"That's not it. To my amazement, I'm feeling resentment."

"Toward Gloria Morgan Vanderbilt?"

"Toward them all."

CHAPTER 12

THEY stopped at the inn to pick up Bedford's things, then proceeded to the garage so Tatty could make arrangements for the stricken Packard.

"Will it ever run again?" she asked the mechanic.

"If you want to spend the money."

Tatty handed another of her cards to the mechanic.

"Do whatever is required and telephone me when it's ready. Send the bill to Mrs. Gloria Vanderbilt."

"The Mrs. Gloria Vanderbilt who has a house here?"

"The very one. If she declines to pay, let me know at once and I'll turn matters over to my attorney."

"But who will pay me?" The man stared dumbly at the card. "You're in New York. And, miss, I take cash."

"You'll have the car," Bedford said.

FOR a long while after they'd crossed on the ferry to Jamestown and started on the road back to New York, they didn't speak. Finally, as though in want of any other, Tatty brought up the subject of the late Czar and his family, and reports now circulating among the membership of New York's Russian Nobility Association of new proof that all of them had been murdered by the Bolsheviks.

"Shot to death with rifles and pistols," she said. "Even the little Anastasia and the family dog."

"When?"

"The last year of the war—somewhere out in the Urals. That horrid Stalin has renamed the town for the thug who organized it—Sverdlovsk, for Jacob Sverdlov. And Mr. Sverdlov has disappeared, doubtless murdered on Stalin's order. I do so hate that man."

Bedford wanted to go to sleep. "A man like that can't last long."

ALBERT drove much faster than Bedford, and by nightfall they had reached New Haven, where they stopped for dinner at a roadside café.

"We'll not make New York tonight," she said. "Where shall we sleep?"

"Bridgeport's just ahead."

"We certainly deserve better than that. How about that lovely little village in Westchester called Cross River."

There were no hotels in or near that tiny town. Only two general stores and a post office. And Bedford's farmhouse.

IT was after midnight when Albert turned the Pierce-Arrow off the North Salem road into Bedford's gravel drive. He'd not been to the house for more than a month, and was displeased to find a window broken, though nothing much seemed disturbed inside.

He had a hot bath, pulled on a favorite old robe, then

let Tatty dab iodine on his cuts and wind a new bandage around his still swollen ankle.

She kissed him on the forehead. "Do you suppose we shall ever get married?"

He felt an unexpected happy glow, but it faded. "A wonderful idea," he said. "But we ought to wait until we're both poor. Or both rich."

"I'd rather the rich. But money shouldn't make any difference?"

"Did you ever read F. Scott Fitzgerald's short story 'The Rich Boy'? 'Let me tell you about the very rich. They are different from you and me.'"

"I don't want to marry F. Scott Fitzgerald."

TATTY had taken a guest room, leaving Bedford to his parents' old four-poster bed in the house's main bedchamber. In the morning, he found her sleeping gently on the counterpane beside him, snug in nightgown and robe, where apparently she had been all night.

After rising, Tatty sent Albert to the general store down by the reservoir and secured the makings of breakfast, including eggs, ham, fresh bread, and jam. Bedford did the cooking. Before serving Tatty her plate, he on impulse sprinkled paprika on her eggs.

"That's interesting," she said.

"It's also Hungarian."

"You're thinking about them again."

"Yes, and if you don't mind, I'd like to make a little digression on the way back to the city."

"Sure. Where?"

"Bronxville."

THEY didn't have to go far out of their way. The town was situated between Yonkers and New Rochelle at the south end of the county along the White Plains Post Road, a route Bedford often took into the city.

The address Bedford had obtained for Paul Howard proved to be that of one of the substantial houses atop the hill that dominated Bronxville both topgraphically and socially. There were supposed to be a number of writers and intellectuals living there, despite the suburban aspect of the place, but Bedford didn't suppose Howard was one of them.

They parked at the curb. The lawn sloped sharply upward and Bedford's ankle suffered for the wrenching incline, but he refrained from complaint.

There was a doorbell, with chimes. No one responded after two rings. Patience ebbing, Tatty went up to the door's knocker and banged it down hard three times, exclaiming loudly, "Halloo! Halloo! This is the Countess Iovashenkova! Are you at home?"

"Aren't you overdoing this?" Bedford asked.

"Nyet," she said, glaring at the door.

Amazingly, as though commanded by her unhappy stare, it suddenly opened. A tall man with pale red hair, large spectacles, and a fleshy face appeared in the opening, looking from Tatty to Bedford and back again.

"Did you say you were a countess?" he asked finally.

"Not were a countess. I am one."

"We've come from Newport," Bedford said. "I'm sorry for the intrusion, but we'd like to talk to you about your wife."

Howard started to open the door wider, then halted. "Who are you? What do you have to do with my wife?" He had large, blubbery lips, and they seemed atremble.

"My name is Bedford Green. I was at the Vanderbilts the night—I'm afraid I'm the one who discovered her—Countess Zala, your wife."

"Zala?"

"Yes. Isn't she your wife?"

Howard was looking at them so uncertainly Bedford began to wonder if some mistake had been made.

"And you?" Howard said to Tatty.

"She is the Countess Tatiana Iovashenkova," said Bedford. "Better known on the New York stage as Tatty Chase."

"Dee-lighted," said Tatty, thrusting out her hand. Startled, Howard stepped back a little as he took it. She seized upon that as an invitation, and moved past him into the hallway after the handshake.

Bedford quickly followed. "We'll only be a minute, Mr. Howard. I do appreciate your taking the time."

They intruded no further than the foyer, but there held their ground. Howard realized he would either have to throw them out or invite them to sit down. He chose the latter, gesturing to a sitting room directly off the hall. It had a fireplace and tall windows, reminding Bedford of the sitting room in his Cross River house.

They all seated themselves, Howard nearest the doorway. He offered no refreshment.

"Are you with the police, Mr. Green?"

It was an odd question. Bedford was wearing his other navy blazer, clean white ducks, and white shoes. His answer wasn't quite the truth, but would have to do for the moment.

"I represent the Vanderbilt family," he said.

Howard's eyes widened.

"Your wife was found just off their beach, and obviously came to harm elsewhere," Bedford continued. "But the Vanderbilts are, of course, concerned."

That certainly seemed true enough.

"What is it you want to know?"

"Is she the Countess Zala?"

"She is a countess," Howard said, somewhat nervously.

"Or believed she was. There have been troubles over there, and . . ."

"Over there?"

"Hungary. What was Austro-Hungary." He fidgeted, his lips trembling. "But her name is not Zala in the United States. It's Kovacs. Margit Kovacs."

"Not Magda?"

"No. Margit, as in Margaret. In America, she calls herself Margaret."

Bedford was curious about Howard's continued use of the present tense. And something else.

"Excuse me, Mr. Howard, but how did you know to go to Newport? How did you learn about her death?"

"I received a telephone call."

"From whom?"

"A woman. I was told to go to the police station."

"But your wife hadn't been identified."

He shrugged. "I don't know. Someone must have known her. We have a summer house near Newport."

"In Bristol," Bedford said.

"Yes. How did you know?"

"The police." An inoffensive lie. "I went there, afterwards. I suppose, looking for you."

Bedford noticed that tears were beginning to well up in the man's eyes. Tatty picked that moment to rise from her chair and go looking at the framed art on the walls of the room. It was all prints, expensively framed—of fox hunting scenes.

"Do you ride?" she asked.

"Uh, no. Well, sometimes."

"Mr. Howard," Bedford said quickly. "It's a long drive to Newport. Yet you were there the next morning. Very early, apparently."

"I told you, someone phoned. I left immediately." He looked to Tatty, who was now examining a small nude statuette she'd picked up from the mantel. Bedford wondered why the man wasn't by this point demanding that they both leave at once.

"Did you bring her back with you?" Bedford asked.

"No. Of course not. I made arrangements—with a funeral home. They put her on a train. The funeral is the day after tomorrow."

"She's to be buried here?"

"At Kensico."

"Without an autopsy?"

"Why should there be an autopsy?"

Bedford had for all of his life been guided by a maxim curiously voiced by both Oscar Wilde and Bedford's high-collared grandfather: A gentleman never insults, except on purpose. Bedford was being inexcusably rude here, and wished he were not. But something was amiss.

"Mr. Green, are you representing the Vanderbilts in some official capacity? Are you their attorney?"

"No."

"Are you a lawyer at all?"

"As a matter of fact, I'm an art dealer. But a friend and neighbor of Gertrude Vanderbilt Whitney. It's on her behalf that I'm making these inquiries."

Howard rose shakily. "I don't think I can help you any further. I'd appreciate it if you would now go."

Bedford wanted to ask the man about the red velvet cord that had been wrapped around his wife's neck, but he'd importuned him enough. He got to his feet. "Yes, I fear we've intruded egregiously. My apologies. And my sympathy for your sad loss. Tatty, it's time to take our leave."

She'd been looking at a framed photograph sitting atop a closed grand piano. "Yes. Thank you." She headed directly for the door.

◆

THERE'S something false about that man," she said as Albert turned the Pierce-Arrow onto the White Plains Post Road.

"What do you mean?"

"I'm not sure. That photograph I was looking at was of a woman."

"Yes. His wife."

"No. Not the woman in the picture you took from the house in Rhode Island. Another woman. Different."

"How different?"

"Not at all as attractive. Not very attractive at all. And blond."

CHAPTER 13

TATTY dropped off Bedford and his suitcase at his art gallery, which he was pleased to find open. He found Sloane in the rear alcove, attending to a broken picture frame. She looked up at him as she might someone returned from the grave.

"Did you think I wasn't coming back?" he asked.

"Of course not. But Bedford, your face? Were you attacked?"

"Had a bit of an accident. Tatty's car is wrecked."

"That beautiful automobile?"

"It's been quite an adventure." He sank into a chair. "Not my fault, though much else is."

"Would you like a drink?"

"No thank you. How about you? Did you find yourself a verse libre poet?"

"Not quite. Edmund Wilson tried to pick me up at Chumley's, but I declined. I'm in no mood to be taking up Edna St. Vincent Millay's castoffs."

"Not even me?"

"Especially not you." She returned to her work, gently removing the canvas from the damaged frame.

"Do you by any chance understand Hungarian?" he asked.

"Paprika. That's about it."

He opened his suitcase, removing the packet of letters. "How about lunch at André Mohar's?"

ANDRÉ was not in his restaurant, as was often the case during the day, but they were given the best available table, nevertheless. Sloane ordered *borjupaprikas galuskaval*, a veal and paprika dish, not realizing it came with *galuska*, or dumplings. She made a face.

"Do you find them unappetizing?" Bedford said.

"No, but I'll certainly be that if I eat too many of these."

"André will be offended."

"Then you eat them. Anyway, he's not here."

"I'm having *szatmari modra*. You see? It has its own dumplings."

She sighed. "Yum."

"Aside from the dumplings, you seem in better spirits."

"I'm back among the living—and real life." She stabbed a dumpling with her fork and took a tiny bite from it.

Sandor Petofi, the waiter, came hovering by. "Everything is all right, Mr. Green?"

"Excellent. When do you expect André back?"

"I don't know. He had to go see the bootlegger."

"I was in here a few days ago, asking if anyone had ever heard of a Countess Zala."

"Countess Zala, yes. Noblewoman. I told you. She was killed."

"I'm talking about a beautiful young woman."

"Beautiful, maybe. But this countess was not young. I think more than forty years old. Very good friend of Admiral Horthy. You know him? Very tough man. A son of a bitch. He put down Hungarian Revolution with what they call 'the White Terror.' Killed lots of Communists and Jews. Made himself regent."

Bedford shook his head. "Sorry, I don't keep up much with Hungarian politics."

"He runs Hungary now. Tough guy. He is why I come here."

"This countess, did she have a daughter?"

"She had children. I don't know about daughter. Maybe."

"Would André know this Countess Zala?"

"Sure. Very famous in Budapest."

"No, I mean the daughter."

Sandor shrugged. "You like dumplings?"

"Yum," said Sloane.

Bedford took the packet of letters from his coat pocket, separating the ones written in Hungarian. "I have a favor to ask, Sandor."

"Sure."

"These letters are in Hungarian, which I'm afraid I don't understand. If you could look through them, when it's convenient, and tell me what they say, I'd be very appreciative."

Petofi took them, glancing at the name and address on the one on top. "It's from Esztergom," he said.

"Esztergom?"

"A town northwest of Budapest. The church is very big there."

"A big cathedral?" Sloane asked.

"No," Sandor corrected. "Important. King Istvan, Hungary's first king, he was crowned there. Is where the archbishop is."

"Is the letter from the archbishop?" Sloane asked.

The waiter looked again at the envelope. "I do not think so." He smiled and slipped the letters into a pocket. "I am busy now with lunchtime, but I will look at them later and let you know."

"I'll come by this evening."

Sloane ate another dumpling.

AFTER lunch, Bedford took his suitcase back to his flat, putting the things he had taken from the Bristol house in a pantry cupboard, setting them behind some canned goods on the uppermost shelf. Then he telephoned the police station on West Fifty-fourth Street, where his friend, homicide Lieutenant Joseph D'Alessandro, was headquartered and could sometimes be found. As the man had not returned from lunch, Bedford left a message.

RETURNING to the gallery, he saw through the window that Sloane now had a customer, a tall gentleman who stood with his back to the street. There was something anxious in Sloane's eyes when she took note of Bedford coming through the door. Stepping inside, Bedford realized the man she was with was the General.

"Mr. Vanderbilt," Bedford said. "This is a pleasant surprise."

The General appeared uncomfortable, as though he had come there reluctantly.

"Mr. Green."

They shook hands politely, Vanderbilt maintaining his stiff stance. His eyes went unhappily to Sloane, who was now the picture of wide-eyed curiosity.

"I am assuming, sir, that you are not here to purchase art," Bedford said.

The General glanced uneasily at an Egon Schiele nude that had been hanging on the rear wall without customer interest for weeks, then shook his head.

"Perhaps you would be more comfortable if we went to your sister Gertrude's. It's just up the street."

Bedford had been planning to call upon her anyway.

"No, actually. I just came from there."

Sloane was an unusually perceptive person. "Bedford, I have some errands to run. Can you watch things on your own for a while?"

"Yes. Thank you. See you later."

"Goodbye, Mr. Vanderbilt. So nice to see you again."

When she'd gone, Bedford placed a "closed" sign in the window and then ushered the General into the alcove and to a chair. He offered coffee—and even a drink—but Vanderbilt declined.

"Mr. Green," he began, "I'm sorry if the tragic occurrence the other night caused you trouble, or if in our reaction to it my family in any way gave you the impression that you and Miss Smith were unwelcome."

"Not at all, sir."

"The incident was very upsetting."

"Indeed. For us, too."

The General's gaze had been unwavering, but now fell away. "Unfortunately, this matter has generated talk. Ridiculous talk, but the sort of rubbish that often finds its way into the less respectable newspapers."

"Like the *New York Day*." Bedford smiled.

Vanderbilt's eyes lifted again. "As I said to you earlier, Mr. Green, my wife and I found your conduct as a journalist exemplary."

"Thank you." Bedford folded his hands in his lap, politely waiting as the General struggled to get to the heart of the matter.

"This talk concerns my son, Neil. There's a presumption of some romantic feeling between him and the lady, and conjecture to the effect that her death was somehow connected to that. One account has it that she drowned herself over the family's inhospitable attitudes toward her. Others hint at foul play. It's all quite outrageous."

"I daresay."

"My son made the lady's acquaintance in Paris, during the war. It was all very innocent. You were there. You know."

Bedford nodded.

"Then she turned up in Rhode Island last year and came looking for my son—rather relentlessly, I'm afraid. He did nothing to encourage her, of course. Neil has friendships with a number of young ladies. But he felt sorry for her. Said she had suffered in the war, and had lost her parents. He befriended her, but that was all . . ."

"I understand, General."

"She was difficult—a highly irrational person. Some of her pronouncements were akin to ravings. A bit frightening. But we wished to accommodate him. He's a fine young man. Quite well intentioned."

"And with a literary bent."

Bedford's observation pleased the General. "Yes. Quite so." A frown intruded. "All this gossip is dreadfully unfair. As I say, outrageous. And if it should find its way into the public print . . ."

"General, I sympathize with you entirely, but I am no longer in the employ of the *New York Day*. I've no influence—"

"Mr. Green, I've come here today to ask your help, but not in the way you think." He shifted in his seat, leaning forward slightly. "Gertrude admires you. She's told me how resourceful you are—and of the wide variety of people you know."

"Just a poor art peddler, General."

A quick, dismissive wave of the hand indicated the General's impatience with false modesty. "Captain Green, the best antidote to irresponsible gossip is the truth. I'd like you to help us discover what really happened to that young

woman—and if foul play was involved, why it happened.
I think something more malevolent than accidental drowning may be involved here, and it may include an effort to
harm my family and its reputation."

"I am not a policeman, General. And I am not a private
detective. If that's what you're in need of, the Pinkerton
Agency has—"

The General raised his hand again to stay Bedford's
words. "Gertrude says you are a gentleman, Captain
Green. An honorable man. And that is what we require—
in addition to your other talents."

He rose, apparently satisfied that the interview had concluded successfully, though Bedford had made no such
response.

"I shall, of course, compensate you for whatever expenses you might incur—and for your time."

Bedford was about to say that would not be necessary,
but caught himself. He'd agreed to nothing, though in
truth, he was interested in the prospect.

"What if I told you I was thinking of pursuing this matter on my own?" he said.

"I shouldn't be surprised at all." Vanderbilt took a card
from his pocket, bearing only his name and a telephone
number. "Let me know what you decide. I'll be in town for
a while."

Bedford rose. "There's something I'd appreciate knowing. Your sister invited the Hungarian woman to your
party—but not as your son's date. Her escort was this Professor Hovarth."

"Dr. Hovarth is a friend of Count Szechenyi. They're
working together on some sort of historical project involv-
ing the Hungarian monarchy. As a favor to the family, he
agreed to accompany the lady to Newport."

"But why from New York? She had a house in Bristol."

"We were told she was going to be coming from New
York, where she also had a residence. But she failed to

meet Dr. Hovarth at Grand Central and she wasn't on the later trains."

He pushed through the curtain that led to the gallery's main room, with Bedford following.

"Something else, General. Just what exactly was her name?"

"She was Countess Zala. Magda Zala. Her title was quite legitimate. Count Szechenyi checked it. The family is a very old one in Hungary."

"Not Margit Kovacs?"

"No." He moved to the door. "Though I believe that is the name under which she entered the United States."

"Her funeral is tomorrow. Will anyone from your family be attending?"

"Would you recommend it?"

Bedford shook his head. "She was married. To a Bronxville man named Paul Howard. Did you know about him?"

"I did not." The General grinned. "You see, you are indeed the man for the job."

He went out the door, happy to leave. Bedford watched through the window as a long car pulled up almost immediately, the driver hurrying to open the door.

BEDFORD sat at his desk as he waited for Sloane to return, idly looking through some unpaid bills. That quickly became too depressing. He watched the traffic on the sidewalk and street for a while, trying to match individual passersby with paintings he had on display they might possibly want to buy. As the passersby kept passing by, this proved depressing as well.

Finally, compelled by what now loomed as inescapable necessity, he fumbled through a desk drawer for a scrap of paper with a telephone number on it he'd almost thrown away.

Liam O'Bannion's New York residence was a suite of rooms in an elegant old hotel on upper Madison Avenue a half block off Central Park. His place of business was quite something else, however.

"Yeah?" said the man who answered. If he looked anything like he sounded, Bedford had small interest in making his acquaintance.

"I'd like to speak to Mr. O'Bannion, please."

"Mr. O'Bannion ain't here."

"Why don't you ask him if he ain't there? Tell him Bedford Green is calling."

A grunt, then silence, though the line remained connected. Finally, he returned.

"Mr. O'Bannion doesn't want to talk to you right now."

"He doesn't know what I'm calling about."

"That don't matter."

"Would another time be convenient?"

Another grunt. While he waited, Bedford took out the photo of the dead countess and Neil Vanderbilt in Paris. She was, he noted, very expensively dressed. No Montmartre good-time girl she. No immigrant named Margit Kovacs. The lady might have just left one of Edith Wharton's teas.

The man of the grunts returned. "He says to come by tonight. Around midnight. He says you know the place."

Bedford knew it too well—a warehouse across the street from Pier 55. It was very close to being the last place in Manhattan he'd want to meet anyone at that hour.

"Very well. I'll be there."

The response was a click.

SLOANE came in a few minutes later, her arms full of shopping. She set her packages down on Bedford's desk, then sat down beside them, swinging her long legs.

"Well?" she said. "Do they think we stole some towels?"

"Not at all. He was most civil and courteous."

"He must want something from you."

"Yes."

"Something to do with what happened up there."

"Everything to do with what happened there. He wants me to find out just what precisely did occur, and why."

"Discreetly."

"Yes."

"What about the gallery?"

"He's offering compensation."

"Yes, but the gallery's your business—on the rare occasion there is any."

"You don't want me to do this?"

She shoved herself off the desk, smoothing her skirt. "Actually, I do."

"Why?"

"Because you're going to do it no matter what I say."

LIEUTENANT D'Alessandro was in Lindy's, as Bedford had hoped, eating a huge pastrami sandwich.

"Don't you ever eat Italian food?" Bedford asked.

"Called you back," the detective said. "Nobody answered."

"At lunchtime?"

"Yeah. Sit down. What can I do for you?"

Bedford slid into the booth. Bedford thought of ordering rice pudding, then reconsidered.

"It's not a very appetizing subject. It's about an autopsy."

"I'm a cop, Bedford." He took another mouthful.

Without naming the Vanderbilts, Bedford told his tale

of the body washing ashore during a party at Newport, and the decision of the local police to declare it a drowning.

The detective continued eating. "Can't blame them, Bedford. You took the cord off her neck."

"But there were marks on her neck. Very well defined. And cuts and bruises elsewhere."

"Would you like to know how many 'accidental drowning' victims we pull out of the East River in the same condition? Sloppy police work, maybe, but it closes cases."

"Joseph. Would an autopsy at this point establish the cause of death?"

"Sure."

"How would I go about getting an autopsy performed?"

"Bedford, we don't have any jurisdiction in Rhode Island. If the cops there stiffed you, you're goin' to have to stay stiffed."

"Her husband's brought her body back here. To Bronxville. They're going to bury her tomorrow."

"We don't have any jurisdiction in Bronxville."

"Could you get a court order?"

"I could try. Would the husband object?"

"Probably."

D'Alessandro wiped his mouth thoroughly with his napkin, then pushed his chair back. "Just how are you involved in this, Bedford?"

"As I say, I found the body."

"And?"

"She washed up on the property of some people I know. They'd like to know what happened."

"Why didn't they ask the local police?"

"It's complicated."

A waiter came by to pour coffee.

"My advice to you, Bedford, is forget about it. You're not going to get anywhere without a court order and we won't ask for one of those unless you can tell me a hell of a lot more than you have. Why do you allow yourself to get mixed up in these things? What do you get out of it except a lot of trouble?"

"I satisfy my curiosity."

"Not tonight, I'm afraid." Joey D stood up. There was no sign or mention of the check.

"Thanks anyway."

"Tell you what," said D'Alessandro as they moved toward the door. "I've got friends with the New York state cops who've got to know guys with the Rhode Island state troopers. We can try them—find out at least what the locals think she died from—drowning, or strangling, or whatever—though I don't understand what difference it really makes."

"I'd appreciate whatever you can find out. I think the local police in Newport are mixed up with bootleggers, if that gives you any leverage."

"Bedford, we're all mixed up with bootleggers. Let me see what I can do." He put on his hat. "You're sure you don't want to tell me who these Newport friends of yours are?"

"It wouldn't make you happy to know."

THE doorman had admitted Bedford without question many times before and did so now, with a tip of the hat and a bit of a knowing grin. After this, he'd doubtless receive firm instructions never to do this again.

Bedford had wrapped the framed photograph in butcher's paper and stood holding it carefully under one arm as he rang the doorbell to the apartment. She took a long while coming to the door, opening it only narrowly, one beautiful brown eye revealing itself to him through the crack.

"I should have known," she said. "What do you want?"

"I really hate to bother you, but once again I need your help."

"Is this about the Hungarian woman?"

"Very much so."

"Haven't you caused enough bother about that?"

"I'm sorry, but I don't know where else to turn."

She sighed unhappily. "Look, Bedford. I'm Italian and Hungarian. That's all there is. What are you going to do if you get yourself mixed up in something to do with Greeks or Norwegians?"

"Have pleasanter conversations than this with you, I hope."

Claire unhooked the door chain and let him in. She was wearing a robe and was barefoot. Her hair seemed damp and he guessed she had just bathed.

"Have you eaten?" he asked.

"Yes."

"Would you like to go out for dessert? Coffee? A cordial?"

"No thank you."

She gestured for him to follow her into her living room. He took a chair by a window; she chose one opposite. The view was south. The glow that was Times Square was visible between office buildings in the distance.

She folded her arms defensively, and sat back, curling her legs beneath her. "What is it you want this time?"

"I've missed you."

"Well, I've missed you—a little. But right now you just remind me of a very bad time."

"I understand." He carefully unwrapped his package. Handing her the framed photograph, he watched her reaction as she brought the picture near.

"Is that the woman you remembered from that party? Something to do with a Prince Skorzeny—at the Astor?"

She held it up. "Is this the Countess Zala?"

"That's what I'm asking you, love."

Claire examined the image more closely. "This is the woman who was at the party. She was totally out of control, a wild woman. Very amorous."

"With what man?"

"No man."

"Women?"

"Yes."

"You?"

"I left." She gave the photograph another look, then set it down on a side table.

"Did you see her body?" she asked.

"I found it."

"Oh dear."

"I think she was murdered."

Claire's face began to pale. She stared at the floor.

"Claire, I need to know some things. I'm helping out the family."

"Hers?"

"The Vanderbilts."

"A bunch of high-hatters."

"Yes, but—anyway, how did you come to be singing there?"

"My bandleader friend Freddy. He said I was requested."

"By who?"

She shrugged. "The lady of the house, I presume. Pretty big house."

"Did she know you knew the Countess Zala?"

"I didn't *know* her. It was an encounter. You've encountered people at bad parties—drunks, bores. That doesn't make them your pals."

"Did she know you'd had an encounter with the countess?"

"Bedford, this is getting to be unpleasant."

"I'm sorry. Just one more thing. Who is this Prince Skorzeny?"

She shrugged. "I don't know. Some rich Hungarian ex-patriate. The party was supposed to be a charity benefit for some Hungarian group."

"Do you remember the name of it?"

She shook her head.

"Do you still have the invitation?"

Claire flushed, then nodded. "It was the first time I was ever invited to anything by a prince."

"Don't let them overawe you. As my friend Dayton Crosby always says, they're just people."

She studied him. "I actually had a good time there. Until . . ."

"Claire, the invitation."

"All right." She went into the bedroom, returning within a minute with the invitation.

Bedford pondered it. "May I borrow this?"

"Okay. Long as I get it back."

"Of course."

He took a deep breath. "Sure you wouldn't like to go out somewhere?"

She bit down on her lip. "Yes, I would. But not now. Bedford? I don't think I'm ready to go on like before."

"I understand. When do you start your tour with Freddy's band?"

Claire grimaced. "That fell through."

"I'm sorry."

"I'm just as happy. But my agent hasn't anything lined up until the fall. Maybe I can find some club dates here in town."

He hated to think of her as a saloon singer, though he'd always had a soft place in his heart for those ladies.

"That was your only engagement with Freddy? The Newport party?"

"Yes." She stood up. Noticing that her robe was loose, she pulled the belt tighter, then led him back down the hall to the door.

"I'd like to see you again," she said. "Sometime. But not until you're done with all this prying and snooping." She opened the door. "So good night."

"Will you be all right?"

"I have money in the bank. And I've been asked to do a little play. It's not on Broadway, and it pays next to nothing. But I may do it. Better than singing to drunken swells."

"I'll come see you, whatever it is."

"After you're done with the Vanderbilts. And the Hungarians." She kissed him, but on the cheek. "Good night."

"Claire . . ."

"Good night."

B EDFORD had carried a gun to Newport, where he'd had no use for it whatsoever. This evening he was walking through Hell's Kitchen toward the Hudson River docks without so much as a jackknife in his pockets, and he felt as vulnerable as when his machine gun had jammed in a dogfight over Ypres with a Fokker D-VII on his tail.

Liam O'Bannion had been his comrade then. They'd saved each other's lives in the air and been drunk together endless times on the ground. But at the end of the war, O'Bannion had told Bedford he was going to kill him—for just cause. In all the time since, he had never explained why. It had been seven years, and Bedford was still alive.

Bedford knocked on the door, which had been much painted over. It was metal, and his raps made insufficient sound. Looking about, he found a piece of broken brick and hammered with that a half-dozen times. Then he stepped back into the shadows, waiting.

The face that appeared in the opening doorway was large—a blob of congealed mush with a cauliflower nose and two beady eyes stuck above it. He wagged a stubby finger, indicating Bedford was to step forward, and when Bedford did, the man reached out and yanked him inside by the arm.

The door slammed shut behind him with a fearsome bang.

"This way, Green."

"I know."

Liam was in his office, a dusty, wooden-floored space with few amenities and a single window so grimy as to be opaque, allowing only a hint of a view of the street outside. His desk was far to the side of it, lest some competitor try to get lucky with a gunshot through the glass.

"Captain Green," he said.

"Captain O'Bannion."

Liam was seated in a wooden swivel chair with a horse-hair seat, his feet up on the desk. Like many in his trade, he was a dresser—as spiffy as New York's mayor, right down to the spats. But he avoided the garish hues so prevalent among the customers at Lindy's. Rather, he took his style from his notion of the proper English gentleman, complete to a weskit.

"Sit down, Bedford. You look nervous. Want a drink?"

Bedford seated himself on an uncomfortable chair to the side of the desk, and out of the way of the grimy window. "Thank you."

Mush-Face, whose real name was Lester, set a bottle of scotch and a small glass on the edge of the desk, but did not pour. Somewhat nervously, Bedford performed the task. O'Bannion's glass was still mostly full.

"You're a bloody amazement, Green," he said.

Bedford, smiled, a little shyly, not knowing what was coming next.

"I told you I was going to kill you," O'Bannion continued, eyeing Bedford over the rim of his glass like someone sighting a gun. "You don't know why. You don't know if I still mean to do it. And if I do, you don't know when. Yet you keep coming round. Are you feeling lucky, or just being stupid?"

"I'm hopeful. Always hopeful."

"Then you're a damn fool."

"Agreed."

"So tell me what's on your mind. Usually find you in posher districts at an hour like this."

"There was a murder—in Newport. A very beautiful young Hungarian woman—the Countess Zala. Magda Zala. Mean anything to you?"

O'Bannion shook his head.

"She washed up at the Breakers while the Vanderbilts were having a party."

"Vanderbilts?"

"Yes. What I need to know . . ."

Liam set down his glass and dropped his feet to the floor, leaning forward.

"What you need to know, Green, is that those people in Newport—the rich ones on the peninsula—they're very good customers of mine. Because of my arrangement with them, the local cops don't get in my way. I unload shipments there all the time. I don't want any trouble out there. I don't want the cops riled up."

"As I said, I'm helping the Vanderbilts. If you don't want anyone riled up, you'd be much better off helping me."

"Helping how?"

"They want to know what happened to that woman. And who was responsible."

O'Bannion poured himself more whiskey. "I'm not getting mixed up in any murders, boyo. Not that kind."

Bedford ignored this. "Do you still run boats up Rhode Island Sound? Offload at Second Beach?"

"Why do you care about that?" A frown darkened O'Bannion's fair-skinned Irish face.

Bedford sat back, folding his hands in his lap. "I'd like

you to inquire of your rum-runner skippers what other boats were on the water when this happened."

"Now how in bloody hell would anyone know that?"

"Your people are always on the lookout for federal revenue cutters. They watch every light on the water. I need to know if they saw one near Ochre Point that evening, especially around midnight. And whether it was a sailing yacht or a motor."

O'Bannion rubbed his chin. "Either way, it could be anybody."

"I'd appreciate whatever you can find out."

"You already owe me, Green."

"I know. I hope I'll be around to repay you."

The Irishman grinned very broadly now. "Have another drink."

MOHAR'S restaurant was closed and dark. Bedford rapped on the door, in case some of the kitchen help might still be on duty, but no sound or movement stirred within. There was nothing left to be done that night. He went home to bed.

CHAPTER 14

"THIS is a really wonderful date, Bedford," said Tatty as Albert drove them north along the parkway. "Arising at dawn to go to a funeral. I shudder to think what entertainment you'll think of next."

"It's nice of you to come along."

She looked at him. "You don't seem very happy this morning."

"We're going to a funeral."

"Just be thankful it's not Russian Orthodox. We'd have to stand for hours."

"I think it's Episcopalian."

"There are Hungarian Episcopalians?"

"Her husband."

THERE were relatively few people in the church. They sat in clumps here and there in the pews, stealing furtive glances at their fellow mourners. Bedford and Tatty kept to the rearmost row, but were quickly noticed anyway.

Paul Howard was up front beside a primly, but well-dressed woman and a younger man who somewhat resembled him. Otherwise, Bedford could not identify anyone. Joe Christopher was not among those present.

Bedford had hoped there'd be an opportunity to view the body, but the casket was closed.

The priest, a middle-aged, pink-faced man who seemed uncomfortable in his obvious unfamiliarity with the deceased, spoke mostly by rote, his remarks largely to do with religion. In his few references to the countess, he called her Margaret.

The eulogy was delivered by Howard himself. He talked about his late wife as though she was a refugee, a victim of the war. He said she was passionate in her beliefs—and liked animals. He cried.

Afterward, Bedford and Tatty remained in their seats, watching the others file out. Howard gave Bedford a dark, unhappy look, but passed on without comment. The woman and younger man who'd been sitting with him eyed Bedford curiously—and Tatty even more so. After them came a few people who might well have been Hungarian, and then a slender woman whose face was hidden behind a very heavy veil. She wore black, her ensemble complete to a black fox fur.

Bedford gave a start. A large man who'd been sitting up front and to the right finally stood and came up the side aisle, passing near.

"Dr. Hovarth." Bedford said.

The professor halted, bowed slightly to Bedford, and then to Tatty, and then moved on, seeming highly preoccupied.

"Can we go home now?" Tatty whispered.

"I want to go to the cemetery."

"Please, no."

"I'll buy you a lovely lunch afterward."

"Where?"

"The Carlyle."

"Done."

I T was a long drive to Kensico Cemetery. At one point they lost their view of the funeral procession ahead of them altogether, and took a wrong turn, arriving finally just as the coffin was being taken from the hearse.

"Let's drive past them," Bedford said to Albert. "We can park over by those trees."

"Should we be afraid of them?" Tatty asked.

"We should be respectful."

They watched the group file down the slope to a patch of brown, freshly turned earth below. Hovarth was the last in the procession, and kept looking behind him—as though for Bedford.

Perhaps that was a conceit. The man may only have been expecting someone who had not yet arrived.

The woman in the heavy black veil was present, but kept her distance from the others. There was something about her height, slenderness, and carriage that struck Bedford as familiar.

"What's the point of being here if we're just going to sit in the car?" Tatty asked.

"I want to see what happens."

"What happens is, they put the casket into the ground, then cover it with dirt. You weren't thinking of digging it up again, were you?"

"I've always said you have a flair for comedy, Tatty."

The clergyman was speaking again. If it was in prayer, Paul Howard wasn't joining in. He was staring across the grave and up the hill directly at Tatty's Pierce-Arrow. But when the cleric concluded, and the attendants began to lower the coffin into the grave, it was Hovarth who started up the slope toward them.

"What do we do?" Tatty asked.

"It's all right. He wants to talk to us and I'd like to hear from him."

The large man was breathing a little heavily as he trudged up to the car.

"Good morning, Mr. Green," he said, putting a foot on the running board.

"Good morning, Professor. Nice day for a funeral. May I present the Countess Iovashenkova."

Tatty waited for Hovarth to bow to her before gracing him with a dazzling, theatrical smile.

"Your presence seems to have upset the family," the Hungarian said. "In great particular, the husband."

"I'm curious about your presence, Professor. You said you didn't know the woman."

"I am here at the request of Count and Countess Szechenyi. They wanted someone to represent them, to express their regrets."

"But no member of the family."

Hovarth ignored that. "And you, Mr. Green?"

"I feel an obligation to the deceased."

"How is that?"

"If you had looked upon her face after we pulled her from the sea, you would understand."

Hovarth nodded sagely.

"Can you clarify something for me, Professor? Why would a Magda, Countess Zala, make herself Margit Kovacs?"

"A name of convenience. That's common with some refugees. Here she was also Margaret Howard."

"But definitely a countess?"

"It's true. She's the daughter of the unfortunate countess of the same name who was killed by Hungarian Communists in Paris. Her father, Count Zala, was a colonel of Hussars who died in an artillery barrage in the war. But she married Mr. Howard—a commoner. Under the laws and traditions of the Hungarian nobility, titles do not confer to the commoner husbands of noble ladies, so in the United States she was merely Mrs. Howard. The U.S. Constitution does not recognize noble titles. In fact, it expressly forbids them."

"Does that make the Countess Gladys Szechenyi merely Mrs. Szechenyi?"

Hovarth fought back a smile. "She is what you would call a special case."

Paul Howard was now coming toward them, along with the prim but well-dressed woman and the younger red-haired man. Albert tapped the steering wheel impatiently with his forefinger.

"Well, I believe we have overstayed our welcome," Bedford said, turning to Tatty. "Countess Iovashenkova, it is time for lunch."

Albert started the ignition—which happily worked, obviating the need for any cranking—and jammed the car into gear. Just as the sweaty, red-faced Howard came trudging up to them, he let out the clutch and pulled away.

"Slow down as you go by their cars," Bedford said.

Albert obeyed. Bedford studied the rear license plates as they glided by the parking area, his eyes staying with one in particular.

Now he knew who the woman in the heavy black veil was.

THEY were halfway through a pleasant lunch at the Carlyle Hotel, near Tatty's Upper East Side residence, when Bedford remembered the letters he had left with Mohar.

"I don't suppose you'd like to have dessert in Greenwich Village."

Tatty looked up from her caviar. "I have a script to read this afternoon. It's rather a dreary play, but they're offering me the lead."

And, he feared, offering her an opportunity for investment.

"I'm sure you will make it a wonderful hit. You may count on me for opening night."

"Let us hope this little Hungarian drama of yours has concluded by then, darling."

MOHAR was at a table near the entrance, reading a copy of the *New York Day*, his restaurant now devoid of customers in the hot midafternoon.

"Letters? You gave Sandor letters? He said nothing about them." He looked about, spotting a waiter named Janos. "Where is Sandor?"

Janos pointed to the kitchen door.

"Have him come here, please."

A moment later, Petofi emerged, clutching the packet of letters, even though he'd not yet been asked for them.

"I am sorry, André," the waiter said. "I read them, but I was waiting for Mr. Green to come back."

"Well, here he is."

"What do they say?" Bedford asked.

Petofi handed them to him. The topmost now bore both wine and gravy stains. "Most say nothing. One asks for money for someone in Szigliget. Another talks about a lack of decent food. Another relates a journey to Trieste." He hesitated. "A few are about love."

"Addressed to her, the Countess Zala?"

"Addressed to Magda."

"And who are they from?"

"Several different men." Petofi then smiled. "And one from a woman."

"The one signed Bella?"

"Yes. That one. Yes."

"A romantic letter?"

"Yes, Mr. Green."

HE stopped on his way back to the gallery at the little park in Sheridan Square, taking out the packet of letters again and looking through them one by one. There were two curious things about the love letter signed Bella. The first, as Bedford now recalled, was that the writer had signed it "Bela," with one "l."

The second was that it was missing. Sandor had not returned it to him.

Bedford went to the pay telephone in the cigar store just across the street and called Mohar's restaurant. The waiter was taking an order and it was several minutes before he came on the line.

"Yes, Mr. Green? Is something wrong?"

"One of the letters I asked you to read has gone missing."

"You sure? I gave you back the whole stack."

"It's not here, Sandor. The romantic one from a lady named Bella. Spelled B-E-L-A."

"Yes. I remember it. I will look. Maybe I dropped it somewhere. I'm sorry."

"It's just that they're not mine. I mean to return them."

"I look, Mr. Green. Don't worry."

Bedford made another call. Happily, after an inordinate number of rings, Claire Pell came to the phone.

"What now, Bedford? Damn it. I was in the bath."

"Sorry. I just had a question."

"Yes?"

"How do you spell the name 'Bella' in Hungarian?"

"Bella?"

"As in Arabella, or Isabella."

"B-E-L-L-A."

"Not B-E-L-A."

"No."

"I see."

"That's a man's name."

"Bella?"

"No, 'Bay-la.' In Hungary, that's a man's name. Bela. As in Bela Bartok."

"Oh."

"Is that all you wanted?"

"I want to see you again."

A sigh. "Glad I could be of help." She hung up.

RETURNING to his gallery, he discovered that Sloane had been having a remarkable day, selling three charcoal sketches by John W. Alexander, a small landscape oil by Ethel Penniwell, and a salacious nude by Kenyon Cox.

"You're an absolute whiz," he said.

"You're solvent," she said.

They celebrated with a dinner in Little Italy and went afterward to a party thrown by someone from the Provincetown Players, who had returned from a stay in Truro on Cape Cod. A writer Bedford knew named Cox, just back from Europe, came up to him.

"You're Bedford Green."

"I suppose so."

"You know the Fitzgeralds?"

"I met them for the first time last month. In Paris. We spent some time together. How are they?"

"Zelda is sleeping with everyone," Cox said. "I could have slept with Zelda whenever I wanted."

"Did you?" asked Bedford.

"No."

Ring Lardner, who'd been standing nearby, had overheard them. "Scott is a novelist," he said profoundly. "And Zelda is a novelty."

Someone nearby applauded the line, raising her glass.

Glasses were being raised with great frequency. A few couples began dancing to a phonograph recording of the Charleston, which required some agility in the small apartment. Bedford thought of asking Sloane to dance, but thought again. She was in good spirits. An inadvertent crash against a bookcase might undo all that.

The mention of the Fitzgeralds planted a seed. When the record was finished, someone called out the name of a song that had been drunkenly authored by Scott Fitzgerald and Bunny Wilson and become all the rage in New York. A few began singing it. By the next chorus, everyone was doing so.

"Larger than a rat!
More faithful than a cat!
Dog! Dog! Dog!"

T**HEY** walked home, and Sloane kissed him good night. After she'd gone inside, he started for his own flat, but was feeling so happy he stopped by Chumley's for a nightcap.

Lee Chumley was at the bar, drinking a beer and writing something on note paper.

"You're in late, Green."

"Went to a party." He ordered a whiskey. "I don't suppose you know anything about a Hungarian countess named Zala?" Bedford asked.

"I am a member of the International Workers of the World, as you very well know, Green. The only Hungarians I consort with in this city are all Bolsheviks."

"How about Bela Kun?"

"He is a very big Bolshevik."

"Is he here in New York?"

"I don't think so. Maybe he was shot. They killed a lot of Communists in Hungary."

CHAPTER 15

THERE were two surprises waiting for him upon arriving at his gallery the following morning. One was an envelope, left by messenger, containing a letter from the General that wished Bedford well in his enterprise and a check for five hundred dollars.

The other surprise came a few minutes later, when the primly dressed woman from the previous day's funeral came walking through the door and right up to Bedford, who was sitting at his desk.

She wore a pale blue, long-sleeved dress with a longish skirt and white collar and facings. Her hat, gloves, and shoes were white as well. She was delicately featured and had a sweetness about her that put him in mind of Mary Pickford. Her hair was a light brown in color that in the sunlight looked blond.

"You're Bedford Green," she said. "You were at the funeral yesterday, but you did not wait to talk to us."

"That's true. My apologies for our abrupt departure but we seemed to be disturbing Mr. Howard. I'm afraid I do not know your name."

"I am Alice Paul, and I am by way of being Howard's sister-in-law."

Bedford responded blankly to this, then said very formally: "How may I be of assistance to you?"

Sloane had poked her head from the alcove, surveying the visitor as she might a painting offered for sale—one she was unsure of buying.

"I'm not familiar with the neighborhood," said the woman, eyeing Sloane warily. "Is there a place where we might have coffee and talk?"

H E chose an inexpensive restaurant over on Sixth Avenue which was open in the morning but did most of its business later in the day. Mrs. Paul said little during their walk, except to comment on the strangeness of the street life they passed. She said she was new to the city, and had never been in this district before.

"I'm from Ohio," she said. "We're all from Ohio originally."

"But not the deceased?"

"Oh no. She's Hungarian."

"There are no Hungarians in Ohio?"

"None like her." She smiled demurely.

She ordered a piece of cherry pie with her coffee. Bedford, feeling celebratory because of Sloane's picture sales, had a dish of ice cream with his.

"Margaret was my sister-in-law," she said. "I'm married to Howard's brother Robert."

Bedford nodded. "So you explained."

"Mr. Horvath said you were working for the Vanderbilts."

"How would he know that?" Bedford, of course, knew very well how Horvath might know that.

"I've no idea. It's what he said. Something about helping the Vanderbilts learn something about Margaret's death."

"Let's just say I'm interested in the matter."

"Well, I'd like to help. So would Robert."

"You and the countess—Mrs. Howard—were close."

"I didn't know her very well, actually. Sometimes she was very nice, very friendly. Sometimes she was difficult."

"How so?"

"Sometimes she would call when Howard was visiting us and ask him for money. She'd scream and wail sometimes. And curse. I assume they were curses. They were in Hungarian. But they sounded like curses."

"You don't seem the kind of lady who would have heard many."

"Howard curses, but I suppose he's had reason."

Bedford finished his ice cream. "What is it you think you can do to help?"

"I've no idea, but if there's anything you'd like to know. . . ."

"To begin with, why is it you are Mrs. Paul and your brother-in-law is Paul Howard? And why do you call him by his last name?"

"Because it isn't his last name. Or wasn't. He changed it. He used to be Howard Paul, but he didn't like the sound of it. 'Too, European,' he said. So he became Paul Howard. My husband—his brother Robert—doesn't mind having Paul for a last name. Neither do I. It's the name on the family business, where the money comes from. What there is of it. My family name is Pfeiffer. I was happy to keep it until I married Robert."

"And what is the family business?"

"My family's? My father was a dentist, in Marion, Ohio."

"I mean the Paul family's business."

"Oh. Plumbing."

"Mr. Howard is a plumber?"

She touched Bedford's hand, as though he'd just told an amusing joke.

"Not a plumber. Plumbing supplies. We have big stores

in Columbus and Cincinnati. Howard opened another one in Yonkers three years ago. He wanted to live in New York. Actually, I think Margaret did."

"The countess."

"Yes. Anyway, all the stores have done very well. Very well. Until recently. I'm not sure what's gone wrong, but the business is in trouble."

One of the artists Bedford represented just then walked by the open door, saw them, and waved. Bedford waved back, wishing the fellow's work had been among the previous day's sales.

"There's no longer a market for flush toilets?"

"There's no longer a lot of profit for some reason." She sipped her coffee daintily. "My husband has never been much interested in the business. He's studying to become a landscape architect. Howard was able to talk him into signing over the voting rights of our stock. We kept the shares, but Howard took control of the company. He's run the whole thing himself for nearly three years now, and he seems to have run it into the ground. Our holdings were worth more than a hundred thousand dollars. Now they're not one-half that. It's been very disconcerting."

"Mrs. Paul, why are you telling me this?"

"You seem like a nice man."

"Sometimes, perhaps, but—"

"And I think you may discover what Howard's been doing with the business."

"But what would that have to do with what happened to the countess—to Margaret?"

"I think Margaret had a lot to do with what's happened to the plumbing company. You should see her wardrobe. Chanel dresses, Mr. Green. Chanel."

"Truth to tell, Mrs. Paul, I hadn't much been thinking about plumbing supplies."

"Well, we've become very worried. And now this horrible thing happening to Margaret. It's quite frightful. She was always strange, but . . . Anyway, we'll be happy to pay you. I have a hundred dollars."

She reached into her purse. He put his hand over hers to stop her. "There's no need, Mrs. Paul."

"Yes there is."

What few customers there were in the restaurant were paying no attention to them, or so Bedford hoped.

"I'm an art dealer, Mrs. Paul."

"That's not why the Vanderbilts hired you."

"I'm really not any good at this sort of thing."

Another sweet smile. She could have been president of the Women's Garden Club of Marion. Probably was.

"Yes you are."

He let her remark pass. "All right. Do you have any idea why she might have been murdered?"

"I don't know. She was always making death threats. Maybe somebody took them seriously."

Bedford recalled the heavy weight of the Wembley revolver, an unwieldy weapon for bedside protection.

"What was she doing in Rhode Island?"

"He gave her everything she wanted, including a house out there she shared with some terrible man she picked up."

"Does your brother-in-law know about him?"

"I don't know. He seldom went out there. Maybe he does. He had a lady friend himself, I think. Someone much more proper than Margaret."

"Where did they meet, your brother-in-law and the countess?"

"Overseas. Howard was in the war."

"An officer?"

"Some kind of officer. I think a second lieutenant—because he went to college."

"Infantry?"

"Something to do with supplies. Were you in the war?"

"Yes."

"What does an art dealer do in a war?"

"Not supplies." Bedford sipped some of his coffee. "You have a very interesting family."

Another sweet smile. "Robert's very nice. His mother is, too."

Bedford signaled for a check. "Thank you for wanting to help. If I learn anything that I think may be of interest to you, I'll contact you. Where do you live?"

"In New Jersey now. I'll write down the address."

PATTY Chase called," Sloane said upon his return. "I told her you were out with a strange woman."

"Thanks." He went to his desk, pulling out the invitation he had borrowed from Claire. The name of the organization was, in fact, the Hungarian Cultural Association of New York. He reached into a lower drawer, taking out the Manhattan telephone directory. He'd written down the phone number before, but had neglected the address.

"Broadway," he said.

Sloane studied him a moment. "What did you say?"

"Do you mind if I take the afternoon off?"

"I think it's a very good idea."

FEELING flush with all the money that had come rolling in, Bedford took a taxi. The address was that of a grimy old office building on the edge of the theater district just a few blocks south of Columbus Circle. He studied the registry of tenants in the lobby, finding nothing unusual. The Hungarian Cultural Association of New York was on the sixth floor.

There was a single elevator of old-fashioned cage construction, with an open stairway making right angles around it. The lift was very slow, so much so Bedford half wondered if he wouldn't make faster progress walking.

Passing the fourth floor, the elevator operator yawning, Bedford noted someone using the stairs to descend—a stout gentleman with highly polished shoes and a walking stick. And a beard.

"Stop, please," Bedford said.

The elevator man blinked at him.

"Stop at the next floor."

They rattled to a halt. The operator grudgingly pulled aside the inner door. Bedford pushed open the other one, then started down the stairs rapidly.

"Professor Horvath!"

The other man looked up. "Mr. Green?"

"Yes," said Bedford, catching up with him. "How are you?"

"What are you doing here?"

"Looking for someone. A patron of the Hungarian Cultural Association." He pointed upward. "Upstairs."

"I'm just coming from there," Horvath said. "I am a patron of the Association. Are you looking for me?"

"No, sir. This encounter comes as a surprise. I'm looking for a Prince Skorzeny. Are you familiar with him?"

"I am indeed. He is a generous benefactor of many Hungarian causes, culture among them."

Bedford took a step upward. "Can I find him at the association?"

"Oh no. He's not here."

Another step. "Perhaps someone can tell me where to find him."

"I can do that. He's in Hungary. What do you want of him?"

"He hosted a party, in the name of the association, at which the Countess Zala was present. This Skorzeny also invited a friend of mine—the young lady singer who entertained at the Breakers. I'd like to know why."

"You would bother the prince about that?"

"Both women were invited to the prince's party, and both were invited to the Breakers. It's an interesting coincidence, considering one of them is now dead."

"You think this singer—Miss Pell, is it?—is involved in the other's death?"

"No, but I thought the prince could explain the connection."

"Possibly, he could. But the one woman is a member of the nobility, and the other is a theatrical entertainer. A connection would be curious."

"Perhaps they can give me his address upstairs. I'd like to write him. Or better, cable him."

"You can try, but I'm not sure they'll give that to you." Horvath reached into his suitcoat breast pocket, removing a slim wallet. "But I have it. Here, I'll write it down on one of my cards."

He produced one and, with an expensive-looking gold pen, wrote out the particulars in a small, neat hand.

"I don't know if there is any possibility of a telephone connection, but I've written down his Budapest number as well." He handed Bedford the card, watching as Bedford placed it carefully within his own wallet.

"May I invite you to a cup of coffee, Mr. Green?"

Bedford accepted, hoping to learn something.

His first question was about the association.

"Just as it says, Mr. Green. The association was founded by Hungarian nobles after the war and the dissolution of the Austro-Hungarian Empire, to advance the idea of a Hungarian nation by promoting its considerable culture."

With that, he launched into a discourse on a nationalist painter named Viktor Madarasz, who had died seven years before. Bedford hadn't quite the time for this.

"Thank you, Professor. I must attend one of your classes sometime."

"In Budapest." Horvath put down money for the check. "Here I do not teach."

REMEMBERING he had neglected to call Tatty, Bedford did so from a drugstore pay phone. Sveta answered, saying Miss Chase had gone out for the afternoon. Bedford left a message, saying he would call again.

After pausing for a cherry phosphate at the soda fountain, he returned to the telephone booth and invested another nickel in a call to the precinct house where Lieutenant D'Alessandro's unit was based. Lamentably, Joey D was not in and had left no message for him.

Bedford set off down Seventh Avenue, eventually turning west and proceeding to the large tourist hotel where he knew Freddy Lange and his orchestra played weekends. Bedford was surprised at his luck. The bandleader and a few of his musicians were in the ballroom, engaged in some sort of rehearsal.

Bedford waited until they'd stopped playing, then came forward. Freddy had been a good source of gossip in Bedford's newspaper days, and Bedford had rewarded him with mentions in his column. He expected a friendlier response than he received.

"We're busy, Bedford. Can't talk to you now."

"I just have a couple of quick questions—about your engagement at the Breakers in Newport."

"That's right. You were the one who hauled that woman out of the sea. Ruined the whole weekend."

"My apologies. Hers, too, I suppose."

"What do you want to know?"

"Who hired you to play there?"

"A Mrs. Szechenyi."

"Countess Szechenyi."

"Okay. Countess."

"Why did she select you?"

"We've played Newport before. And Bar Harbor, Maine. We're a swell orchestra. She must have heard about us and we got hired."

"Did she specify that you bring Claire Pell?"

Lange turned his attention to his saxophone, wiping the mouthpiece with his handkerchief. "I don't remember."

"Very well. Why did you hire Claire?"

"Because she's terrific. Her show was going to close. I thought it would be swell to have her sing with us."

The other musicians began to pass a flask around.

"And you asked her to go on the road with you afterwards."

"Yeah."

"But then you withdrew the offer."

"Well, yes."

"How come?"

"That drowning, the whole Newport thing, it kinda spooked her, I guess. We just weren't clicking after that." He returned his handkerchief to his pocket. "Maybe we'll try again sometime."

"I doubt you'll be able to get her."

Bedford turned to leave, then halted. "One more question."

"I told you, Bedford, we're busy."

"Did Countess Szechenyi call you in person to hire you for the evening?"

"Her? No, it was some Hungarian guy. He said was acting for her."

"His name wasn't Prince Skorzeny, by any chance?"

"Skorzeny? No, it was Hobart. I mean, Horvath."

"Imre Horvath?"

"Yes."

"Thanks, Freddy."

"What's this all about? I mean, what the hell difference does it make? The dame's dead."

"That's why it makes a difference."

BEDFORD went to the little square separating the side entrance of the Plaza Hotel from Fifth Avenue, seating himself on a stone bench facing the circular fountain, with its splendid sculpture of a naked young woman. She was rendered as a mythological figure, but he had met the actual person—an actress and artists' model from the Tenderloin District named Vera. In statue form, she served as something of a muse for him. He seldom came away from these meditations by the fountain without a refreshment of mind or spirit. All F. Scott and Zelda Fitzgerald had done was dance in it.

But there were no great ideas generated that day. All that occurred to him was that, at this point, what he needed from the Vanderbilts was not five-hundred-dollar checks but some answers to questions.

The General and his wife had their principal residence at 640 Fifth Avenue—a large mansion house with broad lawn that would have been far more appropriate in Newport or on the north shore of Long Island than here at the very center of the nation's largest city. Bedford stood before it, wondering if he should have telephoned first. Except for the courtesy involved, he supposed it didn't matter.

A tall butler answered the door, his face set in disapproval.

"I am Captain Bedford Green," Bedford said, hoping the embellishing military rank might prove useful. "I have been engaged by the General on a private matter and need to consult with him." He handed the man his visiting card.

The butler hesitating, his expression hinting that Bedford should have chosen a rear entrance to come calling.

"Please come in," he said finally. "I will inquire whether the General is home."

Without offering to take Bedford's straw boater, he led him into a high central hall, which was dominated by a huge, malachite vase some nine or ten feet tall that stood in the middle. Gertrude had talked of it, but this was the first time Bedford had looked upon the work, which had been made for a Russian nobleman named Demidoff in the early nineteenth century. The Vanderbilts had bought it years before. He walked around it, admiring its ornate perfection, wondering what its fate would have been had it remained a possession of the nobility into the late Russian Revolution.

The butler was back in short order. "I am sorry, sir, but the General is not at home. I will tell him you called upon him. Is there any message?"

"None except that I would like to speak with him as soon as is convenient."

"Very well, sir." He took a step toward the entrance foyer.

"Um, the other Mr. Vanderbilt—the General's son— would he be at home?"

"He is not here, sir. I believe he is at his club."

"Which would that be?"

Another step toward the door. "He belongs to several, sir."

Bedford declined to make a scene. "Thank you, then."

"Good day, sir."

H₁ found Dayton Crosby at the Coffee House Club, playing chess. For the price of a game, which Bedford lost, the older man listened to what Bedford had to say, readily agreeing to help.

"A Vanderbilt would only belong to the very best clubs, so your search will be easy."

"Why is that?"

The old man produced a twinkly smile. "Because I belong to all the best clubs myself. Come with me."

He led Bedford to the Coffee House's small library. On a shelf at the corner were several club directories. Dayton studied the backs of them briefly, then plucked out four of them.

"You should find him in one of these," he said.

"May I use the telephone?"

"Of course, my boy. Of course."

The desk attendant at the first club Bedford called informed him that young Neil Vanderbilt was not on the premises, a response he got from all the numbers he called. But the last one added that the young man had left only a few minutes before.

"My name is Captain Green," Bedford said. "I work for General Vanderbilt and it's important that I speak to his son. Do you know where I might find him?"

"I believe he said he was going to Newport."

"Newport? Rhode Island?"

"Yes, sir. He often goes there."

Bedford stared at a painting on the wall. It was modern, a jumble of shiny machinery. "Thank you."

Crosby had gone into the main room. Bedford sat a moment, then picked up the telephone one more time, speaking quietly when the connection was made.

"This is Bedford Green. I'd like to speak to Mr. O'Bannion."

"You would, would you?"

It was Mush-Face. Bedford supposed he was being civil. When he was being uncivil, he'd likely begin conversations by discussing the imminence of the caller's demise.

"I would. He was going to make an inquiry for me. I'm wondering if he has an answer yet."

"He was going to do something for you?"

"You know that he was. You were there when we talked. Please tell him I'm on the phone."

There was a long silence. Bedford heard a chair being pushed back across a rough floor.

"Hold on," Mush-Face said.

A much longer silence ensued.

"Mr. O'Bannion ain't available," Mush-Face said, returning finally to the telephone. "But he says to tell you that when he's got a message for you, you'll know it."

"Sorry?"

"He'll let you know." He hung up.

BEDFORD returned to his gallery and found it closed, though Sloane had left a message on his desk informing him that Tatty had called again. He tried to reach the lady once more, but not even Sveta answered.

He had time. He picked up the phone and asked for the overseas operator, placing a call to Budapest. It proved an arduous process, and ultimately an unsuccessful one. An hour later no connection had been made. He gave up in disgust.

Chumley's beckoned. The establishment was nearly empty, though Lee Chumley was on the premises, reading a Socialist newspaper at the bar as he drank a beer.

Bedford ordered gin.

"Rough day, Bedford?"

"A frustrating one."

"You should work with your hands."

"I do. I'm hanging paintings all the time."

"Hmm."

"Lee, you know pretty much all the radical groups in town."

"But I'm not talking."

"Do you know any Hungarian ones?"

"I'm not talking."

"Lee, I'm not going to inform on anyone. I'm just curious if you know of any radical Hungarian groups who have it in for the nobility."

"I know a lot of radical groups who have it in for the nobility, and then some. All radical groups have it in for the nobility." He sipped his beer. "But I'm not talking."

WISHING to elude a gathering weight of frustration and defeat, Bedford returned to his apartment, poured a drink; enjoyed it in the process of a long, cool bath; and then had a ham sandwich and a second drink by way of dinner. As he stood before his closet, wondering how to dress for the evening, an idea occurred to him he heretofore would have instantly rejected and disdained:

He'd go see Elsa Maxwell.

A tiny, dumpy, yet indefatigably irrepressible woman, she bore with ease the unofficial title of New York's most aggressive and ambitious social climber. Happily for New York, she was more usually in Paris, but she was back in the city that summer.

He'd depended on her as a source of gossip when he was writing his newspaper column, in return granting her a few favorable mentions about her own activities or those of people she was promoting. But he found such arrangements unseemly and unsavory and they had been a factor in his deciding to abandon that trade.

Now, however, he needed information doubtless only she could provide.

Consulting his calendar, he then rummaged through the desk drawer where he put mail he'd wanted neither to read nor discard, sifting through a number of engraved social invitations sent him recently by people still unaware that he was no longer a society columnist. Elsa, of course, knew of his withdrawal from the trade and had been upset by it, but had continued to pester him with invitations, as though in the hope or belief that he'd return to the fold.

There were actually three from her in the stack—all for social gatherings organized by her on behalf of one cause or another but paid for by someone else. Two of the events had come and gone, but the third, as he had vaguely remembered, was on for that evening—and at the Plaza Hotel.

Setting down the remnants of his second cocktail, he began dressing himself in black tie.

LISA had posted herself by the ballroom door, and saw him the instant he started up the thickly carpeted grand staircase. He had declined what must have been two-dozen invitations in a row from her, so her surprise and enthusiasm were quite genuine.

"Bedford Green!" she exclaimed in her raspy, booming voice. "You're here!"

"Why, so I am," Bedford said, reaching the landing. "How nice to see you again, Elsa."

A brief nervousness came into her eyes, as though she feared he was actually bound for another engagement in the hotel and come her way by mistake.

"Are you back with the *New York Day?*" she inquired, without giving him a chance to respond. "Do you know who's here? Serge Obolensky! At least, he will be. And Anita Loos!"

"I'm sure you're all having a wonderful time," he said, "but it's you I came to see."

"And it's marvelous to see you, Bedford. Now come, I want to introduce you around."

"Elsa, I'm not back with the *New York Day*. Or any paper."

"Well, you will be. Come on." She tugged at his arm, pulling at him as she might a puppy on a leash.

He disengaged himself. He'd been afraid that he'd have to pull her away from some gaggle of arrivistes. Now she was bent on dragging him into one. He needed only one word to stop her.

"Vanderbilts."

He might just as well have struck her between the eyes with a hammer.

"What did you say?" she said.

"I need to talk to you about the Vanderbilts. Is there some place we might go?" One thing he hated about the Plaza was its lack of public places to sit.

She retook hold of his arm and led him down the corridor, turning through a set of mirrored double doors into someone else's party—from the look of it, a wedding feast.

Elsa plopped down on a velvet-covered bench to the side, pulling him next to her. If she'd been a puppy, now she was an intensely curious cat.

"Tell," she commanded.

"Nothing to tell. Just something to ask."

"That's as good as telling, Bedford, as you very well know."

"What I'm interested in, Elsa, is gossip. All the gossip you've ever heard about the Vanderbilts."

"All of them? That could take weeks."

"Not all of them."

"Reggie Vanderbilt alone. Did you know he went through his entire fortune? Fifteen million! All he left his wife with was a hundred and thirty thousand—plus a trust fund for little Gloria."

"Tell me more."

AS Elsa had been so helpful, Bedford felt duty bound to linger at her party. She thrust upon him a new friend of hers named Mimi Phlug. He danced with her—and talked with Mr. Phlug about the stock market. He was introduced to a woman named Holly from New Rochelle who was boring and a couple from Nyack named Hecht who were not. A languorous French woman named Zoë danced with him three times. He thought her interesting until he realized she was drunk. It finally occurred to him that he was getting that way, too. Everyone was beginning to seem interesting.

The newspaper columnist Cholly Knickerbocker turned up, looking uncomfortable. Both men expressed amazement to find the other present.

"I'm retired from all this," said Bedford. "I just came by to ask Elsa something."

"I was told Serge Obolensky was coming," Knickerbocker said.

"Not here yet."

"What did you ask Elsa about?" Knickerbocker had been Bedford's clear superior in the column writing game, but was not above wheedling out gossip, if it came to that.

Bedford set down his champagne glass, and leaned near. "It has to do with the Countess Zala."

"Who?"

"The Hungarian woman who was murdered up in Newport."

"Was that her name?"

"Yes. You never heard of her before?"

Knickerbocker looked at his watch. "No."

Bedford pondered this. "If I asked you to name a single member of the Hungarian aristocracy living in the United States, could you?"

The other man thought upon this. "It would take a while."

"You're slipping, old man. What about Gladys Vanderbilt?"

"That's right. Szechenyi. I sometimes forget he isn't Russian."

"Did you ever hear of a rich American named Howard? Paul Howard?"

Knickerbocker treated this as about as weighty a matter as the Hungarian question. "Actually, no. Who is he?"

"Plumbing."

"Plumbing?"

"Plumbing supplies."

"Society is dead, Bedford."

"That's what Dayton Crosby says."

"Good night, Bedford."

He persuaded himself he would stay to see if Serge Obolensky arrived. When the Russian failed to materialize by midnight, Bedford bid Elsa adieu and went out the Fifty-ninth Street entrance to the taxi line there.

"Have you seen Serge Obolensky tonight?" he asked the driver, as the man made a U-turn back toward Seventh Avenue.

"Never heard of him, pal," he said.

"Proves my point exactly."

The driver said nothing more, presumably thinking he'd picked up another inebriated good-time Charlie, whom he'd have to remind to tip, if not pay.

"How about the Countess Zala?"

"Yeah. She's dead." The driver reached on the seat

behind him and picked up a copy of the *New York Daily News*, handing it to Bedford.

The story was headlined, "COUNTESS FOUND DEAD." It was hard to read, especially with so much champagne to contend with, but Bedford managed. The article did not involve any Vanderbilts personally, and made no reference to romantic relationships, but treated the countess as a sort of posthumous party crasher, and went into great detail about the entertainments at the Breakers.

No wonder the General had been so swift and generous with his expenses. He would doubtless be very keen on a return on his investment soon.

According to the story, the Newport police were still calling the incident an accidental drowning.

I was much too late to call Tatty when he got home, even with the hours she often kept, but certainly not to try Joey D. The sergeant at the station house said the detective had gone out again, but would return before he went home for the night, as was his custom.

Bedford told him he was now himself at home, and would appreciate a telephone call at any hour.

He turned on the lights in his living room, which had a tall bay window overlooking the street. Bedford's apartment was on the fourth floor. Looking over the rooftop opposite, he could see the tower of the gigantic Woolworth Building to the south. He looked down at the street. A young couple were strolling arm in arm toward Hudson Street. There was someone standing in the doorway opposite.

There was a sudden flash. An explosive sound he remembered from the war came ripping through the air, followed by a crash of glass and a sharp, stinging, expanding pain in his chest.

CHAPTER 16

YOU'RE the luckiest man in New York," Lieutenant D'Alessandro said, staring in wonderment at Bedford's wound.

Bedford looked down at his bloodied chest, and the clean spot below his heart with a diagonal cut running across it, a dark canal of congealed crimson. He reached to touch it, but a nurse pushed his hand away and pressed a gauze dressing upon it. With that in place, she began to wind a long bandage around his chest.

"If I were a lucky man," Bedford said, "I would have gone directly to bed and not stood there by my window."

"The bullet just missed you," said the detective, who was wearing a green suit. "We dug it out of your ceiling. Forty-four caliber. Would have killed you real dead."

According to the doctor who had treated him, Bedford's wound had come from a large shard of window glass. It had penetrated his flesh but struck a rib, falling free. They'd cleaned the cut and sealed it, but the injury still hurt, a throbbing, steady pain.

"I wonder why they didn't take a shot at me when I was getting out of the cab."

"Maybe it was in the way. Whoever it was, it looks like they used a pistol. Which is pretty stupid at that distance and angle. Four stories up. Tough shot from the street."

"You're sure it was from the street?"

"That angle. Had to be. Maybe from an open car. Do you remember a car?"

Bedford shrugged. "No. I remember a man across the street. But he was just standing there. And a man and a woman, walking down the street, looking amorous. That's all."

"We'll canvas the street for witnesses."

"Do you know about this hospital?"

"All too well."

"No. Another reason. This is where Edna St. Vincent Millay was born. It's why she got the middle name 'St. Vincent.' She's named after this hospital. At least, that's the legend in Chumley's."

"She's a writer?"

"Joseph. She won the Pulitzer Prize for poetry. She's the queen of Greenwich Village. Or was. Spends a lot of time in Paris now."

The policeman shrugged. "I tried to reach you earlier. I finally got through to the cops in Newport. Guess what? Your victim was a genuine floater."

"Sorry?"

"The dead Hungarian lady. Those coppers aren't fools. They called in a doctor to examine the body after all—just to make sure they got that on the record in case somebody beefed. He said she drowned. No doubt whatsoever."

"But she had a cord wrapped around her neck—as I told you."

"Maybe she did. But that's not how she left this world."

The nurse finished her bandaging, then stepped back, proud of her accomplishment.

"Do they still have her listed as accidental?"

" 'Presumed accidental.' "

"Hmmm."

"But we're treating your case as an attempted homicide."

"I won't quarrel with that."

"Any idea as to who's that mad at you?"

Bedford thought upon that seriously. "There'd be a few, I suppose."

"You want to give me a list?"

"Not yet. I think I may narrow it some."

"Would Liam O'Bannion be one of the finalists?"

"I don't know."

"You want me to go have a talk with him?"

"If you do that, I'll be sure to perish."

"I'd sure as hell like to bring that cocky Mick in. Just to sweat him a little."

"Not just yet, Joseph. Thanks anyway."

The detective put his notebook back in his pocket.

"There is something I'd really like you to do, though," Bedford said. "You told me you didn't know of any Hungarians in the rackets."

"Right."

"How about subversives?"

"Huh?"

"Your flatfoot chums on the Red Squad have been hot after every Bolshie and anarchist and what have you in the city—including some friends of mine. Surely they've got a few Hungarians on their list."

"You mean arrest records?"

"I mean any kind of list the Red Squad has got. But just the Hungarians."

"This is necessary?"

"I don't know. It depends on who might be on the list. But it could be very useful."

"Okay. I'll see what I can do. Uh, you've got two lady friends waiting for you."

"Two? Who?"

"I'll send them in."

TATTY and Sloane, looking improbable together, entered the emergency room in a rush.

"My poor darling!" Tatty gave him a hug and a kiss, producing a delightful form of agony. Bedford took a deep breath as she stepped back.

"What on earth is this all about?" Sloane said, standing off a little and eyeing Bedford's wound with disapproval.

"I wish I knew."

"Maybe you should stop doing whatever you're doing."

"What I'm doing at the moment is thinking of moving to Iowa."

"Not tonight," said Tatty, gingerly touching his bandage, then looking for his shirt. "You're going to stay with me."

"I was going to have you at my place," said Sloane, "but I'm just around the corner from you and they might try again. Tatty's on the Upper East Side. They don't allow this sort of thing up there." She grinned, being a pal.

"That's very kind of you both," said Bedford, "but I can stay at home. I doubt they'd strike twice in the same place."

"Even lightning bolts do that, dearie," said Tatty. "You're coming with me, and that's that. Besides, I have news."

He looked at his wristwatch. "What could that be?"

"They've fixed my car."

THERE was no traffic on Fifth Avenue and Albert drove fast.

"This is no longer amusing," Tatty said. "Art dealers aren't supposed to be shot."

"Though many of them should be."

"You don't suppose that horrible Howard person had something to do with this?"

"Pistols in the middle of Greenwich Village after midnight doesn't quite seem his style."

She patted his knee. "Do you still hurt?"

"Not there."

She touched his chest. "There."

"Yes."

"It hurts?"

"Yes. But I'm getting used to it."

"You poor dear. You must be frightened."

He thought upon that. "A little."

"Do you have any idea why this happened?"

"No. I suppose I may have severely annoyed someone with my inquiries about the Countess Zala, but I'm not sure it's that. For all I know, it's some socialite wreaking vengeance for a column I once wrote about her. Or something more worrisome."

"And what would that be?"

"Something to do with the war."

"The war ended seven years ago."

"I know."

"Bedford, I truly do want to help you with this."

He took her hand and held it gently. "You're first cabin, Tatiana Chase. And I do certainly appreciate your providing me a roost for tonight, but for the rest, I think it's best you stay out of harm's way."

"We could go abroad."

"Where? Hungary."

"They were a corrupt and rotten old empire, those Austro-Hungarians. Look at all the trouble they got the world in."

"It's what comes of having archdukes."

As they turned off Fifth into Tatty's street, a car that had been following them closely made the corner as well. Bedford's anxiety lessened when it kept going after Albert had pulled up at the curb by her entrance.

She came around to help Bedford to the door.

"I'm fine," he said as Albert drove off to the garage.

"Ha." Tatty pulled his arm around her shoulders, which made him hurt more than it helped.

They'd made a mistake. The other auto came roaring back in reverse. The front and rear doors on the right side flew open and two men jumped out, grabbing hold of both of them. The one who seized Bedford had an automatic pistol in his free hand. He dug it into Bedford's ribs.

Bedford cried out profanely. The man jabbed with the barrel again. "Shut up," he said. "Get in the car."

"Leave her be," said Bedford. "She doesn't know anything about anything. She just gave me a ride from the hospital."

"In the car. Both of you. In the back."

It was very cramped in the auto. Tatty, recoiling from the inadvertent touch of the gunman after he followed them inside, climbed up onto Bedford's lap. He put his arm protectively around her, then moved her away from his bandaged chest.

"Who are you?"

The driver turned around. It was Mush-Face. He grinned, in his case, an extraordinarily grotesque manipulation of facial tissue.

"This lady is Tatiana Chase," Bedford said. "She is an extremely well-known actress and the daughter of one of the most important men in this city. If you harm a hair of her head, there will be Hell to pay all the way to City Hall. The mayor himself will be after your scalps."

"Just shut up and enjoy the ride, palsie."

He turned into Central Park.

◆◆◆

THEY followed the curving drive to the reservoir, pulling up next to a long Cadillac touring automobile parked by some overhanging trees.

"Get in that car," Mush-Face said.

"Front or back?" Bedford replied, calculating the chances of a run into the trees until reminding himself what might happen to Tatty.

"Backseat." Mush-Face looked to Tatty. "You stay here."

Bedford walked to the Cadillac, measuring his life in steps. The rear door opened just as he reached it. With a glance to the trees, which now seemed miles away, he entered.

"I just want you to know, laddy buck," said O'Bannion from back in the shadows, "that I had nothing to do with what happened at your place tonight."

"How do you know about that?"

"I've got friends, including a few in the police department." There was a clink of glass, and Bedford found himself offered a small tumbler full of whiskey. He took it, tasting first-rate scotch.

"Perhaps they'll be kind enough to inform you that kidnapping at gunpoint, like attempted murder, is a violation of both state and municipal statutes, punishable by lengthy terms in prison."

"Listen, Green. If it had been me, you'd be dead now."

True enough. "Then why this late-night ride in the park?"

"A friendly get-together, boyo. I've got something you want."

Bedford sipped and waited.

"You're in luck," O'Bannion continued. "Turns out I did have a shipment come in at Rhode Island Sound that night. And my crew saw a boat near the Breakers. A motorboat. Not a big steam or sailing yacht. My boys kept an eye on it."

"There were a lot of boats out there."

"Aye, but only one that close to the Breakers. And there

was something funny about it. It would move, stop for a long time, move again, then stop. We thought it might have been a federal revenue boat. But maybe not. It had only one running light—a green one."

"On the port side."

"I know about boats, bucko. My father was a County Clare fisherman. It lay right off the Breakers, jerking around like that. My skipper got a good look at it. Small cabin. Not a yacht. More likely a fishing boat. Eventually it took off."

"Headed south?" Bedford was thinking it would most likely go on down and around the Brenton Point peninsula and then make for the Newport waterfront.

"No, east—at high speed, past the stern of my boat and then around Sachuest Point. After that, it turned north, right up Sakonnet Bay."

"To Fall River?"

"Fall River. Portsmouth, Providence, Bristol—one of them."

"Bristol."

"Sure. Right up the bay."

"None of those towns are very posh."

"Like I told you, Bedford. A fishing boat."

"Well, thank you, Liam."

"I want more than 'thank you,' boyo. Whatever you find out about that boat—or how that woman came to wash up at the Vanderbilts' party—I want to know. Fast, and first. Just like we were still friends." His smile shone in the shadows like the Cheshire cat's.

"Of course."

"And if I find out who put a bullet through your window. Well, I'll take care of it."

"That could interfere with your other request of me."

"I'll decide what interferes with what."

Across the way, Bedford saw Tatty turn toward him, though he couldn't make out her expression. "Why did you have to bother her, Liam? She's probably scared half to death."

"My apologies. Meant no harm. I only wanted to meet the lady." With that, he snapped open his door and stepped outside, then casually strolled to the other auto.

Bedford, moving slowly, followed. Watching O'Bannion open the car's rear door, he feared Tatty was going to take a sock at the Irishman. Instead he heard the word: "Dee-lighted."

TATTY had a comfortable bed prepared for him in her guest room. She showed no inclination to join him on it as she had in Cross River.

"It is very, very late—even for crazy people like us," she said, kissing him on the forehead. "The doctor said you need rest."

"I know. I have to get back to my gallery first thing in the morning."

"You'll do no such thing. Those fiends out there will be trying to get you."

"Not if they think they succeeded."

"How can they think that if you show up at your gallery?"

"It will only be for a few minutes. And I have to stop at my apartment."

"I told you. I'll get your window fixed for you. I'll send Albert over in the morning to get whatever you need. Can't have you seen in black tie in the morning." She kissed him again, then stepped toward the door. "Such wonderful fun tonight, darling. Not simply funerals. Hospital emergency rooms—and rides with gangsters."

The door closed quietly.

BEDFORD awoke very late in the morning to find Tatty gone and her maid Sveta and driver Albert in sole residence, the latter eyeing Bedford with some impatience.

"Miss Chase went to have lunch with one of her producers," he said. "She told me you need some things picked up from your apartment."

"Yes," said Bedford: "I'll go with you."

"But she said you were to stay here."

"You won't know where to look."

Sveta prepared him a bowl of oatmeal, ignoring the fact that he was dressed in evening clothes, though with a chest bandage in place of a formal shirt. He was nearly finished with his breakfast when she returned to the kitchen, holding up the shirt as though it were a dead animal.

"Is blood?" she said.

"Is, indeed."

"I wash?"

"No, you may throw away."

"Okay."

It was only when he was in the car with Albert that he realized he had failed to tell her to remove the cufflinks and studs.

ALBERT stood idly and uncomfortably by.

"What do you want me to do?"

"Stand by the window and let me know if you see anything funny going on in the street."

"This is Greenwich Village. Always something funny on the streets."

"Please."

With Albert standing with his back to him, Bedford went to his bookcase and reached around the back, removing a cigar box that contained four fifty-dollar bills and his pistol, which he put in his tuxedo jacket pocket.

"I'm going to wash up and change clothes now," Bedford said. "I won't be long."

"There's a woman in an apartment across the street," Albert said.

"Often the case," said Bedford from the bedroom.

"She's not wearing any clothes."

"He's a painter, that fellow over there. She's probably posing for him."

"No, they're doing something else."

"Just keep watch."

Clean shaven, hair combed, teeth brushed, and a fresh blazer, striped shirt, and white duck trousers in place, Bedford packed up his toiletries and then dug out his old Royal Flying Corps kit bag. He put the gun in it, along with enough carefully folded clothes to last several days. He was ready.

"Very well, sir," Bedford said, returning to the living room. "Let's be off."

"Be right with you, Mr. Green," said Albert, without budging.

He'd almost fogotten the countess's letters, but looking to the side table where he'd left them, he saw they were gone. He held out the hope Joey D or one of the other policemen had taken them, but he guessed that was not the case. The intruder hadn't bothered with anything else in the apartment. There was no sign of any search. The Hungarian book was still where he'd set it down, and the photograph of the countess and young Vanderbilt still inside and intact. Both went into the kit bag.

"All right, Albert."

Reluctantly, the other turned and followed.

It wasn't after anything specific at his gallery. But he wanted to go through his mail and check with Sloane in

case anyone had tried to contact him. As he came through
the door, Sloane indicated that someone had done exactly
that—and pointed to her.

Mrs. Paul was sitting behind his desk, holding an envelope much as she might a fan.

"Good day, Mrs. Paul."

"Hello, Mr. Green," she said cheerily. "Miss Smith said
you'd been injured. I hope you're feeling better. I'd appreciate it if I could speak with you."

"Before we go that far," he said, "is that my mail?"

"No, it's not." She glanced about the gallery unhappily.
"Is there somewhere we can go? Besides that apple pie
place we went last time?"

Bedford was just as happy to be gone from Greenwich
Village in the circumstance.

"There's a car outside with a driver. Tell him you're
with me and I'll join you presently. Then we'll go uptown."

"Uptown?" She acted as though she feared he meant
Harlem.

"A few blocks. Not far."

He waited until she went through the door, then turned
to Sloane, who shook her head.

"I really would like things to get back to normal, Bedford."

"Can you manage things for a day or two longer?"

"It's easier, really, when you're not here."

"How reassuring. You can reach me through Tatty."
She patted his chest. "Don't bleed to death."

BEDFORD had Albert take them to Fourteenth Street and
Luchow's, a German restaurant of his long acquaintance. At his request, they were given a table at the back,
away from the door and the windows.

"I always thought this place was Chinese," said Mrs. Paul, taking up a menu. "I'd no idea it was German. It doesn't bother you, eating German food, after the war and all?"

"The war wasn't about food."

"Well, it was horrible. I'm so glad Robert was too young." She flushed. "I'm sorry. That must sound dreadful. You were in the fighting, weren't you?"

"A bit."

"I'm sorry." She lowered her lashes.

"What's the reason for this visit, Mrs. Paul?"

"Well, now, I'm not sure. I've come across something. I don't know if it's important. I don't even know if I should be showing it to you. But it may mean something."

"That letter you were holding?"

"Yes." She took it out of her handbag and handed it to him. "It's from Howard's girlfriend. Mr. Green, I believe they've gotten married."

Bedford read through it, and sat back. It detailed arrangements for a motor trip to be made to a justice of the peace in Maryland. "It is a bit soon after his wife's death. He might have waited a few more hours."

"He's made an honest woman out of her."

"Where did you get this?"

"I was at his house, picking up his mail for him, when I saw this. I didn't want to pry, but he's away in Ohio and I didn't know if it was important."

"But it was already opened, wasn't it?"

"Very well. I snooped."

Bedford handed it back.

"Very ardent stuff," she said. "It's hard to believe she was talking about Howard. He's not what you'd call a very romantic fellow. Her name's Theodosia. Theodosia Hastings. From Greenwich. In Connecticut. See, look at the envelope. That's very posh, isn't it?"

"Greenwich. Yes."

"I think she's probably just the sort of woman Howard always wanted," Mrs. Paul continued. "Very much like the lady who works for you."

"Sloane? I've never met anyone like Sloane."

"What I mean is, well brought up. And . . ."

She puzzled over her next word.

"Rich," said Bedford.

"It would seem so." A Mary Pickford smile.

The waiter came and they ordered. She wasn't very hungry.

A FTER they had dropped Mrs. Paul at Pennsylvania Station for her return trip to New Jersey, Bedford asked Albert to drive him to the offices of the *New York Day*. Albert did so grudgingly.

"Miss Chase will have come home by now, Mr. Green. She'll wonder where we are."

"This won't take long," he said, and exited the car, heading for the paper's loading docks.

He returned more than an hour later, a large manila envelope in his hand.

"Now?" asked Albert.

"Just one more stop. Just off Central Park West."

B EDFORD found himself relieved that the several rings of the doorbell went unanswered. He had absolutely no idea what he could at this point say to Claire that might persuade her to help him yet again—or even to speak to him. He feared he'd only bring on a nasty row.

But a note would certainly be much easier—and might prove far more effective. He wrote a lengthy one on the back of the envelope—carefully, so he wouldn't harm the contents—then slid it under the door.

TATTУ had changed into a less formal frock and was in her living room, sipping a cocktail and reading *Vanity Fair*. She did not look up when Bedford entered, waiting until he had seated himself opposite her in a chair near the window.

"And where have you been?" she asked. He felt married.

"Tending to Hungarian matters."

"I can ask Albert where you went, you know."

"He'll tell you that I went to my apartment, gathered some things, stopped at my gallery, and had a late lunch with the dreadful Howard person's pretty sister-in-law, stopped at my old newspaper, and hurried back here." He left out the digression to Claire's apartment.

"You were wounded. You should be recuperating in bed."

He pressed against the bandage with his hand. It still hurt. "I'm doing just fine. In fact, I was going to suggest we go out tonight."

"To dinner?"

"Yes. And then a drive in the country."

"Where?"

"Bronxville."

"Whatever for?"

"To commit a burglary."

CHAPTER 17

ALBERT'S usefulness extended beyond motorcars. Overhearing Tatty and Bedford plot their nocturnal assault upon the Howard residence as they drove north on the parkway toward Bronxville, he volunteered the fact that he had once served time in Ossining's Sing Sing Prison for an accounting malfeasance of some sort, and while there had acquired a knowledge of breaking and entering, among other skills.

"Why, Albert," said Tatty. "I don't recall your putting that with your references."

"No, ma'am."

"Is it easy, breaking and entering?"

"The trick is in breaking as little as possible when entering," he said.

And so he demonstrated, deftly opening a basement window at the rear of Howard's house. Helping Bedford and Tatty climb down inside—with Bedford requiring far more assistance than Tatty in his banged-up state—Albert handed them each an electric torch and then returned to his post as lookout behind the wheel of Tatty's Pierce-Arrow, which they'd parked in the street.

Three blasts from the horn and they were to flee.

They went quietly together up the stairs to the main floor, then stopped in the central hall.

"There seems to be no one home," she said, whispering.

"Ohio, the sister-in-law said," Bedford whispered back. "What shall we look for?"

"I'm going to find his study and browse for letters and a bankbook. I'd be interested in any photographs you can find. Anything of hers."

"Zala's?"

"Yes."

She gave him a nudge and then, with her inimitable sang froid, sallied forth. Bedford went down to the other end of the hall and looked about that end of the house, then retraced his steps and turned upstairs, finding the chamber he sought up there.

There was a rolltop desk against one wall of the study, kept open a crack by some papers that stuck out at the bottom. Quietly sliding the rolltop back into its recess, Bedford set about pulling open the multitude of little drawers, one by one.

Howard had an apparent penchant for souvenir collecting—restaurant matchboxes, theater ticket stubs, invitations to posh parties. There was a clutter of such stuff almost everywhere Bedford looked. He was surprised to find a few invitations to parties he had himself attended. Somewhere in those crowds of boiled shirts had been Paul Howard—though possibly, back then, the man had been Howard Paul. Bedford wondered if they had spoken.

A wide, lower drawer, which had to be pried open with his folding pocket knife, yielded contents more to his liking: personal letters, and bankbooks. Many of them.

He'd gotten through most of them when he heard Tatty coming up the stairs, the dancing light of her electric torch preceding her.

"Find anything?" she said, peering in.

"Yes. You?"

"No. Nothing. I'm going to check the master bedroom."

"Right."

Bedford had seen enough. He returned the bankbooks, then stood up, playing his light around the study. There was a bookcase, with three small framed photographs on the shelves. Holding one close, he found himself looking at what must have been a fairly recent photograph of an extremely beautiful and well-dressed young Countess Zala, standing with an anxious-looking Howard in front of an expensive automobile.

The second picture was of Howard, in his wartime uniform. The third was of a young woman in a shirtwaist with an old-fashioned coif. She was slender and had excellent posture, but her neck was scrawny. She had a thin, bony face and long, beaky nose. New England had grown such women like trees.

Picking up the photo, he noticed something behind it— a small stack of papers. He put down the picture and took up an envelope on the top of the stack, holding it close to the light.

It was in Hungarian. He recognized it as one of the letters he had had in his apartment. The others were there, too.

"Yikes!" Tatty cried.

He looked up. "Tatty?"

"Bedford, come *here*!"

She was in the master bedroom across the hall, standing stiffly at the foot of a canopied bed. Lying across it was the body of a young woman. She was naked, and there was something tied around her neck.

"Is she dead?"

Bedford went to the head of the bed, playing his own electric torch upon the grisly visage. "Yes. Very."

An auto horn sounded three times, quite loudly. Bedford went to the draperies, pulling one close and peering out the window.

"Out the back," he said. "Now."

T**HEY** hurled themselves down the stairs, along the hall, and out the back door, through the kitchen.

"Run," he said. "Don't stop for anything."

Crossing the lawn, Tatty halted briefly to remove her shoes. Then they pushed on, crashing through a following hedge.

"Where now?" she said, still moving.

"Through these yards to the next street. Then down the hill."

"What about Albert?"

Bedford was huffing along, his chest hurting. "He'll have to fend for himself." He could hear a siren approaching, then another.

"How could anyone know we were there?" She slowed down to accommodate him.

"Maybe it was our lights."

He tripped on the next hedge, and went sprawling. She helped him to his feet, and they went on. A dog started barking, then others. Confronted by a fence, they turned and ran alongside it, past a garage and then down a driveway. A long, dark car was waiting just up the street. Bedford shrank back a moment, then realized who it was.

"Saved," he said.

Albert had left the right rear door open for them.

T**HEY** returned to the city via the back streets of Yonkers, crossing the Bronx line in a surprisingly large amount of traffic.

"I really think we should contact the police," Tatty said.

"That would only complicate matters."

"But we didn't do anything."

"We're burglars."

"That woman. What a horrible look on her face."

"She didn't appreciate what was being done to her."

"I wonder who she is."

"I found some pictures," Bedford said. "One was of a very plain, beaky-nosed woman."

"Yes?"

"It was her."

CHAPTER 18

Y OU know, Bedford, I'm spending a hell of a lot of time here on a case that's not in our jurisdiction," said Joey D as he prepared to bite into his *ka csirke galuskaval.*

"So am I," said Bedford, "and I don't even have a jurisdiction."

"The captain finds out, I could find myself transferred to Sheepshead Bay or something."

"Manhattan without you, Joseph, would be like New York without Mayor Walker. At all events, I'm helping out a man with an address on Fifth Avenue, among a number of prestigious other places. If he's pleased, you won't have to worry about your captain. At all events, this may all relate to my attempted homicide—and you are investigating that."

The lieutenant took another bite. "This is good."

"Yes it is. Was the Red Squad helpful?"

D'Alessandro glanced both left and right, then pulled a sheaf of folded paper from the breast pocket of his magenta suit. He hesitated, looking to either side again. "You want to do this here?"

"It's why we came. Let me see it, please."

The detective put the papers swiftly into Bedford's hand, then sat back, as though trying to distance himself from them. "Cost me a couple of favors."

"I think you'll find this a worthwhile investment of your time." Bedford began reading down the column of names on the first page.

"It's all the names that looked like they might be Hungarian—including a lot of them they say definitely belong to Hungarian radical groups. With some of the others, it's hard to tell. Could be Romanian or Italian or something."

Bedford removed his Mark Cross fountain pen from his pocket and circled one of the names, and then another. Then he turned to the next page.

"This will do just fine," he said.

The policeman leaned close, and pointed to an entry.

"Funny to see that noble name on the list."

"Not unprecedented. Think of Felix Dzerzhinsky."

"Who the hell is that?"

"The head of Lenin's Cheka, the Soviet secret police. He was brought up quite differently."

"All a bunch of screwballs, if you ask me."

"Screwballs with guns."

André Mohar appeared, towel over his arm. "Everything is okay, Captain Green?"

"Excellent, André. As always." Bedford nodded at the towel on the man's arm. "Are you waiting tables tonight?"

"I'm shorthanded. Sandor Petofi quit."

"He quit?"

"He called up. Said he is leaving New York. Too dangerous here."

"Where'd he go?"

"Maybe back to Hungary. I don't know." Mohar shrugged. "He was doing well here."

"Well, that's too bad." Bedford gestured to his companion, who was eating with great gusto. "André, I'd like you

to meet Detective D'Alessandro. Our city's finest crimi-
nologist and a man of Epicurean taste."

"Epicurean." Mohar shook Joey D's hand. "I hope you
have Hungarian taste, too."

"Excellent meal," said the detective.

"Good, good. I'm glad you enjoy. See you later, Captain
Green."

Bedford waited until Mohar was out of hearing. "Did
you hear anything about a murder up in Westchester?"

"They've had a bunch of murders up there. Two bootleggers were shot to death in Ossining. They're worried
about some kind of Hudson River gang war. You'd think it
was Jersey."

"I'm talking about a woman in Bronxville."

"They don't have murders in Bronxville."

"Check it out. It may be in connection with a burglary."

"How do you know about this?"

"I don't know all about it. What I do know is that the
house they found the victim in belongs to the man who was
married to my Hungarian countess."

D'Alessandro shook his head. "Once again, Bedford.
Out of my jurisdiction."

"I believe her name is Theodosia Hastings. I could be
wrong, but at all events, duty compels us to let the local au-
thorities know that."

" 'Us' meaning who?"

" 'Us' meaning you."

"Should I tell them it's something a noted former gossip columnist picked up at a tea dance?"

"I should prefer you told them it came from one of your
many anonymous tipsters."

"Anything else I don't know about?"

"There's something more I need to find out, if I could
impose upon you one more time?"

"Jeez, Bedford, you owe me favors the way you owe
Arnold Rothstein money."

"You don't threaten me as much. It's a simple thing. I'd like you to contact the Coast Guard in Rhode Island and find out if they've cited any boat owners for having only one running light in the last week or two."

"What?"

"Night lights on a boat. You're supposed to have two—a green for port and a red for starboard. I'm interested in one showing a green only."

"That's all?"

"It's a lot."

More chewing. Then the detective nodded at the list of subversives still sitting beside Bedford's plate. "Mohar saw that, you know."

"I know."

BEDFORD stopped by St. Vincent's Hospital for a change of bandage, as he'd been instructed to do, then headed crosstown. Dayton Crosby didn't answer his doorbell, but turning to descend the steps, Bedford noticed the old gentleman walking along with his dog in the small, gated park across the street. Going up to the fence, he called to him. The dog started to bark.

"Bedford!" Crosby said, coming closer. "Still chasing countesses?"

"I'm afraid so, and I need to call upon your expertise again."

"Keep this up and the firm will make me charge you by the hour."

"You'd bankrupt me within the week."

"You know the small extent of my knowledge of Hungarians."

"I'm interested in an American family. In Greenwich. Hastings. A young woman named Theodosia Hastings."

Crosby puzzled over the name for a moment while his

dog quietly relieved himself. Then both animal and master turned for the gate.

"Wait there," Crosby said over his shoulder. "I'll come around. I think I know those people, but I want to check my Social Register."

The name was there. The girl's was listed below her parents', along with a sister. She'd gone to Sarah Lawrence, not far across the New York line from Greenwich. He guessed from the dates that she was nearly thirty.

"Thank you," said Bedford, writing down the address and telephone number on the back of an envelope.

"Are you inviting them to one of your Greenwich Village soirees?"

"No. It has to do with my Hungarian countess."

Crosby picked up a cat. They seemed to be lying around for just that purpose. "Well, they're a respectable old family, as memory serves, though it's a wonder they're still in Greenwich."

"How's that?"

"Reduced circumstances."

"How far reduced?"

"Depressingly reduced. A game of chess?"

TATTY was in bed by the time he returned to her townhouse, but was sitting up, reading.

"I'm going to do the play," she said.

"That's wonderful. I'm sure it'll be a tremendous hit."

"I hope so. I'm investing in it."

"I think that's called putting your money where your mouth is."

"Hee hee hee." She set down her magazine. "Your dear friend Claire Pell called. I don't know how she knew you were here."

He sat down in the chair by her dressing table. "Probably Sloane. I trust you explained."

"You mean did I tell her that we're not having an affair and that I've simply taken you in like a sick puppy? No, I did not. You can supply your own explanations."

Bedford crossed his legs. "What did she say?"

"Very cryptic. She said to tell you, 'It's him.' And you're not to bother her or her relatives about this ever again."

"Thank you." He picked up one of her hairbrushes. It was silver, inlaid with some sort of Russian Imperial design on the back.

"Are you about to ask me for something?"

"I wonder if I could borrow Albert and your car tomorrow."

"To go where?"

"Greenwich."

She took a deep breath, exhaling slowly, thoughtfully. "All right. Anywhere else?"

"After that he can drop me at the train for Newport, and I'll go fetch your car."

"Tomorrow morning?"

"Yes."

"Good night," she said. She left off the "darling."

"Good night."

She turned out the light as he reached the door. "I'll go with you."

CHAPTER 19

A WOMAN wearing a cook's apron answered the door—hardly a sign of prosperity in such a large house. Her eyes went immediately to the crimson and black Pierce-Arrow parked in the circular drive, then returned to Tatty and Bedford.

"Yes?"

"We'd like to speak to Mister and Mrs. Hastings."

"Not home." Another glance at the Pierce-Arrow.

"Do you know when they will return?"

"No sir. But Miss Hastings is at home."

"Miss Hastings?"

"Who shall I say is calling?"

Tatty stepped forward, presenting a visiting card. "Tatiana Chase. And this is Captain Bedford Green."

"We would like to speak to her about a man named Paul Howard."

The cook examined the card dubiously. "Just a minute, please."

She left them there, reappearing after more than a minute. "This way, please."

They were led into a sunroom just off a large sitting room.

It was filled with a variety of potted plants and had large windows with a view of the lawn. Seated in a white wicker chair by one of the windows was a young woman who was as singularly attractive as the woman at Howard's house had not been. Yet she bore a strong resemblance.

She wore a pale pink summer dress with little bows on it and white shoes and stockings. Her tearful eyes were almost the color of the dress and her pale skin nearly as white as the stockings.

"Please be seated," she said, indicating two chairs opposite her. She looked again at Tatty's card, then set it down. "I'm Delia Hastings."

Bedford repeated their names. "I'm so sorry to intrude at such a time."

The woman weakly waved her hand to dismiss the courtesy, then rubbed her eyes. "Are you with the police, 'Captain' Green?"

"We're here in a private capacity," Bedford said. "I've been making some inquiries concerning Mr. Howard on behalf of a family in Newport. It was off their place that Mrs. Howard drowned."

"Mrs. Howard?"

"The Countess Zala. His wife. A Hungarian countess."

"What does any of this have to do with my sister?"

"We understand that Mr. Howard and your sister were married very recently."

"But now she's dead."

"Yes. So I've been informed."

She sat up straighter in the chair. "Informed by who? We were only told this morning."

"A police detective friend discussed the matter with me," Bedford said.

"I really should ask you to leave, you know," she said, a bit of color returning to her face. "I've just been told my sister has been murdered. My parents are over in Westchester having to deal with that. And you complete strangers show up to ask questions on behalf of some other strangers in Newport who are concerned because someone drowned near their house."

"You're quite right," said Bedford quietly. "This is an inexcusable intrusion. We should have come at a different time. I do apologize."

He rose. Tatty hesitated, then did the same. They were about to go through the door when Delia Hastings said, "She was going to leave him. They were married two days ago—in Maryland. But one day was enough."

Bedford turned. "Sorry?"

"Theo and Paul Howard, or Howard Paul or whatever his name was, were married by a justice of the peace in Bel Air, Maryland, two days ago. She moved into his house that night and the next morning she called here to say she was coming back home. Now she's gone."

She put a handkerchief to her face, looking away. It was then that Bedford noticed she had a large glass of what looked to be sherry on the table beside her.

"We want to help," Tatty said. "We think the deaths of both these women are related. We'd like to ask you a few things about Howard."

Delia Hastings dabbed at her eye one more time, then took a drink of sherry, swallowing with some difficulty.

"We know little about him. Theo met him at an Episcopal Church gathering a few months ago. He was very nice to her, I will say that. And he was extremely generous. I wouldn't have put him on my dance card but Theodosia . . . she was more susceptible.

Bedford nodded. "She didn't mind his being married?"

"She didn't know there was a wife until they called about the drowning."

"Your sister was with him?"

"She was at his house. He was in the city on business. She answered the phone and they told her his wife had drowned. Just like that. She was devastated. She came home at once. He telephoned here looking for her, and when Theo told him what happened, he left immediately for Rhode Island. The next thing I know, he turns up again and they run off to Maryland."

"Have you heard from him today?"

She shook her head and then drank more sherry, nearly finishing it. "No. Not a word from him—unless my parents talked to him."

"I was told he was in Ohio."

"Then perhaps you should go there and look for him." She swallowed the rest of the sherry.

"Do you think he's the sort of man who might have done this? Did she ever speak of his mistreating her?"

"No. My parents disapproved of him. Intensely. But he was no fortune hunter. Quite the opposite."

"How do you mean?"

"Let's just say he was very generous."

"Do you know why your sister wanted to leave him?"

"Aside from the obvious reason, no."

"WHAT do you think of her?" Bedford asked as they descended the steps to the car. "She didn't seem terribly distraught."

"Yes, she was. Just too well bred to show it."

Albert started the car, then looked over his shoulder. "Back to the city, Miss Chase?"

Tatty stretched out her legs, admiring her pretty shoes. "What do you think, Bedford? Should we go to Ohio and look for Mr. Paul? Or should we go back home and forget that your friend Gertrude ever said the word 'countess'? Or shall we go on to Newport?"

Bedford thought a moment, then put his arm around her—stiffly, but affectionately. "I think the answer to all this can be found back in Newport."

"Along with my Packard. The Boston Post Road, Albert."

CHAPTER 20

AFTER obtaining lodgings for themselves and Albert at the waterfront inn, they went to the garage where they'd left the damaged Packard. The repairs had been extensive, but the repainted fender did not quite match the yellow of the rest of the automobile and there were other signs it had been in a fight. Nevertheless, it ran. The bill came to nearly four hundred dollars.

"I'll drive," Tatty said.

THE peach-colored roadster was not in view at the big house in Portsmouth and the servant who answered the door said Gloria Vanderbilt was not at home. Bedford dropped the General's name.

"You have a message from General Vanderbilt, sir?"

"Not a message. I'm making inquiries on his behalf and I've been reliably informed by friends in New York that Mrs. Vanderbilt has returned to Newport. If she is not presently in the house, I am prepared to wait."

"Me, too," said Tatty.

"The Countess Iovashenkova," said Bedford.

"One moment, sir."

Tatty seated herself on a bench by a large granite urn. "Is there such a thing as an affable servant anywhere?" she asked.

"Sveta is affable."

"Sveta is impossible—though I love her dearly. Her mother was in service in the household of the Grand Duke Michael, did you know?"

Bedford moved to where he had a view of the sea. "I hope she fared better than he did."

The servant had returned. "Mrs. Vanderbilt will be pleased to see you now."

They were ushered into a bright, sunny, high-ceilinged chamber that faced the Seaconet River and was furnished in a style Bedford could only call languorous. Gloria Vanderbilt received them reclined on a chaise longue near a double door that opened onto the terrace. She wore a blue satin dress and matching shoes, and was sipping tea or coffee while she went through her mail.

They reintroduced themselves.

"Are you here about that car?" she said, not looking up. "You shouldn't have bothered General Vanderbilt about that. I'll have someone send you a check."

"I'm taking care of the car," said Bedford.

"I have absolutely no recollection of any accident," she said.

"You may not have been aware of it," Bedford said. "Perhaps it was my fault. I should have let you by earlier."

"This was on Ocean Drive?"

"It's not what I've come to talk to you about."

A certain, inexplicable sense of indelicacy came over the conversation. The young woman kept her eyes demurely averted, waiting. Bedford watched her without speaking further. Tatty looked from one to the other, then sat back, finding herself in a scene for which she had no script.

"Mrs. Vanderbilt," said Bedford finally. "I should appreciate it very much if you could show me the view from the terrace. I've been curious about it."

He stood up. "If you'll excuse us, Tatty."

"Oh indeed. You can tell me all about the view later."

He bowed to her.

THE breeze played with a strand of Mrs. Vanderbilt's dark hair and the ruffles along the bodice of her dress as she leaned upon the terrace railing. A large sailing yacht was moving across the water in the distance but she had no interest in it.

"My sister Thelma says I can trust you," she said.

"I've never found it useful to betray confidences."

"And you think I am going to confide in you?"

"I hope that you will. I am here about the Countess Zala, as I gather you have surmised."

"In the name of the General?"

"In the name of protecting the family from any undue embarrassment or injury to its good name. Gertrude is a friend of mine."

"Magda was a friend of mine."

"You call her Magda."

She turned to face him. Her youth and extraordinary beauty, at this close proximity, came at him like a rush of wind. "Magda is her name. The others—were conveniences. She has been—had been—through many difficulties, as you know."

"You were a good friend of the countess's?"

"I was very fond of her, Mr. Green," she said, her voice cool with sadness. "I cherish her memory. And that's all that need be said."

"I understand. And I agree."

Now she looked back to the water, this time watching the large sailing vessel, which was gliding through the channel to the south. "I asked that Magda be invited to the party. She asked me to. It would have been her first time at the Breakers. Countess Szechenyi objected. Young Neil—he had known her in Paris—took Magda's side, as did Professor Horvath, who is a friend of Count Szechenyi."

"And the General?"

"He always wants what is best for his son. I believe he was worried—about Magda, what she might do—though there was no cause." She turned her back to him now. "You understand."

"I do. So she was invited, then?"

"She was uninvited, and then reinvited, I guess you could say. But in the end, she didn't come. I talked to her on the telephone. She was very agitated. She said it would be dangerous for me if she came. Magda was a highly emotional person. She drank too much. She sometimes made threats—spoke in very dramatic terms. I never took it seriously."

Mrs. Vanderbilt wiped at her eye, then turned to lean back against the railing, facing the huge house her marriage had brought her.

"I think she was trying to come to us," she continued. "In the water. I think she was trying to reach us. Life can be very hard at times, Mr. Green. Anyone's life."

"You're very young," said Bedford. "Life will get better."

Something close to contempt came upon her countenance—not for him, but for that notion. "You're said to be a worldly man, Mr. Green. How can you say that?"

He saw Tatty through the window picking up what looked to be a Paul Manship sculpture of a young woman as though it were a child's toy.

"I have just one more question, Mrs. Vanderbilt. To your knowledge, could Countess Zala swim?"

She put her hand to her mouth, then frowned. "I don't know. I took her to the Bailey Beach Club several times, as my guest. I think this is what upset Gladys. I don't recall her swimming, though. She'd wade into the water, but only a little."

"Even when you would swim?"

"Yes."

"Thank you, then. I'm sorry to have intruded, and I see no need to bother you any further."

"What will you tell the General?"

"That he has no need to worry about the reputation of his son—and that he is fortunate in his relatives."

She glanced at an upper window of her house. "You're kind. Kinder than . . ." She declined to finish.

"How is your daughter, Mrs. Vanderbilt?"

"Little Gloria? She is happy, I'm sure. She's in New York—with her nurse. I wouldn't want . . ."

The child would be all of a year old. "A little young for parties."

"Yes."

Recalling her European upbringing, Bedford kissed her hand—regretting it, for Tatty was now staring at them through the window. He feared she might now "accidentally" drop the statue.

"I like her pearls," said Mrs. Vanderbilt, fingering her own. "Do you know how I got these?"

Bedford shook his head.

"When Reggie and I were first engaged, we went to lunch with his mother. She asked him if I had 'received' my pearls yet. He told her he couldn't afford the kind of pearls I deserved. So she summoned the waiter and had him bring her a pair of scissors. She had this double strand of pearls that went to her waist. She cut off a length that was enough to make a necklace and handed it to me.

'There you are, Gloria,' she said. 'All Vanderbilt women have pearls.' "

"They become you."

"Reggie said they were worth at least seventy thousand. I swore I'd always keep them—but now I don't know. Seventy thousand."

Bedford took a step toward the open double doors. "My best to Thelma."

"Goodbye, Mr. Green."

Reentering the room, he noted that Tatty had returned the statue to its pedestal and was staring at the entry to the house's central hall. There stood a very handsome young man in gray flannels, unbuttoned silk shirt, and espadrilles, slouching against the wall.

"Good morning," he said, with a decided German accent. Bedford had had a great deal of respect for the German airmen he had flown against in the war, and after it he had befriended a couple. But this fellow's arrogance was instantly apparent—and unbearable.

"This is Captain Green, Fritzi," said Mrs. Vanderbilt. "He's a friend of Thelma's."

"Captain? Hauptmann?" The young man was still smiling.

"Royal Flying Corps," said Bedford.

"And the lady?"

"Countess Tatiana Iovashenkova."

"Prince Gottfried Hohenlohe-Langenburg," said Mrs. Vanderbilt. "A friend."

Tatty did not say, "Dee-lighted."

W HERE now?" said Tatty as she started the Packard.

Bedford waited until they had pulled out of the drive, as if Gloria Vanderbilt and her "friend" could hear. "I'd like to drive up to Fall River."

"Isn't that supposed to be a rough town?"

"Not as rough as New York City."

"What's in Fall River?"

"I need to see a man about a boat."

THE boat dock was just south of the long bridge that led from Fall River across the estuary to South Swansea and near a clump of smokestacks that would serve as singular landmarks for any mariner coming up the bay and ship channel. The office was at the north end of the dock in a clapboard shack. The proprietor, a balding, heavyset man in a fisherman's cap and sleeveless undershirt, sat on a stool beside his counter, flicking at flies with a rolled-up chart while eating a thick sandwich. A half-full stein of beer was at his elbow. Tatty did not seem dee-lighted to make his acquaintance, either.

"You want to charter a fishing boat?" said the man, looking with some wonderment at Bedford's white duck trousers and blazer.

"Yes. A cabin boat. The one just down the dock with the black trim will be fine."

"You want to take it out today?"

"Right now, if we could."

"Sorry, I got no one to crew for you this afternoon. The only hand who'd be available is out on another charter."

"I won't be requiring a crew, thank you. I know boats and I'm familiar with these waters."

"Y'are, are you? Where's Spar Island?"

Bedford turned to the open window. He could see it, directly southwest, in the middle of Mount Hope Bay. He pointed to it.

"And where's the ships' channel?"

The red buoy just downriver indicated that. "Runs right along this shore. About thirty feet deep at this dock."

"You got to be careful. I rented a cabin boat to this son

of a bitch last week who ran it aground on the rocks down at Fort Barton. Just left it there."

"I know the waters."

"Where you planning on going?"

"Down the bay a bit. Maybe to Common Fence Point."

"You don't look like you're going fishing."

"I'm not. I just want to go out on the water."

"For how long?" The man took an enormous bite of his sandwich, chewing as loudly as he had spoken.

"The rest of the afternoon, into the evening."

"But what are you going to do out there?"

Bedford gestured toward the street alongside the dock, where Tatty sat behind the wheel of the yellow Packard. "I want to take my girlfriend out."

The other nodded, his chews turning into a sort of grin.

"It'll be twenty dollars for the day, what's left of it."

Bedford figured that to be perhaps twice the going rate.

"And I'll need a deposit."

Bedford put two ten-dollar greenbacks on the counter. "We'll leave the car. If you'll keep an eye on it."

"Car like that, the whole neighborhood will be keepin' an eye on it."

"We'd like a picnic lunch."

"That I don't got. Just bait. You can get sandwiches in the restaurant across the street."

"All right. Give me the rental form and I'll sign it."

The man did so, showing some wariness.

"You'll leave the keys to that car?"

"No. Just the car." Bedford signed the agreement at the bottom, then paused. "I was told one of your boats had a running light out. That's not this one, is it?"

"No. It's the one that son of a bitch ran aground at Fort Barton."

"What did he look like, this person?"

The man shrugged. "Young guy. He was wearing a

hat—some kind of yachting cap. And he was dressed a little like you."

"What color hair?"

"Can't remember."

"Did he wear spectacles?"

"Yeah. What do you care who he was?"

"I was wondering if he was somebody I know. What was his name?"

"Pierce. Richard Pierce."

"Oh yes. Terrible sailor."

"You know where to find him?"

"He has a place in Rhode Island. Somewhere on the bay."

"He owes me."

"I'll keep an eye out for him." He picked up the motor starter keys from the counter. "Where's the boat Pierce foundered?"

"I have it hauled up on the bank upriver."

"See you this evening."

T HE boatsman came down on the dock to cast them off and observe Bedford's seamanship, which, unlike other of his attributes, was excellent. Making a neat turn, he marked the smokestack that would be his bearing on their return that night, then opened the throttle heading out into the bay, staying precisely within the channel.

"Shall we eat now?" Tatty asked.

"I daresay."

"Too bad we don't have any wine."

"Lemonade is fine."

"Where are we going?"

"Down to Newport. I want to take a look at the Breakers from the sea."

"Whatever for?"

"I'm hoping that will occur to me once I get there."

"Don't get too close," she said. "If they get a look at this filthy old tub, they'll faint."

THEY breasted Sachuest Point just as the sun was sinking behind the low hill of the Newport peninsula. After lunch, Tatty had gone below to sleep. She now returned, yawning. She had removed her shoes and stockings and came beside him barefoot.

"Ah, such a romantic cruise," she said. "Have you noticed how this boat smells?"

"Merely of fish. Like the sea."

"I may never eat caviar again."

"That, I do not believe." Bedford took out his chart, holding it up to the fading light, then set the boat on a course west by northwest.

"It's unmistakable even from here," he said.

"The Breakers?"

"Yes." He throttled back, looking at the chart once more. "There are rocks offshore. I want to see how close I can come to the beach there."

"Why?"

"I want to make certain whoever it was didn't intend simply to drop her off."

"What if you hit a rock?"

"Then we'll have a long walk—and maybe swim. Can you?"

"Circles around you," she said, standing on tiptoe to better see the approaching land mass over the cabin roof.

"I hope it will not be necessary."

"Shouldn't you have the running lights on?"

"Not just yet."

Gauging the tide, Bedford drew within fifty yards of the shore and then killed the engine, letting it drift. The boat turned sideways to the current and moved along, its progress easily measured by the passage of trees and rooftops. Coming by the Breakers, he saw many windows already illuminated and could make out several people on the terrace. Their number was small enough to be only family and servants.

They could not have told who he was at this distance, of course, but their boat was certainly obvious.

Ochre Point extended out into the Sound just ahead. Bedford restarted the engine and steered away, heading southeast.

"Back to Fall River?" she asked.

"Yes. With a brief stop enroute."

"It's going to be dark, you know."

"We have a clear night."

THE boat, drifting shoreward with the motor idling, came to a stop with a swoosh and scrape of wooden hull against mud and gravel. Bedford dropped over the bow, feet going into muck, then called softly for Tatty to lower the anchor and line to him. He took it forward onto dry beach, digging the anchor point in hard. Then he went back to help Tatty onto the shore. After a couple of painful bare-foot steps, she stopped to put on her shoes.

"Where are we going?"

"To that house just up the beach."

"The countess's house?"

"I'm not sure now who should be called the owner. But this is where she was living."

"There are no lights on."

"Let's hope it stays that way."

He started walking up the shore, moving as quietly as possible. Holding on to his arm, she followed.

"You're going to break in?"

"I've already done that once before. I'm afraid I wasn't able to give the place as careful a look as I should have done. I'm going to attend to that now." ·

"I must say, Bedford Green, I'm not very keen on this at all. Especially after what we found in her husband's house."

"I don't want you to come with me inside. I want you to wait outside. If someone comes along, warn me. If I run into trouble, run like hell down the beach."

"I don't like this."

"It's unfortunately necessary."

They went the rest of the way without speaking, their feet crunching on oyster shells exposed by the tide, which was now returning. When they reached the scrubby bushes near the house, he crouched down, bidding her to do the same.

"Wait here. If anyone comes up the lane, give a shout."

"What if they come after me?"

"I'm leaving you this." He reached beneath his coat, taking his pistol from beneath his belt at his back.

"Good God, Bedford."

"*Shhhhh.*" He slipped away into the shadows.

T**HE** house appeared to be without a light, but Bedford made a circuit of it just to make sure. Coming around the front, he made the unfortunate discovery of a car parked in the yard, but it proved to be the Ford Speedster that had been there on his earlier visits.

As before, the windows were open but for screens. He lingered by one at the side, listening, then crept back to the screen door at the front, pausing once again. Pulling it open, he winced at the sound the rusty spring made, waited, then stepped inside.

Everything seemed as he remembered, except the

wicker furniture in the main room had been moved closer together for some reason. Creeping down the hall, he entered the kitchen and struck a match. To his amazement, it had been cleaned up. There were a few dirty dishes on the counter by the sink, but otherwise it was quite orderly.

The match came close to burning his fingers and he blew it out, quickly lighting another. Beneath the white kitchen table was the case of whiskey he had bought Christopher. Bending close, he noted that only two of the twelve bottles had been taken. Standing straight, he saw that one of them was standing atop the old-fashioned icebox. It was nearly full.

Blowing out the second match, he stood still a moment, listening, sorting out the night sounds. Then he proceeded back down the hall, this time heading for the cellar, which he had left unexamined the last time.

The door opened noiselessly enough, but the stairs leading down squeaked with every step. He had descended no more than four of them when an unmistakable sound made him freeze.

It was an automobile, approaching up the lane.

Moving back, he stood in the doorway. The car was coming fast. Above his head, he heard the unmistakable sound of two human feet hitting the floor, and then footsteps. Just then, Tatty called out his name in warning, just as he had instructed her to do.

Bedford reached the kitchen just as the headlamps of the auto flared over the side bushes and the car pulled up before the house. Proceeding out through the pantry, he found that the back door for some reason was closed and locked. There was no key.

The front door opened, and a light came on. He heard someone come down the stairs. There were voices, several, speaking a foreign tongue.

There was no more sound from Tatty. Bedford presumed she had run like hell down the beach.

Joey D had once shown him the simple art of lock picking, but he was unsure how much he'd remembered. As he
had no choice, he closed the door separating the pantry from
the kitchen then groped his way through the darkness to the
outside portal. Taking out his pen knife, he felt his way with
his fingers to the lock and inserted the blade, applying pressure by turning the knob as he probed and fiddled.

The voices elsewhere in the house became louder,
sharper, imparting great earnestness about something. They
came closer, a light going on in the kitchen. He hoped they
weren't attending to hunger.

But they were. As he crouched, withdrawing his knife
from the lock to hold it as a last, desperate weapon, the
kitchen door he'd closed opened and a man stepped into
the pantry, turning to the shelves along the wall to the side.
He took several items, including something in a large
paper bag, then returned to the kitchen, unfortunately leaving the door ajar.

Bedford figured he'd have one last chance. Inserting the
knife blade again, he tilted the point more to the center of the
lock and felt, joyously, the pressure ease as the knob turned.
Pulling the door slowly open, admitting a freshness of
breeze and the sound of crickets, he withdrew the knife and,
still at a crouch, made his way outside. Poised on the stoop,
he closed the door, then slowly stood up.

The voices were still loud. There was anger about something.

He moved to the other side of the bushes, lifting his head
above them to peer at the brightly illuminated kitchen window as he went by, glimpsing three faces inside. If they were
looking out the window, they appeared not to notice him.

Crouching low, striving to quiet his heavy, nervous
breathing, he moved on along the shore. For some reason,
all the injuries he had suffered in this dubious enterprise
now began to hurt, most tellingly his right ankle, which he

had badly stressed in his crouch. He was limping by the time he came up to the boat.

He'd thought Tatty might have kept on down the beach for the sanctuary that was the town of Bristol, but she was by the boat, struggling with the anchor. The rising tide had loosened the craft from the muck a little and it was almost afloat.

"Hello, darling," she said, amid grunts. "Give me a hand."

"Get aboard," he said. "See if you can start the engine."

"They'll hear," she said. "Wait till we're both aboard."

The anchor struck his left shin as it came free. Swearing, he tossed it over the bow into the boat and waded around the side, wondering what his white shoes must look like. He boosted Tatty onto the boat, and once there, she helped pull him over the railing. Without further hesitation, he rushed to the motor, turned the key, primed the fuel intake, then tried starting. It took four tries before the engine finally coughed into life.

Looking back up the beach, he saw the play of a hand-held light up by the house. It seemed to be moving toward them.

Jamming the gear lever into reverse, he gave the motor full throttle. The engine roared and thrashed in the water, but the bow seemed still held by the bottom. Bedford shoved the control back into neutral, then into reverse, and then repeated the process three times. On the fifth try, there was movement, and then the boat pulled loose, turning sideways to the beach.

The hand-held light was coming closer.

Bedford spun the helm to port and gave full throttle, steering south on a heading for Hog Island and the passage that would take them back to Fall River. He half feared there would be gunshots, but there were none.

Tatty put her arm around his waist, and he put his around her shoulders.

"I just love these romantic cruises," she said.

THEY were able to dock and tie up without much difficulty. The charter man had given up waiting for them and gone home. Bedford set the starter key to the boat on the threshold of the office door, and then followed Tatty to the street. The Packard sat unmolested.

"Wait here," he said. "I'm going down the shore to check out the boat he pulled ashore."

"What can you expect to find there at this late date?"

"Probably not much, but maybe something useful."

He was right in both respects. Clambering aboard the craft, which was up on blocks, and prowling its interior with a succession of hand-held matches, he found nothing suspicious or out of the ordinary. There were small curtains inside, but they were brown and had no cords. One pushed them along their rods by hand.

Climbing back down to the ground carefully, he limped back to Tatty, who had the motor running.

"Oh dear," she said as Bedford got in beside her, "the long drive back to Newport."

"There are motor lodges along the way. We can stop at whatever's open and has a vacancy." He thought a moment. "And a telephone."

"Telephone! Bedford, it's the middle of the night."

"That's when I'm most likely to reach the people I need to."

CHAPTER 21

Like birds realighting in a tree after a sound had startled them, a number of the Vanderbilts who had fled after the unfortunate incident at the Breakers had now come back to Newport for the remainder of the season—which in their terms meant only the month of August.

The General was at home. Bedford was received inside so swiftly it seemed almost as though he was expected. Ushered into the General's library, he found him with eye-glasses on nose, a cigarette in hand, and a diagram of some railroad device on the desk before him. He stood to shake Bedford's hand.

"I received your message, Captain Green, and I must say, I was pleased to do so." He gestured to a chair on the other side of his massive desk. "Would you like coffee?"

Bedford seated himself, crossing his legs. "Yes, please."

The General pushed a button that rang an electric bell elsewhere in the house. "I'd like my son to hear what you have to say. He's keen on taking part. He was in Russia, you know, fighting the Bolsheviks."

"I thought he was in France and Flanders."

"That, too. Enlisted as a private, though he was offered

a commission. Served through the war, then went to Archangel in 1918 with the expeditionary force. Terrible time up there."

A butler, different from the man who had welcomed Bedford at the front door, entered and bowed at being asked to bring another cup and more coffee. The General pushed another button, then sat back, cigarette tilted up in his mouth.

"It's a nasty business, even a little frightening," he said. "We are obliged to you for your enterprise."

"I hope the truth is not as bad as it looks," said Bedford.

"It can't be, because now we're prepared." The General thumped the desk. He seemed to be enjoying himself. Bedford found the whole matter chilling in the extreme.

Private Vanderbilt, as Bedford now thought of the youth, came in, immediately followed by the butler, bearing a tray.

"Would you like coffee this morning, Mr. Vanderbilt?" the butler asked the son.

"No thank you." He pulled up the footstool from his father's reading chair, turning it lengthwise and seating himself astride it as he might a saddle. He looked to Bedford. "Tell us everything. Bolsheviks in Rhode Island. Who'd have thought it."

"It's a different world, I'm afraid," Bedford said.

"You're persuaded Magda was one of them?"

"Yes, but I'm not sure if it was willingly."

"And her husband?"

"Here's what I know."

He was extremely thorough in his presentation, so much so that the General had only one question.

"We must strike at them first," he said. "When do you suggest we do it?"

"Why not now?" said his son.

"They'd see us coming," said Bedford. "I think we wait

until tonight. There are some preparations I need to make, and the darkness will favor us."

"You don't think they'll lam out beforehand?" The General grinned, enjoying his use of criminal jargon.

"No. These people are fanatics. They'll be waiting for another opportunity."

"Then we'll have time for a small dinner party this evening."

"I should think it an excellent idea," said the son.

"Done," said the General, and he thumped his desktop again.

I T was nearly noon when Bedford rapped on the door to Tatty's room at the inn.

"Whoever you are, no thank you," she replied.

Bedford rapped again. "It's Bedford."

"All right. Just a minute."

She took her time coming to the door, opening it only a few inches. She was wearing a dressing gown, and perhaps nothing else.

"Bedford," she admonished. "It's the middle of the morning."

"Actually, the morning's all gone. If you like, I'll come back in the middle of the afternoon, but I hope you won't sleep much later than that, or you won't be ready for this evening's entertainment."

She stepped aside to admit him, blinking. "What entertainment is that?"

"We're invited to dinner, at the Breakers. A number of Vanderbilts will be there, and some other guests."

"*Quelles frissons,*" she said. "What's the occasion?"

"I think we may be at the end of our inquiry."

"How nice. Does this come from our interesting voyage of last night?"

"In part. Though one more voyage may be in order."

"But instead of doing something about these Magyar miscreants, we're all going to a dinner party?"

"It's the Vanderbilt way of doing things."

"This is all just too, too amusing, Bedford." Without another word, she went back to bed.

T**HE** Vanderbilts were a family who dressed for dinner— meaning black tie—but Bedford had ruined his white dinner jacket getting shot at and had brought no replacement. Consequently, he settled for a fresh shirt, white duck trousers, and a clean blazer, with a red, white, and blue striped tie.

Tatty, as always, was perfectly appropriate, this evening wearing a black, short-skirted dress with taffeta trim and her habitual pearls, which would now be facing stiff competition.

T**HE** Breakers was as aglow and aglitter as it had been the night of the big party, though there were far fewer automobiles. Once again, Bedford parked Tatty's Packard next to the peach-colored Hispano-Suiza roadster.

Albert wheeled the Pierce-Arrow into place beside him, leaving the engine running while he got out to open the door for Tatty, who alighted with a nimble hop.

"You know where to go?" Bedford asked.

"Yes sir. Went up there this afternoon, just so I'd know it."

Bedford reached into his coat, pulling forth his old Savage automatic. "Do you want to take this?"

Albert gently pushed the offered weapon aside. "No thanks. Got my own."

THE dining room at the Breakers was a mere forty-eight feet by thirty-two feet, and included twelve rose alabaster columns with gilt bronze capitals among its overpowering decor. But its most impressive aspect was its ceiling, which was no fewer than fifty feet above them. The central portion was decorated with a life-size painting Countess Szechenyi described as "Aurora Heralding the Dawn" by the artist Paul Baudry.

Tatty sat staring up at it after the soup course, finally lowering her head and pronouncing: "Bully ceiling, Countess. First cabin."

"Baudry did the ceilings of the Paris Opera."

"Miniatures compared to this, I'm sure."

The Countess Szechenyi made no retort. She had been quite deferential to the actress this evening, perhaps aware now of Tatty's far longer and more genuine pedigree in the roosts of European nobility.

It was for the Vanderbilts a relatively small gathering, though the guest list would have impressed New York society writers. In addition to the General, his son Neil, his daughter Grace, and the Count and Countess Szechenyi, there was Professor Horvath, Gloria Morgan Vanderbilt, Mr. and Mrs. Henry Cooke Cushing, the Countess Iovashenkova, and a society artist named Howard Chandler Christy. Mrs. Cushing, a lady of decidedly exotic dark-haired beauty named Cathleen, was Reggie Vanderbilt's daughter, a product of his first marriage. This made her young Gloria's stepdaughter, though she was only a year her junior.

Bedford found himself seated next to Mrs. Cushing. Chatting with her, he recalled a charcoal and watercolor sketch of her done a year or two before by an American woman artist named Olive Snell. He'd loved it and tried to buy it, but it had not been for sale.

"I have it," she said with gentle voice. "It was done just after my marriage. I'm afraid it stays in the family." She smiled, as though wishing it were otherwise.

"Perhaps it shall be in a museum one day."

"More likely one of these houses."

"Perhaps one day they'll be museums."

"I don't think that's quite what the old Commodore had in mind."

Professor Horvath, on the lady's other side, leaned close. "Do you have an interest in Hungarian art, Mr. Green?"

"I don't know much about it. There's an artist named Tivadar Kosztka I've heard of, though I've never looked at his paintings. Postimpressionist, I understand. Picasso calls him a genius."

"A Postimpressionist, but hopelessly outdated. Decadent fantasies."

"But very popular."

"Señor Picasso misplaces his admiration."

The General, eyes merry, stood up. "Gentlemen, we must excuse the ladies."

Tatty shot Bedford an unhappy look, astonished at so anachronistic a suggestion. But she voiced no complaint.

When the women had moved on—to the Great Hall and beyond—the men reseated themselves. Count Szechenyi, Cushing, and young Neil Vanderbilt accepted cigars. The others opted for cigarettes, except Bedford, who contented himself with cognac.

"Captain Green here has made an interesting discovery," said the General. "That poor woman's drowning may not have been a random occurrence. Apparently, she had violent designs upon us."

His remark instantly commanded everyone's attention. Count Szechenyi sat stiffly, moving his eyes from one to another of the guests as though he were a guard keeping watch on them. Bedford wondered how much the General had told him.

"She appears to have been a protégé of Bela Kun, the Communist revolutionary," said Bedford.

"That's impossible," said Horvath. "She was a member of the nobility. Her mother was a close friend of Admiral Horthy. Her mother was, in fact, murdered by the Communists."

"That's true," Count Szechenyi added. "An outrageous atrocity. Admiral Horthy was compelled to take harsh measures in reprisal."

"I'm not all that well acquainted with Hungarian history or politics," said Bedford. "But the daughter had a letter from Kun. He was trying to convince her that her mother had been killed on the Admiral's order, and encouraged her to take revenge."

"That's simply preposterous," said Count Szechenyi. "The House of Zala is an old and respected one. Centuries old. The family has been a defender of the throne going back to King Matthias Corvinus in the fifteenth century. With all respect to you, General, this man of yours is speaking nonsense."

Bedford restrained himself from replying to this humiliating reference as he might have done in a different circumstance and setting. He was grateful Tatty was "with the ladies," and not witness to his embarrassment. She was fully capable of striding up and socking the man—a sizable impediment to Bedford's plans for the night.

"Felix Dzerzhinsky was a Polish nobleman," Bedford continued. "He abandoned all that—and even the cause of Polish independence—to become head of Lenin's secret police. There were aristocrats who joined the French Revolution. Many of the Zalas were liberals. They supported Lajos Kossuth and a Count Istrvan Szechenyi in the 1848 Hungarian Revolution. The New York police have a Hungarian Prince Skorzeny on their list of dangerous leftist radicals and revolutionaries."

"Now that is truly ridiculous," Horvath said. "The man is a major benefactor of the Hungarian Cultural Association."

"I've never heard of him," said Szechenyi. "Is Skorzeny even a Hungarian name? It sounds Czech—or German."

"Nevertheless, I believe he is Hungarian, sir," said Horvath.

Young Neil Vanderbilt leaned forward, addressing Bedford directly. "She was nothing at all like that, you know. Didn't have a lot of money. The war had been hard on her. But she never talked like a Bolshie."

"You have this letter?" Horvath asked. "If what you say is true, it will someday have great historical value. To have a dictator like Kun put these things down on paper in his own hand—it would be very interesting to a collector. Certainly a Hungarian collector."

"Professor, I fear the revenge he sought from her was to be directed at this house, at people in this house."

"You are talking like a madman," said the count.

"I believe the principal victim was to be yourself, Excellency," Bedford said.

"Nonsense!" Szechenyi brought his brandy glass down to the tabletop with such vehemence Bedford was greatly surprised it didn't break.

"I would like very much to read this letter," Horvath said.

"I don't have it anymore, sir. Unfortunately, I gave it to another person to translate—someone perhaps more knowledgeable about radical revolutionaries. He said he lost it. I've no idea. But it's gone."

"Why didn't you take it to the police first?"

"You met the local constabulary the night of her murder, Professor. They would understand none of this. Especially written in Hungarian."

"Even if what you say is true, she's dead now. What is the worry?"

"I believe there are several of these people working out of the countess's house here in Rhode Island. It's in a town called Bristol."

"Not far from Reggie's house in Portsmouth," said the General.

"I went there last night. I don't speak Hungarian and could only look through the window. But they had guns."

An uncomfortable silence came upon the gathering. The count then attempted to change the subject, but no one at the table was interested.

"Captain Green, do you think this Countess Zala was murdered?" said the General, returning the discourse to its intended track.

"I don't know how she came to be in the water."

"Perhaps she was trying to crash the party," said Mr. Cushing.

"She was invited," said young Neil. "In the end."

"Yes," said Horvath. "She was to have come with me."

"She wasn't trying to crash the party," Bedford said. "She couldn't swim."

"Shouldn't you now go to the police?" said Szechenyi. "Why haven't you?"

"I wanted to speak with the General first."

"And so he has," the General said. "I think we should talk to the police. I intend to do that first thing in the morning. But not these local fellows. I'm going to telephone the commander of the state police up in Providence." He rose. "And now I think we should join the ladies."

Tᴀᴛᴛʏ and Bedford left in the Packard just after Gloria Vanderbilt and the Cushings departed. Insead of heading up Bellevue Avenue toward town, they took Victoria

Avenue to Lawrence, went a block south, and turned east again, following Ruggles Avenue to its dead end by the sea at Ochre Point. Bedford turned off the motor.

"We're supposed to be spooning," Tatty said. "You'd better kiss me."

She leaned back against the seat, moving closer and turning toward him. Bedford leaned closer still and did as she ordered.

"That should convince anyone," she said at length.

"Not a lot of acting required."

"Is that a compliment, or a reflection upon my theatrical abilities?"

They let a few minutes pass. Finally, Bedford restarted the car and, with headlamps off, pulled it up to the corner, stopping far enough into the intersection to have a good view of Ochre Point Avenue and the route north.

More minutes passed. Then more. "I'm getting bored, Bedford. You'd better kiss me again."

When he turned his eyes to the street once more, he saw a figure emerge from the bushes by the gate and turn in the direction of Newport's downtown. He waited until the man had progressed another block, then started the Packard.

"The time has come for you to return to the house, love," he said.

"But as I'm not going to," she said, "that doesn't matter."

"Please, Tatty. This could be dangerous."

"More dangerous than our little adventure last night?"

Quietly, he put the car in gear and slowly rolled forward.

BEDFORD waited until the man was nearing the town center, then turned on the Packard's headlamps and came roaring down the street, pulling ahead of him and bouncing the automobile up on the curb.

"Stop right there—Your Highness!" Bedford shouted.

He had felt uncomfortable and not a little nervous lugging his automatic pistol around all this time, but now he had an actual use for it, for Horvath looked as though he was about to run.

Hoping that the man was able to see it, Bedford brought the gun to bear as conspicuously as possible. Happily, reinforcements arrived just then in the form of a large Rolls-Royce touring sedan with young Neil Vanderbilt at the wheel. Stopping alongside Horvath, he leapt out the door, coming around the rear of the Rolls to block Horvath's escape. A little less nimbly, the colonel got out the other side. Bedford exited the Packard to join them.

Horvath seemed more confused than frightened.

"General," said Bedford, "allow me to present His Highness 'Prince Skorzeny.'"

"What are you talking about?" said the Hungarian, still

indignant. "Why have you accosted me in this manner? I demand an explanation, Mr. Vanderbilt. I am your guest!"

"Actually," said the General, grinning. "You're Count Szechenyi's guest."

"I don't know if you're an imposter or whether there never was an actual Prince Skorzeny," said Bedford. "But it was as 'Prince Skorzeny' that you hosted a party last year that the Countess Zala attended. You also invited a friend of mine who has identified you as 'the Prince' from a newspaper photograph that was taken on Hungarian Independence Day."

"And you're on the New York police list of Red subversives," said young Vanderbilt.

"Those idiots probably have President Coolidge on that list because he was seen talking to foreigners," Horvath protested. "This is insane. You've no right to be running people down on the street and waving guns at them. Have you forgotten where you are? Who you are?"

"Where were you going?" the General asked.

"Out for a walk."

"You've changed from black tie," said the General, noting the professor's dark cotton trousers and black Jersey. "You told no one you were going out. And you didn't leave by the front door."

"I went down the lawn to the water. Then I decided to take a walk through the town."

"What for?" said young Neil.

"I believe you were going to make a telephone call," Bedford said. "A discreet call. One you wanted no one to overhear." He heard the sound of an automobile engine, but it was at some distance.

"Where I was going is entirely my own business. Now let me go."

"You were going to make a call to a house in Bristol," said Bedford.

"What house in Bristol?"

There was the flare of headlights as the approaching car made a turn onto the street. Horvath took note of it, and began edging away from Bedford and his pistol.

"Put that away," he said. "What are you going to do, shoot me with Vanderbilts here? You know very well you won't use that weapon. Now let me pass before I start shouting for the police."

The car sped toward them, accelerating, then abruptly slowing as it came near. Bedford wondered why it was arriving so late.

He looked down at the gun he was holding, then put it back into his pocket. "You're quite right, Professor. I wouldn't use this. And you needn't shout for the police. For here they are."

"General Vanderbilt?" said the state trooper in the front passenger seat of the sedan.

TATTY had taken the wheel of the Packard and refused to budge—unperturbed by her lack of a driving license and the fact there was a police vehicle traveling just behind.

"I'm enjoying the entertainment," she said. "I just wonder what's next in the script."

Bedford stared at the sandy road ahead, the headlights burning through a wispy mist. "In the best of all possible worlds," he said, "we will arrive at the house and Professor Horvath will inform the inhabitants that they have been found out. Then they will peacefully surrender."

"You sound like Voltaire's Dr. Pangloss."

"Not all optimism is misplaced."

"Tell that to the Countess Zala."

"I don't think she was much of an optimist."

He looked behind them, making sure the Rolls-Royce and the police automobile were still in formation.

"Not to be pessimistic," Tatty said, "but what if you're

wrong? What if these people are just a bunch of political crackpots, like your friend Mr. Chumley?"

"None of Mr. Chumley's associates have turned up dead with red velvet cords around their necks."

"But you could be in very big trouble if you're wrong, Bedford."

"It won't be a new experience."

ALBERT had pulled the Pierce-Arrow off the lane just past the boatyard, having parked it so that the headlamps could illuminate a long stretch of the roadway that led on to the gray house by the water's edge.

Bedford pulled the Packard up just behind it, motioning to the following automobiles to come up alongside.

"We should block the way," Bedford said.

"You want to put state property at risk but not these fancy cars," said one of the uniformed cops.

"If something happens to it, the state will be compensated, I assure you," said the General.

The other policeman said something to his comrade. Without further comment, they backed their sedan around into place—front end aimed back toward Bristol.

"Now what?" said young Neil Vanderbilt.

"We walk up to the house," Bedford said. "Very carefully."

"What did you do in the war, Green?" Neil asked.

"I flew aeroplanes."

"I was in the infantry. And intelligence. Best I go first."

Bedford and the General followed. Behind them came the two policemen, holding on to Horvath, with Albert bringing up the rear. Bedford looked back to wave reassuringly to Tatty, who sat unmoving behind the wheel of the Packard.

There were no lights on in the house. As they drew

nearer it, they could hear no voices—just the summery sounds present the night before. Bedford slowed, easing his step on the gravel. Young Vanderbilt continued on ahead, then stopped in a crouch, moving behind a clump of bushes just shy of the house's scrubby yard, which contained a sedan as well as the Model T Speedster.

The sky was largely free of cloud but a haze of mist hung over the low ground, and thickened almost to fog out on the water of the bay.

The others were looking at Bedford. Hearing more footfalls in the stone, he turned to see Tatty coming up from the parked cars. He waved her back, uncertain how obedient she'd be.

Wanting to wait no longer, he tapped Vanderbilt on the shoulder, indicating he was going back to the others.

Reaching them, he showed the policeman his Savage automatic, whispering, "I have a permit to carry this in the city of New York." They accepted the lie. Bedford then took Horvath by the arm and, holding the pistol on him with his other hand, began walking him up toward the house. As he passed Neil Vanderbilt, he motioned to him to follow.

Without further impediment, they reached the front door and stood to either side of it, holding Horvath in place facing it directly. The two policemen moved over into the shadows behind the Model T. The General and Tatty shrank back as well. Bedford had no idea where Albert had gone, but hoped it was somewhere useful.

From the window above, he heard now the unmistakable sound of snoring. The notion of simply stepping inside and accosting these fellows in their beds was inviting, but as he thought upon, it, probably stupid. People startled from sleep reacted in unpredictable ways—especially when involved in dangerous enterprises.

"Call to them, Professor," he said quietly. "Tell them to come down. Whatever is going to happen here, it will be much worse if they don't cooperate peacefully. We have the police here, for God's sake."

"This is absurd. Nothing is wrong."

"If you're correct about that, we shall know shortly. Now, please. Speak."

Horvath took a step away from the door, took note that Bedford's pistol continued to be aimed at him, then looked up to the second floor and began shouting something in Hungarian.

There was a mix of squawks, grunts, and shouts in response. Then a sudden quiet.

"Tell them to come down," Bedford instructed.

More Hungarian. Seconds later, they could hear through the screen door the sound of hurried footsteps descending the stairs, then running feet. But no one came near the door. Bedford saw shadows flitting across his murky view of the interior.

"They're going out the back!" Bedford shouted.

He and Neil Vanderbilt turned and ran to the corner of the house, then along the side until they had a view of the shoreline. Listening, Bedford thought he heard noises to his left—possibly muted cries of pain from someone running on the stones and oyster shells barefoot.

The sounds diminished, supplanted by a rustle of brush to Bedford's rear. Horvath, who should have known better, was running away, cutting diagonally through the scrub to join the others in their flight.

A small burst of light shimmered in the mist ahead of them, followed by the muted crack of gunfire. Bedford aimed his pistol in that direction, but was unsure what he'd hit. Neil Vanderbilt stood up straight, tugging at him.

"Come on, let's get them!"

"Right," said Bedford.

They moved along the beach at a slow trot. There was another gunshot, and then the whine of a bullet.

"Shame you're not armed," Bedford said.

"Don't worry. I am."

Two more flares of muzzle flash. The bullets came much closer, prompting Bedford to drop to the ground. Vanderbilt took a few more steps forward, then did the same.

Then all at once the sky to the immediate southwest lit up like a small town fireworks display—with strings of firecrackers going off. A few gunshots down the beach were fired off in reply, prompting another, more intense staccato from out on the water.

"Submachine guns," Vanderbilt said. "Thompsons."

"Stay down," Bedford cautioned.

"I'm the infantryman, remember?"

"Sorry."

The battle sounds ceased. In their wake came some muffled screams, and then the thrum of a large, powerful boat motor. It rose in volume and then began to recede. Through the mist, Bedford saw a faint glimmer of light, moving fast. Then it was gone.

More screams, fainter now. Then voices behind them. The state troopers were approaching, carrying electric lanterns.

"Don't shoot," said Bedford. "It's us!"

He stood up, as did Neil Vanderbilt. They listened cautiously a moment, much like animals in the wild. The screams had become moans. The large motor boat was barely audible now.

"Let's take a look," said one of the troopers.

The policemen took the lead. Neil, in soldierly fashion, moved out to the side. Bedford did the same, finding himself walking almost in the water.

Within a very short distance, they came to the place. There was a man lying on his back on the beach—the source of the moans. Another lay half in and half out of the water. Holding one of the lanterns high, the state trooper examined one and then the other.

Bedford went at once to the moaning man, kneeling on the gravel.

"Sandor?"

The onetime waiter opened his eyes, focusing with difficulty. "Mr. Green?"

"Yes, Sandor. It's me."

"Why you kill us, Mr. Green?"

"We didn't," Bedford said, realizing the falseness of his words. "We didn't fire a shot."

"Then who?"

"These are dangerous times." Bedford shifted his weight, relieving the pain in his knee. "I need to know why you killed her, Sandor. The woman whose letters I showed you. The Countess Zala. Why?"

The man's eyes were turning watery. "We did not kill her. They took her away." His voice was weaker.

"Who took her?"

"Don't know. We were going to take her to that party. But they came for her. Took her away in a boat."

"Who?"

"Don't know. Maybe Szechenyi."

"Why were you taking her to the party?" Bedford said. "She could have gone by herself. Why would she need a gang of leftists for escorts?"

Petofi started to mouth a word, but his lips abruptly ceased their labors.

"What were you going to do there, Sandor?"

The man's eyes widened, looking hard at Bedford.

"You idiots were going to do something to that place, weren't you? And blame her, a member of the nobility."

"We . . ." The word remained solitary.

"What were you going to do? Were people going to be hurt?"

"They are very bad people, Mr. Green. Very bad."

"Who? Who's so bad?"

"All of them." The words came as an exhalation of breath. There was not another.

Bedford stayed motionless for a long moment, then wearily stood. Someone was coming up behind them. He turned to look, expecting Albert or the General. Instead, it was Tatty, cursing.

"Ruined my shoes," she said. She stopped. "These men are dead."

"You've asked me what the war was like. This is a very small taste of it, only it happened every day. Thousands of times a day."

She stepped back. "Did you shoot them?"

This time an honest answer. "No. Now please stay back, love. They're not all accounted for yet."

As if to second his argument, there came the crack of a shot from landward. Bedford pulled Tatty down to the ground, rolling over on top of her to protect her and then raising his head. A figure was coming out of the brush, firing at them with a pistol.

A policeman was hit and went down. The other shot at the onrushing attacker until his pistol was empty. Bedford feared he'd have to use his Savage on the man as well, but the gunman faltered, twisted to the side, and then landed in the sand and gravel with a thud.

Then it was absolutely quiet.

"Bedford. I can't breathe."

He got up, and helped her to her feet. All of them rose, including the wounded trooper, whose injury was to the arm, and apparently slight. They all stood around the man who'd been trying to kill them. He'd been hit several times, and the bullets had been destructive. Tatty turned away.

"I wonder who he was," Neil Vanderbilt said.

"His name was Joe Christopher," Bedford said. "Or more accurately, Jozsef Krystofi. That's how it appears on the Red Squad subversive list. The man I was talking to, the one who just died, he's Sandor Petofi."

"You know them?"

"Krsytofi was the Countess Zala's supposed boyfriend," Bedford said. "Lived in the house with her. I took him for a useless rummy, barely able to stand, half the time. But I was wrong. He was certainly nimble tonight. The other gentleman, he was a waiter at a Hungarian restaurant in Greenwich Village. They were all mixed up in this—whatever it was."

The state troopers were both looking out over the water. "Who in the hell did that shooting?" said one of them.

"Tommy guns," said Neil Vanderbilt. "Like in the war."

"They were bootleggers," said Bedford, presuming they were well down the bay.

"All this shooting over liquor?" said one of the cops.

"Happens in Chicago all the time," Bedford said.

"Horvath's gone," said Neil Vanderbilt.

They peered into darkness.

"He was on foot," Bedford said. "He can't get far."

T**HEY** were not interested in pursuing Horvath in the darkness, and so returned to the gray house. Dividing themselves, they began to look through it, turning on lamps as they progressed. Bedford, with Tatty following, headed upstairs to what had been the Countess Zala's bedroom.

The bed was far more rumpled than it had been, indicating that one of the men had been using it. Bedford looked under it, finding nothing of interest, then turned to the drawers. The Wembley revolver was missing from the night table, but the dresser still contained her things. He went through them quickly, then went to a closet, finding it full of dresses.

"She had expensive taste," said Tatty.

"Not exactly a plumber's wife," Bedford said. He began moving the hangers along the rod to better look at some of the frocks. "She could have worn any of these to the Vanderbilts' party."

He pulled one out from the others, examined it carefully, then took it out into the bedroom and laid it on the bed.

"That would look very nice on a woman with her dark hair and fair coloring," Tatty observed.

"The color is red—crimson."

"Yes. As I said, doubtless very flattering to her."

"Tatty. It's velvet. Red velvet. It matches what was around her neck—what I thought was a red velvet drapery cord. And look." He lifted the short skirt of the dress, displaying the hip-low waistline. "It came with a belt. A tie belt. See here. It was torn loose."

She looked where he indicated. *"Je ne comprends pas."*

"Whoever did this was intimately acquainted with her wardrobe."

There was a commotion downstairs. Some shouting, and then quiet. Bedford went to the top of the stairs, just as the ruckus commenced again.

"What's wrong?" Bedford asked, coming down the steps.

"Look what we found in the cellar!" said Neil Vanderbilt.

He held up a large, heavy-looking cylindrical object as though it were some fabulous treasure.

"What's that?" Bedford said, coming nearer.

"It's a bomb! Like the one that killed all those people in Wall Street five years ago. There's a whole crate of them down there."

The General stepped up to take the deadly object from his son's hands and carefully look it over. "Captain Green," he said finally. "You have saved this family from far more than embarrassment."

CHAPTER 23

HORVATH was picked up the following morning, walking toward Providence from Bristol and trying to thumb a ride. The state police who found him obliged him with a trip to the Rhode Island capital in the back seat of their car. He was locked up, pending formal charges, in the Providence city jail.

"Are they going to charge him with murder?" Bedford asked.

"I wish that were the case," said the General. "There's not sufficient evidence for that."

They were seated on the terrace of the Breakers, sipping cocktails in the sunshine as blissfully as though they'd done nothing these past many days but enjoy their summer leisure. Scott Fitzgerald had written a sarcastic yet winsome line in his new novel, *The Great Gatsby*, about the rich "being rich together." Looking at Tatty, as she sat in her pearls and fresh summer dress, chatting with young Neil Vanderbilt, Bedford understood perfectly.

"What can they charge Horvath with, then?" Bedford asked.

"I've had one of my attorneys make inquiries," said the

General. "In the immediate instance, there's the Volstead Act. There was a nearly full case of scotch whiskey on the premises—and the gunfight on the beach had all the marks of a bootleggers' quarrel. That's enough to justify prosecution, if not a conviction. The bombs would seem to offer a better prospect. Unfortunately, in both regards, there's no proof that he was an actual denizen of the house. After all, we brought him there. In fact, he's been ranting on about having been kidnapped."

Bedford sipped his gin. There were two sailboats out in the sound, apparently racing. But their movement seemed so slow at this distance they might have been swans, gliding on a pond.

"Do you think there's a possibility he'll escape justice?" Bedford asked.

The General gave his master jewel thief's grin. "Not a chance, Captain Green. His appearance on the New York police's subversive list, combined with those bombs and the exposure of his dual role as the so-called Prince Skorzeny—our attorney feels certain it's enough for the federal government to deport him, which we shall see to in short order. But in the meantime, we must keep him incarcerated."

"Do you mean deported to Hungary?"

"Of course."

"Horthy will have him killed. Your brother-in-law will make certain of that."

The General became quite serious. "Two young women are dead, Captain Green. Those three men, dead on the beach. The threat implicit in those bombs. Imagine what would have happened if one of them had gone off at the Breakers?"

"Wall Street all over again."

"On our lawn. Horvath must pay for that. You have police friends in New York. Whatever assistance they can render in this regard—it will be most welcome, and appreciated."

"I'll apprise them of the situation."

"Perhaps they can explain these. They were found in the pockets of the dead men."

He dropped three coins on the table. "Count Szechenyi says they're Hungarian."

Bedford examined one. It bore the same diagonal cross scratches as the one he had found among the Countess Zala's possessions.

"I can only assume this is their membership badge," he said. "I found one on your beach."

"Horvath."

"Probably."

The General thumped the table, more gently than he had the desk. "But that's the end of it." He looked from one to another of his guests. Bedford was just finishing his drink.

"Would you care for more refreshment, Miss Chase?" the General asked.

"No, I think we must be off, General," she said. "We've a long journey." She set down a glass still half full, and stood, extending her hand. "I must say," she said. "This has been just dee-lightful."

WITH Tatty riding with him in the Packard, and Albert following in the Pierce-Arrow, they made the five o'clock ferry to Jamestown and had reached the Connecticut line by sundown.

"The General is quite a gent," said Tatty. "He gave me a check to cover the repairs for this car. A thousand dollars."

"But, Tatty, they didn't come to that much. And I said I would take care of it."

"No, no. I told you, Daddy will. You keep your money. You've earned it. As for the General, don't worry. I'm not going to cash his check. I'm going to frame it. I think it will be just too, too amusing to have that in my library."

Bedford shook his head, saying nothing. Tatty snuggled down in the seat. She tilted her head back, looking up at the sky. "Bedford, would you like to go sailing on Thursday?"

"I fear not," he said. "I've got to get back to work at the gallery. Poor Sloane's been shouldering the entire burden."

She scrunched down further, putting her knees up against the dashboard. "Just thought I'd ask."

T**HE** three of them had a late dinner together at an inn at Old Saybrook, eating quickly and saying little. As they returned to where the cars were parked in the gravel yard, Bedford was about to ask if Tatty wanted to spend the night there. But before he could speak, she halted by the Pierce-Arrow and, yawning, precluded the suggestion.

"Albert," she said. "Are you up to driving straight through tonight?"

"Yes, ma'am. I had a couple of naps today."

"Well, then, I think I'll ride with you. There's much more room in the back than there is in the Packard." She went up to Bedford and took his hand. "You don't mind, do you, Bedford? You can stop at your farm in Cross River. I need to get back and start work on that play."

"Are you sure? I don't mind driving."

"It's for the best, Bedford." She stood on tiptoe and kissed him, then touched his cheek, then went to the Pierce-Arrow, where Albert stood holding the door.

"Good night, darling. And goodbye for now," she said. "Keep the Packard as long as you want." She got in. Albert drove much faster than Bedford was willing to, and was gone from view within a few minutes on the highway.

BEDFORD did not stop at Cross River, but nevertheless did not arrive outside his apartment until late the next morning. He found a parking place a half-block away, then lugged his suitcase to his building.

There was considerable mail, but he left it unexamined on his hall table. He made one telephone call, to Detective D'Alessandro, who was not at his station house. Bedford left a message to be called at home, then lay down on his couch, in the hopes of two or three hours' sleep. When he awoke, it was night.

And his telephone was ringing.

Bedford sat up, rubbing his eyes gently, then went to the living room and picked up the receiver. "Hello? Tatty?"

"It's Joey D," said the bemused voice on the other end. "When did you get back?"

"This morning. How come you're calling so late?"

"Been out of town. Up in Westchester. At the invitation of the county sheriff's police. We found the guy you said we should go looking for."

Bedford rubbed his head. "Howard Paul," he said.

"Down on the books as Paul Howard. We found him dead. His car was found in some woods near Tuckahoe. The body was in some weeds alongside the Bronx River. Single gunshot wound to the head. Right through the temple. Died instantly."

"How long had it been there?"

"Very ripe. My guess is he probably did it right after his second wife was murdered."

"He?"

"Paul Howard."

"Suicide?"

"As clear a case of that as I've ever seen, much as you could see anything with the condition the body was in with all this heat. There was a note, saying how much he loved his two wives and how sorry he was he had to kill them."

"Did he explain why?"

"Something about his first wife being a terrorist. And his second one deserting him."

"Did you find the weapon?"

"The gun? Sure. It was in his hand. One shot fired."

"A Wembley military revolver?"

"Yeah. How'd you know?"

"It belonged to his first wife. Very symbolic gesture. You might want to check the bullet. I'll bet it matches the one you found in my ceiling."

"I'll let you know. You want to join me at Lindy's, for a nightcap?"

Bedford looked at his watch. "How about breakfast? Meet you at Pierre Hilliard's coffee shop."

"The Carousel. Right. When I get off watch. Say seven A.M."

"See you then."

He hung up, then sat staring at the phone. Tatty never worried about the hour she received or made calls, but she was doubtless as tired as he.

There was one more call to make. It saddened him that he so well remembered the number.

"Yeah?" said the unmistakable voice of Mush-Face on the other end.

"This is Bedford Green. I'd like to speak to Mr. O'Bannion."

"That so?"

"Tell him I'm just back from Rhode Island."

There was a silence. Then a faint blur of voices on the other end.

"Mr. O'Bannion wants to know what you want?" Mush-Face said, returning to the phone.

"Tell him I appreciate his help but all I asked was for him to stop them. Not shoot them to pieces."

"Just a minute." Another exchange. "Mr. O'Bannion says to tell you that stopped them."

"I didn't want anybody killed."

"Mr. O'Bannion says to tell you you're lucky you weren't among 'em."

An actual pause followed.

"Mr. O'Bannion wants to know if everything is hunky-dory now with the Vanderbilts and all their swell friends."

"Yes. Hunky-dory."

"Then Mr. O'Bannion says thank you." Mush-Face hung up.

Bedford sighed, then went to his living room window, standing precisely where he had been when the gunshot had fractured the glass and wondering if he was being foolish. The pane had been replaced. Everything looked as normal.

Nothing moved in the street below. Yet he sensed an inexplicable menace. Perhaps, henceforth, he always would.

CHAPTER 24

SLOANE had opened the gallery and gone through her morning routine by the time Bedford arrived. She was seated at his desk, reading the paper, when he entered, and did not look up until she'd finished the short article she was reading.

"Welcome back," she said. "Did you have a simply marvelous time?"

"Ernest Hemingway would have called it a marvelous time," he said. "He would have particularly enjoyed the gunfights."

"Gunfights?" she said with arched brows. "Sounds a bit jejune for the Vanderbilts."

He sat in the chair beside the desk. "How are you, Sloane?"

"I'm just ducky," she said with a now friendly smile. "And I actually missed you."

"Have you sold any more paintings?"

"No. In fact, one of our buyers returned one. The old lady in Patchin Place. But Gertrude dropped by and said she had some clients in mind for a number of our things. And she said she'd like to see you."

"I'm very popular with people named Vanderbilt
lately."

"Tidy up their little problem, did you?"

"Yes, but not very tidily. There were more killings."

"That I do not wish to hear about." She stood up, relin-
quishing the throne. "Tatty Chase called. She wanted to
make sure you were all right. You were supposed to call
her when you got in, you cad."

"Yes, I have her Packard. It was much too late to call.
Anyone else?"

"Mrs. Paul. She called several times. Yesterday and this
morning."

"Did she sound upset?"

"I suppose so."

"She has reason to be. Claire Pell?"

"Lovely lady."

"Did she call?"

"Not a tinkle. Are you going to return Tatty's car? I
could use a lift uptown to the Fuller Building. The Wilson
Gallery has some sculptures they want us to handle on con-
signment. Very modern. Should sell quickly, I think."

"I'll have to leave them to your judgment. I need to be
elsewhere for a bit."

"Elsewhere where?"

"New Jersey. I have to call on Mrs. Paul. Her brother-
in-law was found shot to death."

"No you don't." There was a hint of humor in her eyes.

"No I don't what?"

"Need to go to New Jersey. It has come to you."

As Sloane had observed, Mrs. Paul was outside, approaching from across the street. She noted Bedford
through the window but made no sign of recognition until
she had come through the door.

"Hello, Mr. Green," she said softly. "I'm glad you're
back safe."

He took her gloved hand and ushered her to his chair, lowering her into it gently.

"I was going to call you, but I've only just now returned," Bedford said. He hesitated. "The police . . ."

"I spoke with them. I know." She took a handkerchief and dabbed at her eye. "Truth to tell, Howard and I never really got along, but this is so horrible."

Bedford put his hand on her shoulder. She was wearing another of her demure, long-sleeved dresses despite the heat. He could feel the warmth of her flesh beneath the thin material.

"Would you like something to drink?" Sloane asked. "Water? Iced tea?"

"No thank you."

Bedford and Sloane stood awkwardly a moment, waiting.

"You were trying to reach me," he said finally. "Is it about your brother-in-law?"

Mrs. Paul wiped her eyes again and then put her handkerchief away.

"I wanted to ask you about Margaret. And about what you found out up there with the Vanderbilts. I want to know what they had to do with Howard's death."

A middle-aged man and woman, well dressed and looking interested, had paused at the window and were contemplating some framed prints on display there. Sloane took a step closer to the door.

"I'll tell you what," Bedford said to Mrs. Paul. "It's almost noon. Let me take you to lunch."

She smiled wanly. "You're very kind, Mr. Green."

"Let me telephone and make a reservation. I'll meet you outside. I have a car."

He drove her to the restaurant in the Packard, which seemed to impress her even more than the Pierce-Arrow had done. André Mohar came to the door to welcome them personally, taking him to his best table, which impressed her also, though the restaurant was only half filled.

"You heard about Sandor," Bedford said.

Mohar nodded. "It's very sad. But they have to learn that they must leave all that revolution craziness behind when they come here. It's always trouble. Big trouble. Always."

"The police said it was bootleggers who did them in," Bedford said. "I believe that to be the case."

"One must be careful with bootleggers, also."

He left them with menus and headed toward the kitchen.

"What were you talking about?" Mrs. Paul said.

Bedford set down his menu. "Your late sister-in-law Margaret was mixed up with some Hungarian revolutionaries, including one who used to work here as a waiter. They moved into her Rhode Island house after she—after her drowning."

"How could they do that?"

"Joseph Christopher? Her boyfriend? He was one of them. His real name was Jozsef Kristofi."

"Was?"

"He was killed. The Hungarians fell afoul of some rum-runners. There was some shooting."

"Oh dear." She reached to touch his arm. "Were you there?"

"Yes."

"And you're all right?"

"Yes."

"Good." She sat back. "Joseph was a Red. Gosh. Then she was mixed up with them from the beginning? Before she married Howard?"

"Apparently so."

"But why did they kill her?"

"They didn't."

"You mean . . . you said she drowned. Do you mean she wasn't murdered?"

"No, Mrs. Paul. I very much believe she was murdered. But it wasn't the Hungarians. Your brother-in-law left a note. It said he had killed her. Would you like to order?"

She glanced over the menu. "What is *belszin kedvesi modra?*"

"Beef and goose liver in mushroom sauce."

A queasy look came over her face. She closed the menu. "Maybe I'll just have soup. Do go on, Mr. Green."

"We found some bombs at the house in Bristol. Terrorist bombs. I'm persuaded the Hungarians meant to use one or more of them at the Breakers. I don't know if they intended only to damage the place, or to kill some people, but if it was the latter, they could have killed quite a few."

"Including you."

"Possibly." He looked about the room for a waiter. Finding none, he returned his attention to Mrs. Paul. She was very pale. "Are you all right?"

"Yes. It's just, all this death. All this talk of it. After what's happened to Howard. What you've just told me . . ."

Bedford took her hand. "I'm sorry. Let's change the subject."

"No. Please go on. I'll bear up. I need to know what happened."

"I believe they planned to use Countess Zala to discredit the Horthy regime. To use her as a scapegoat. She was going to the party at the Breakers. As best I've been able to put things together, I think their plan was to set off their bomb and leave evidence that would implicate her. There was enough of it lying around her house—letters, a gun. She was a member of the nobility, mind. Her mother was one of Horthy's mistresses. It would have caused quite a political stir back in Hungary."

"But why would they want to attack people like the Vanderbilts?"

"Not the Vanderbilts. Count Szechenyi. He's a high-ranking official and his family is one of the oldest in the Hungarian aristocracy."

She covered her face with her hands, her sleeves falling back a little from her hands. "I don't understand any of this. It's so confusing."

"Revolutions are like that."

Her hands came away. "But you said they didn't kill her."

"No. Certainly not. They wanted her to attend that party. She could have gone. That had been arranged. But she was taken away from her house by someone else, using a boat. She was naked when we found her, not in evening clothes. There was a red velvet belt around her throat, but the dress it came from is still in her closet."

"You're sure it wasn't the Hungarians?"

"No. Not naked. I believe she was being taken out to sea—to be thrown overboard out there. With no clothes or anything to identify her by. She'd simply disappear. The Hungarians didn't want her to disappear."

"But she wasn't thrown overboard far out at sea. You said it was right off the Breakers."

"My guess is that there was a struggle and she was able to break free and fight off her kidnappers. She jumped overboard in the desperate hope she might reach the Vanderbilt house, or at least call out to someone to rescue her. But there was a jazz band, and no one could hear her. And unfortunately, she could not swim."

"This is all so tragic. And so strange. If not the Hungarians, who could have done it?"

"Someone she knew well enough to let into her bedroom. Someone who knew her well enough to know she couldn't swim. Someone who, needing something to bind her hands, knew she had a red velvet dress with a cord in the closet."

Mrs. Paul stared at the table top. "Howard," she said.

"He certainly fits the bill, doesn't he?" Bedford searched again for a waiter. "A fishing boat was chartered that day in Fall River by a man who may very well have been Howard. He had Howard's flair for inappropriate dress—wearing a yachting outfit with a billed cap and an Ascot to rent an old fishing boat, clothes that might be appropriate for J. P. Morgan or one of the Vanderbilts on one of the America's Cup class sailing yachts but not for a Fall River charter. Forgive me, but that sounds very much like your brother-in-law. Also, the pistol he was found with was hers. It had been taken from her night table."

She reached for her purse. "I promised you money if you would find out what happened—and so you have. I'm very grateful." She produced two fifty-dollar bills. "Please take this."

Bedford shook his head. "I cannot."

"Please."

"No, Mrs. Paul. It's not necessary."

"Are you sure?"

"Very."

She returned the money to her bag. "What I don't understand is why Howard would kill his new wife—Theodosia? He loved her. He'd just married her!"

"She was leaving him. Perhaps he'd just found out that her family had no money. And that they were mostly interested in him for his. Which was why she was leaving him. As you say, he was milking the plumbing supply company dry. There wasn't much money, was there? Not by Hastings standards."

"They're very socially prominent people. Howard liked that. I think he would have done anything to stay in their good graces."

Bedford nodded. "Their good graces required money." He saw a bus boy walk by and caught his attention, asking for water.

"I still can't believe Howard was in such a state he'd do these things," Mrs. Paul said. "You've no idea how unlike him this all is."

"Actually, I believe I do."

She fidgeted with her hands. Over her shoulder, Bedford noted the bus boy approaching with a large pitcher of water.

"What do you mean, Mr. Green?" she said.

"I don't believe he killed anybody."

The bus boy came rushing up, stumbled, and fell forward, dumping the entire contents of the pitcher upon Mrs. Paul's neck and shoulder. She shrieked, rising as she did so, shaking the water from her arms and hands.

"I'm sorry, so sorry," said the bus boy.

"You damned idiot!" she cried.

The water had soaked most of her blouse, rendering it translucent. One could see in almost perfect detail the slip beneath, the bruise on her shoulder, and the scratch lines on her arm. Bedford stared at them, aware suddenly that she was staring hard at him.

"What's going on here, Mr. Green?" she demanded.

Mohar came up, appearing very anxious.

"Would you tell Mr. D'Alessandro I would like him to join us now, if it's convenient," Bedford said.

"Yes, Yes." Mohar dabbed absurdly at Mrs. Paul's sodden blouse with a napkin for a moment, then, as though reminding himself of the realities that obtained, scurried away toward the kitchen as fast as his bulk would allow.

Mrs. Paul used the napkin herself, pulling the sleeve away from her flesh. Then her eyes returned to Bedford.

"You arranged that, didn't you?" she said, backing away.

"Calm down, Mrs. Paul."

"You made him do that. And you're supposed to be the great *gentleman*. Look what you've done."

She moved further away, compelling Bedford to step closer. To the right, he saw Joey D and Mohar coming out of the kitchen door.

Mrs. Paul saw him, too. Turning to the next table, she picked up a knife and jabbed it down as hard as possible into Bedford's arm, then let go of it, flinging herself toward the restaurant's front door.

Wincing against the pain, Bedford pulled the knife free of his blazer's sleeve and started after her, but D'Alessandro reached her first, grasping one arm, then both together, having cuffs on her in a trice.

Mohar began telephoning quickly.

"You need a doctor, Green?" D'Alessandro asked.

"No. She used a bread knife. I'm barely stabbed."

"Just so you're stabbed. Now I officially have jurisdiction."

A COP off the beat responded first. Then a car from the precinct house in the neighborhood pulled up, with two uniformed officers inside.

Holding a napkin to his arm, Bedford followed the prisoner and her captors to the vehicle. She was placed in the back, between Joey D and one of the uniformed men. The other patrolman got back behind the wheel.

Bedford leaned in over the door. "Was it just the money, Mrs. Paul? Or did you really hate him?"

She glared at him, then looked away, lips tight.

"We have to talk to your husband," D'Alessandro said.

"You can't," she said, a near snarl obliterating every hint of her former sweetness. "He's in Ohio."

CHAPTER 25

Tatty met him at the door in her dressing gown, pearls in place, full champagne glass in hand.

"You're a vision," Bedford said.

"You're very, very late."

"I'm sorry. I was in Yonkers."

"You poor thing. Let me get you a drink, and you can tell me all about it." She led him into the living room of her townhouse, but halted without inviting him to sit. "I have a better idea. It's a lovely night. Let's go up to my roof garden."

She asked Sveta to bring champagne and whiskey, ice, water, and fresh glasses, then led the way up the three flights of stairs. There were two chaises longues among the other furniture and many potted plants on the terrace. Pushing them next to each other, she reclined on one and patted the seat of the other. They sat a moment, not speaking, holding hands and looking out over the soft darkness of the park at the twinkly lights of the apartment buildings along Central Park West on the other side.

Sveta completed her task, then retired for the night.

"Tell me about your fascinating trip to Yonkers," Tatty said.

"A visit to the Paul Plumbing Supply Company. They found the body of Robert Paul there under a pile of toilets that had fallen over."

Tatty sipped her champagne. "And that nice little woman from Ohio did all this herself?"

"I think all three of them had a hand in taking Countess Zala from the house in Bristol, though I'm not certain they had murder in mind at the outset. I don't know if Mrs. Paul got those bruises and scratches trying to throw the countess overboard, or trying to stop her from jumping. But the countess drowned all the same. Our dockyard friend in Fall River identified Howard from a picture as the man who rented the boat, and a filling station attendant remembered seeing three people in Howard's car."

"What about Theodosia?"

"She was in the Social Register. Howard didn't care if she had any money or not. Mrs. Paul and her husband were the ones worried about what her family's financial straits would mean for the rest of the assets of the plumbing supplies company."

"And the unfortunate Howard?"

"I'm pretty sure he was shot by someone in the rear seat of his car while he was behind the wheel. The angle was a bit off for someone trying to shoot himself. Whether there was someone beside him in the front seat, I cannot say. I suspect there was. They must have been going to those little woods for a private chat."

"Then she killed her husband Robert?"

"Lieutenant D'Alessandro thinks he was probably hit on the head first and then had the stack of toilets pushed over on him."

"And then there was one."

"The heiress to the fixtures fortune—what was left of it."

"Has she admitted to any of this?"

"No. And she's only been charged with attacking me with a knife. But she'll doubtless stand trial for complicity in the death of the countess. Beyond that, who knows? At all events, I can't imagine a jury sending anyone that pretty and winsome to the electric chair. But a lady like her will not enjoy prison at all."

"All this just for money."

"Of course."

"I'll never understand."

"Mrs. Paul was from Marion, Ohio. It's a long way from there to here."

Tatty crossed her legs. She had taken off her shoes. "New York is so lovely when you look at it from here," she said. "It's rather like a beautiful garden. You've no idea of all the creepy crawly things going on in it."

"The people across the park may be thinking the same thing about us."

"They wouldn't dare." Tatty finished her wine and set down the glass. She lay back, putting the back of her hand over her brow. "You know, I'll never feel quite the same about Newport or Hungarian food again."

"I trust your displeasure will not extend to plumbing fixtures."

She laughed. Tatty had the most wonderful laugh of any woman he knew.

"I was just thinking," he said.

"Too late at night for that." She put her hand in his.

"No. I was thinking that Sloane is entirely right. You and I really ought to be married."

She did not respond. Finally, her hand came away and in a moment she poured herself more champagne.

"Bedford, I want you to have the Packard."

"No, Tatty, I couldn't. I've brought you a check. To cover the repairs."

"Forget that. And take the car. They won't give me a

new driving license for another year. I have my Pierce-Arrow, and Albert. The Packard will just sit. And the front fenders don't match anymore anyway."

"I couldn't. It's too much of a gift."

"Not for me."

"But for me."

She said nothing for a long time. When he turned to her, he saw that she was looking at him—with some seriousness.

"Actually," she said finally. "Sloane is wrong. We probably shouldn't be married."

"And why is that?"

She fingered her pearls, looking away from him. "Ask me again when you *can* go sailing on Thursdays."

AUTHOR'S NOTE

THIS is a work of fiction. Bedford Green, Sloane Smith, Tatiana Chase, and Lieutenant D'Alessandro are fictional characters, as are the Countess Zala, Imre Horvath, the Howard family, and Theodosia Hastings, among others. Consequently, none of them could have been at the Breakers in the summer of 1925, and the Vanderbilt family could not possibly have been involved in such a story.

But the Vanderbilts of that generation were a singular family, in accomplishment as well as wealth. I have involved them in this tale of greed, murder, and deceit, rendering them as true to life as possible, because they so vividly represent the Newport that was and the highest echelons of American society in that glittering era. Their inclusion also provides the reader with an opportunity to visit, not only that long-ago time, but behind those mansion walls where so few once were allowed to tread.

ACKNOWLEDGEGMENTS

CHRISTOPHER Haynes, William Thorn, Margaret Schwarzer, and especially the late Cleveland Amory contributed significantly to the knowledge of Newport and American society that I drew upon for this book. I am grateful also to Paige Price and Tammy Grimes; my splendid editor, Gail Fortune, and tireless agent, Dominick Abel; and to my wife, Pamela, and sons, Eric and Colin, as only they can know.